Search for the Summer Stone

Book Five
The Hercynian Forest Series

Reba Birmingham

Launch Point Press
Portland, Oregon

www.LaunchPointPress.com

Praise for the
Hercynian Forest Series

Search for the Summer Stone (Book Five)

"Merryville might look like an ordinary town at first glance—with ordinary people living their lives and the usual cast of characters and various factions of leadership and issues. Then we discover that there's a parallel universe of magical creatures, fairies, and elves interwoven with the lives of Mitzi, Panda, Val, and Juniper! Welcome to the world of the Hercynian Forest. Reba weaves all of this together in a most elegant frame of relationships—mystery—imagination—with a bit or romance and intrigue to boot. You are sure to recognize yourself in at least one of the characters as they grapple with the issues of good and evil that arise. How do we connect with each other? How do we discern the forces of power in our lives? What can we learn from those who came before us, our ancestors? These questions are embedded in the story-telling of this marvelous series." **~Kay Lindahl, author of *The Sacred Art of Listening***

Circle of Stones (Book Four)

"Ms. Birmingham made us wait for a while (ok, ok, there was a pandemic) for Book Four, but it's well worth the wait. All her delightful characters, including humans, elves, fairies, and other mystical creatures, are well drawn and entertaining. I'm looking forward to the next volume." **~Tina B. Tessina**

"Loved the unexpected twist and turns and always keeping me on my toes. A great fun read! Highly recommend to all!" **~Melinda Elmer**

The Wolf You Feed (Book Three)

"Quirky and engaging characters, plot twists, adventure and fantasy, humor and thrills, all put together flawlessly " **~Carolyn Weathers, author of *Crazy* and *Leaving Texas***

"The settings are vivid and real and the characters loveable. The plot's interesting and contemporary. Highly recommended for those who want a true "beach read"—especially a Long Beach one!" **~Marie Cartier, author of *Baby, You Are my Religion: Women, Gay Bars and Theology Before Stonewall***

"I dare to add Reba Birmingham's name to the distinguished list of fantasy writers who use magic, myth, and mystery to discover new meaning in old truths. It was truly inspiring to see lesbians, a Native American, and fantastical forest creatures join together to defeat an evil that is as ancient as the Bible and as modern as today's headlines." **~Mel White, author of *Stranger at the Gate: To be Gay and Christian in America* and *Holy Terror: Lies the Christian Right Tells Us to Deny Gay Equality***

Words on a Plate (Book Two)

"Tired of fantasy that features the same old wizards and dragons and knights on a quest? Reba Birmingham has just the antidote for you. *Words on a Plate* introduces us to an enchanting mix of magical powers, elves, mysterious happenings in a Peruvian jungle, ravens delivering messages via thumb drives, a horticultural society and its politics—and a main character who is a tax preparer. Not your usual Tolkien clone! Funny and suspenseful by turn, this delightful fantasy brings new life to an old genre. I enjoyed it. You will too." **~Sheila Finch, author of *A Villa Far From Rome***

"An exciting adventure with unique characters navigating their way through fantasy and reality...[*Words on a Plate* is an] easy read, writing is crisp, and the mystical characters are interesting with creative powers." **~Katie Cotter, former news editor, *The Advocate***

Floodlight (Book One)

"As an avid reader and writer of YA Fantasy, *Floodlight* hit so many of those elements that I love about fantasy—the mysterious heritage, the unseen world that parallels the one we know, the amazing characters and creatures that we encounter, the adventure, the impending doom, and the fun. But I loved getting to enjoy all those elements with a fully established relationship. I love Panda, the hard facts-and-figures person, and her free-spirited. kind wife, Mitzi. These two balance each other completely. Panda is joined by their friends, Juniper and Val, as they whisk away to another country to save Mitzi...oh, and maybe the world while they're at it! **~Debbie McQueen, author of The Dragon King Series**

"In this first novel in a projected fantasy series, debut novelist Birmingham's LGBTQ representation among the cast is refreshing. She parallels the fictional cult with the patriarchy, and she compares inter-species relationships in the fantasy world with LGBTQ relationships in ours." **~Kirkus Reviews**

"I love me some wacky plots and characters, and between the thrills and chills in *Floodlight*, this book has a lot of humorous stuff in it. Besides, there are elves and griffins and dwarves—oh my!—who could ask for anything more? If you like the funny urban fantasies of Charlaine Harris or Jim Butcher's Dresden Files, you'll likely enjoy Birmingham's new series." **~Jessie Chandler, award-winning author of The Shay O'Hanlon Caper Series**

"Likable main characters...(and) sweet elf characters. Having two lesbian married couples was refreshing to read. The balance between supportive and not supportive of lesbian relationships (was) realistic." **~Bookloverblogs.com**

The Hercynian Forest series

Floodlight

Word on a Plate

The Wolf You Feed

Circle of Stones

Author Notes

Thank you for reading this series. Why do I write these stories? First and always, I hope you are entertained and find Merryville and the magical world a good escape. Perhaps you are lying in bed reading, near a fireplace, on a train, or have one of my books in your bag waiting for you. If you are new, welcome! My Hercynian Garden and Merryville characters are kind, pretty down to earth, and have adventures in their regular and magical worlds. They have been drawn into the fight with *Lupus Imperium*, a great stand-in for every oppressive regime in our current world. As you are reading, know that books like this are being banned! Reading the series is becoming part of the resistance. Thank you.

As you follow Panda and Mitzi, notice how they grow with each new book release and get stronger. As for LGBTQ content, I love representing a lesbian married couple with healthy female friendships. It's not a romance story, as they are already committed to one another. These free creatures simply live their lives and have adventures with their friends while part of the diverse landscape we call the United States. Representation is important. I want us all to see ourselves fighting evil and overcoming our inner stumbling blocks. For those who have been with me since the beginning, I hope you enjoy that in book five, some characters from earlier in the series circle back to take part in *Search for the Summer Stone*. Enjoy.

Dedication

To Layla Jo

a dragon warrior.

Characters

Alaric—Youngest member of Ehren's council in the Hercynian Garden.

Alexandra Stephanovsky—Formerly of Merryville, living in the Hercynian Garden as an attorney on Ehren's council; married to retired detective Charlie Potts.

Ali Badawi—Hercynian Garden agent from Egypt, running Taggart's Emporium with Panda's sister Puddle while the Browns are away.

Aurora Brown—Co-owner of Taggart's Emporium in Merryville, CA; married to Ralph Brown.

Brother Bruno—*Lupus Imperium*, lives in Schwarzwald Castle, Germany.

Charlie Potts (aka "Dr. Charles Copley" when undercover)—Retired detective; married to Alexandra Stephanovsky; lives in the Hercynian Garden.

Dominique—Tour guide for Azari Safari Company in Namibia.

Dr. Edith Roswell—Expert on Namibia from the UK on tour with Azari Safari.

Dr. Mot—Chief Medical Officer in the Hercynian Garden.

Dr. Rick Bush—Professor from Texas on tour with Azari Safari.

Ehrenhardt "Ehren" Winter—Leader of the Hercynian Garden; father of Mitzi Fowler.

Ekkhard "Ekk" Schmidt—Married to Elsa and Elvin guardian of the Fowlers.

Elsa Schmidt—Married to Ekk and Elvin guardian of the Fowlers.

Enid—Welsh, a Shade from the past who oversees the Hercynian Garden Library.

Fetu—Brave Samoan on the cargo ship.

Frederick Winter—Mitzi Fowler's deceased father.

Gary Smithers—Former city councilman for Merryville; agent of *Lupus Imperium*.

Geoff & Simon—Brothers from Australia on tour with Azari Safari.

Heloisa—Chief Guardian of the Hercynian Forest.

Hortense Miller—Former president of the Merryville Horticultural Society.

Jack Johnson—Owner of Johnson Global Shipping and other companies.

Jay Winter—Human barista from Merryville; married to Ehrenhardt Winter.

Johannas—Driver for Azari Safari tour bus.

Juniper Gooden—Curator of Merryville Museum; married to Valerie Gooden.

Karla—Historian; member of Ehren's council in the Hercynian Garden.

Lorelei Pinck—U.K. academic accompanying Dr. Edith Roswell on tour with Azari Safari.

Lulu—Police officer working with LAX; an old acquaintance of the Fowlers.

Mitzi Fowler (aka "Miranda" when undercover)—Married to Panda; daughter of Ehrenhardt Winter; half-griffin; tour guide.

Nathan—Namibian gas station worker.

Panda Fowler (aka "Dr. Hannah Panover" when undercover) —Our narrator; married to Mitzi; "Caller of Ravens;" tax preparer.

Puddle Fowler—Sister of Panda Fowler.

Ralph Brown—Co-owner of Taggart's Emporium; married to Aurora Brown.

Rena Bush—On tour with Azari Safari; married to Rick Bush.

Sally Johnson—Member of the Merryville Horticultural Society; married to Jack.

Sam—The Colonel's soldier.

Sergei—Viktor Volkov's right-hand man.

Shrumm (first name Popkin)—Ehrenhardt's "First Person" in the Hercynian Garden.

The Colonel—A *Lupus Imperium* agent.

Twyla—Juniper and Valerie's guardian fairy.

Valerie Gooden—Native American healer; best friend of the Fowlers; married to Juniper.

Viktor Volkov—New leader of *Lupus Imperium*.

Virginia Merry—Long deceased matriarch of one of Merryville's founding families.

Wit Storieman—Meaning "white story-man," a local who can be hired for a few bucks to entertain with stories in Luderisk.

Woda—Chief Magical Officer in the Hercynian Forest.

Terminology

Free Creature—Those who believe in the dignity of all living beings and freedom for each individual to choose their path forward, as long as they do no harm.

Hercynian Garden—A magical headquarters hidden in the Black Forest of Germany.

Lupus Imperium —The current manifestation of an ancient religion dating back to the myth of Romulus and Remus and seeking control of all free creatures.

"Magic is believing in yourself. If you can do that, you can make anything happen." Johann Wolfgang von Goethe

Prologue

The sun above the Namib Desert of Africa beat down unmercifully. All around me, as far as I could see, was hot sand. The soles of my feet burned, even through my new REI boots. My legs felt as heavy as lead while I slogged through golden sand toward a ghost town barely visible on the horizon. A glance at our tour bus was all I needed to spur me on. It was the only shade for miles but was permanently out of commission. The tan bus lay pitched to one side—bullets riddled the Azari Safari Tours sign, windows shattered, and heavy tires flattened. I knew at least one unfortunate soul was still belted into his seat, beyond human aid. Eventually, sand would claim the site and be his grave. My head hurt. I wanted to sink to my knees and weep, but there was no time for self-pity. Mitzi was somewhere ahead with the others in the clutches of some nasty men and creatures. I prayed she was alive as I wiped the blood from my cheek, which mixed with tears, and pushed forward. Someone else's sweat ringed my floppy hat, and my long sleeves burned against my arms under the merciless sun in a cloudless African sky. I trudged on, swatting tsetse flies from my face, certainly not laughing now.

Chapter One

Merryville, California

Thistle Drive was full of houses like ours. Most were two stories, built post-WWII, with an asphalt driveway and a decent-sized yard. My wife and I lived a few blocks from Merryville's downtown, arranged around Main Street. When you walked south down Main Street, on your left was Merryville Park, a green space with trees, benches, and a statue of Virginia Merry, for whom the town was named. On the right, you could grab a coffee at "Not Your Mother's Coffee House," a gay hang-out, or pick up some tools at Taggart's Emporium. Our good friends Ralph and Aurora Brown owned Taggart's, and my crazy sister Puddle worked there. My wife and I bought our home in Merryville years ago with the insurance proceeds after my parents died.

Mitzi and I happily married, and until a year ago, we were blissfully unaware of all that went on just out of sight of our idyllic town. Our lives were turned upside down when I was working late at my tax office one night and found an elf hiding in the bushes. Against all odds, Ekkhard Schmidt and his wife, Elsa, now lived in a treehouse in our backyard. Go figure. We called him Ekk. They introduced us to the Hercynian Garden, ground zero for magical creatures and the ongoing fight for the freedom of beings of all kinds from an evil organization called *Lupus Imperium*.

Since that day, our lives were busy, scary, and, truthfully, kind of fun, but I always thought it would be over at some point. Now, Mitzi's father, the leader of the Hercynian Forest, wanted to send us on another mission. His order made me resentful because he expected us to drop everything and obey. He didn't seem to care that, along with being dragged into fighting *Lupus Imperium*, I still had to work, doing taxes. He also didn't seem to care that our absences decimated Mitzi's travel business last year. Because of this war, she had to cancel several tours as we traveled to Germany and Peru. I felt we'd done our bit and was glad we survived. I was ready to return to "normal."

I lay on the couch in our living room this Saturday, drinking coffee and watching the news. Our local anchor appeared in our downtown park as "Breaking News" rolled across the bottom of the screen.

"Mitzi!" She was in the kitchen and didn't hear me. I was riveted as a group of young men and women gathered near the statue of Virginia Merry. They were in a yelling match with two men, both surrounded by uniformed officers in our downtown park. People carried signs with various slogans such as, "This is California, not Mexico!" and "Merryville, not Merida!" Waving US flags filled the screen. The two men the group yelled at looked vaguely familiar, and I thought one might work at "Not Your Mother's Coffee House." I almost spit out my coffee when Hortense Miller walked by the camera holding a sign that proclaimed Preserve Our History!

"Honey, Hortense Miller's on TV!" Hortense was well-known to us and a member of our local horticultural society. There was no response from the kitchen.

"Oh my god, Mitz, something's happening at the park!"

"Be there in a sec. I'm on the phone."

I watched the melee unfold as Mona Morgan, the Channel Five talking head, spoke breathlessly into the mic. "Since Mayor Francisco Gonzalez came into office, some citizens have revived the old controversy about renaming Merida into Merryville, with some saying the city should tear down the statue of Virginia Merry. This protest by the group," she glanced down at a piece of paper, "Native California Patriots, was peaceful until some folks from the coffeehouse crossed the street and confronted them. While the protest was allowed, controversy erupted when coffeehouse patrons got physical. Police were called, and the protest turned into the confrontation you see right now."

In the background, I saw police break up the crowd. Mona put a manicured nail over her earpiece. "Police are ending the protest and sending everyone home. There will be quite a traffic jam. We'll come back to this after the sports news. The Merryville Dolphins are—"

I tuned it out. Merryville used to be boring, but people seem riled up about everything now. I missed boring.

I wished Ekk was with us and that Mitzi would get off the damn phone. The news cycle started to repeat a business segment, so I shut it off. Even with things boiling over at home, I needed to stay focused. We had a part in the fight for good and had a mission before us. Mitzi's father decided we were *perfect* to go undercover on a safari to Africa, Mitzi would be our tour guide. Our mission was to determine if a magical "Summer Stone" might be hidden somewhere in Africa.

I started to scroll social media while I waited for Mitzi, and I made the mistake of reading comments under a post about Virginia Merry's statue removal. They weren't pleasant. Our local college, Merida University, had never changed its name, and much of the push to remove the statue came from there. The youth were unfiltered in their opinions, and the war of words was on. According to them, if you didn't want to change the name of the town back to Merida, you were a racist, period. In times like these, the magical world seemed better than the one here. I would have loved to be able to add comments about some magical meditation, but I would be thought crazy. Obviously, we're not supposed to talk about magic, or these missions, with ordinary civilians.

My siblings, Brooke and Puddle Fowler, knew about the Hercynian Garden, as did our best friends, Juniper and Valerie Gooden. All four had played a part in various magical shenanigans over the last year. So did Ali Badawi, a magic creature who now managed Taggart's Emporium for the Browns. Aurora Brown was magical, too, and was currently in the Hercynian Garden in Germany, helping Garden scientists and magic workers find remnants of the ancient stone. None of them were here right now to talk to.

My magical circle at home was getting bigger. We had Ekk and Elsa Schmidt, who we considered family now, and Twyla, a fairy who was tasked with protecting Juniper and Valerie Gooden.

I sat up and stared out the front window at our overgrown yard. The sun shone, cars trundled down the street, and a skateboarder rolled by on our cracked sidewalk. Violence was rare in Merryville, and I wondered what the world was coming to. It seemed to me we didn't need to fly across the world to fight evil. It was already here. Any thought about our upcoming mission halfway across the world caused me stress.

Search for the Summer Stone

Five weeks ago, a piece of an ancient magical stone, long forgotten in the storeroom of Taggart's Emporium, got "switched on." The effect on my hometown was enormous and frightening. This was how we got to know Ralph and Aurora Brown better. A *Lupus Imperium* agent, Gary Smithers, activated the stone, and it would have killed everyone if Aurora and the elves hadn't been able to stop it. Merryville's temperature dropped to freezing, and ice and snow covered our whole town. I shook my head; it seemed like a dream.

The "Winter Stone," as we call it, was safely tucked away in a vault at the Hercynian Garden. We needed to get the Summer Stone in there, too, and away from the bad guys. Gary Smithers was also tucked away, in a jail cell somewhere, and good riddance. Now, Mitzi's dad, Ehrenhardt, had prioritized rounding up other remnants of the circle of stones. Intelligence placed the stone in Tanzania.

Our cat, Brutus, jumped on the couch, and I petted him. There was no hurry to get the Summer Stone, right? If all these stones had been hidden all these years, what was the big rush?

My personal need to delay was due to a trivial matter of me first learning to control my apparent ability to call "the ravens," who were a fickle bunch of birds. They used to be allied with *Lupus Imperium* in the past but now have come to our side. They switched sides because Ehren's Hercynian Garden ideals held the best chance for their continued freedom, which was self-serving. Astonishingly, they chose me to be their point of contact and were valuable to our cause because of all their eyes in the sky.

This was my struggle: how to work with these ravens. I wondered why me. My magic seemed like the least of those around me. It would have made more sense for any unique magical role to be bestowed upon my wife, who, as a half-griffin, could fly. However, her flight ability wasn't entirely in control, just like my alleged ability to call the ravens. In an attempt to be some type of raven master, I had spent weeks in the Hercynian Garden in a failed training. So far, this TV remote in my hand was about the only thing I could control at will.

Mitzi walked in. "I was on the phone with Val. What happened?" Val was the wife of Juniper Gooden and our best friends. Mitzi stood at the end of the couch and looked at me.

"There are Nazis in the park."

"*Our* park? *Merryville* Park?" She looked incredulous.

"Well, perhaps not actual Nazis but a group that calls themselves 'Native California Patriots.'"

"They have the nerve to call themselves Native? What does that even mean?" She flipped her beads over her shoulder.

Her eyes were wide, nostrils flared. Even so, she was always beautiful to me. Her offense at right-wingers calling themselves native was not because my wife was Native American. The beads were just her thing. We went on a cruise years ago to Roatan (one of the perks of being married to a travel agent), and the locals beaded two thin braids of hair on either side of her face. She liked it and has kept up those beads all the years since, decorating them with color and unique beads for specific occasions. She was offended on behalf of Val, who was born on the Ute Reservation in Colorado and was Native American. Mitzi's most beautiful quality was her compassionate heart. She sat next to me on the couch. "We gonna talk about it?"

"What?" Uh oh. "How's Val?" I tried to deflect what I knew she was going to bring up.

"She's fine. I just wonder if we'll get to the Ute exhibit before it closes." Mitzi looked at my nest on the couch. "You look like you're here for the day."

"I was about to get up and shower." We both knew I was lying. I'd avoided anything that moved us closer to our mission.

"Bullshit." Mitzi, lithe, wearing shorts and a polo shirt, breathed heavily through her nose and ran her fingers through her short, sticky-uppy hair. "Panda, it's been weeks since you returned from training in the Garden." Her expression was severe. "I just downloaded our tickets to Tanzania. We leave two weeks from today."

The stress I'd been trying to avoid landed on me like a weighted blanket. "Oh." I hadn't done much to prepare. Calling the ravens was something I had no idea how to do, but it was critical to the success of our new mission in Africa, or wherever we were, as long as the threat from *Lupus Imperium* existed.

"Panda, no matter how much you want to, you can't forget what we now know." The sun still shone into the living room, but everything changed.

"Hortense was marching with those guys in the park," I said. "There was a fistfight, and some coffeehouse people were involved."

"I'm not surprised. Haven't you noticed? The whole world is roiling with hatred." She would not be deterred. "And you and I have been offered an opportunity to do something about it."

I hadn't put these *our world* things in the context of the larger fight we were engaged in. A light bulb came on. "You think this has something to do with *Lupus Imperium?*"

"I talked a lot with Alexandra Stephanovsky while you were training. *Lupus Imperium* is worldwide, and of course I do." She made a biting motion with her hand. "They feed on everyone fighting each other. There's a new guy on the council named Alaric in charge of technology. He says *Lupus Imperium* is all over social media." She warmed to her subject. "Deep fakes, misinformation—"

"Alexandra should never have retired. She was the best defense attorney." I had personal history with her since I'd been framed and arrested for arson. Alexandra and her friend Donna Dunkin cleared my name.

"Think about it. That was a local thing, too, but *Lupus Imperium* was behind it. Alex's now using her talents to do great work for my father in the Garden." Mitzi pointed at the TV remote. "Just like we have a chance to do if we get off our butts."

"You should run for office. Or preach," I said and started to get up. "I'm motivated."

"Okay. So?"

"I, ah. I hate your father telling me what to do." I sometimes wished Mitzi was an orphan; her mother was a pill too.

"So we let the world fall to shit because you're pissed at my dad?" That pierced my excuse for trying to delay.

"Of course not." The blanket fell to the floor. "But summer's over," I said weakly. "How can we find the Summer Stone?" my last argument for delay, "If it's not summer?" It sounded stupid even to me.

"Panda, we're going to Tanzania, on the African continent. It must be before *their* summer, which starts this December. It's too dangerous to go after the hottest season starts. No one knows what it would be like if the Summer Stone switched on." We stared at each other as her words sunk in. "We need to go in two weeks, which means—"

"Which means I need to get off the stick and figure out how to do something I have no clue how to do." Instant grumpiness. Even Brutus jumped to the floor with annoyance. She was right. I shook my head. "Honestly, I don't even know how or where to start. Mitz, my Garden training was a disaster. I've lit candles, prayed about it, and talked to Ekk and Elsa, but the ravens don't respond. I'm a failure at this."

Mitzi, used to my mood swings, sat down and put her arm around me. "I've been talking to Valerie, and we've come up with an idea about how to help. I told her we might come to the museum and talk to her and Juniper, and see that Ute Native American exhibit, okay?"

I looked at her, grateful for the kindness, and knew my time of procrastination was over. I stood and stretched as I nodded. "I guess it's time to take off my pajamas." My pj's with a goofy print suddenly felt juvenile. I had to rise to the occasion, for Mitzi if nothing else.

***

Merryville Museum

I put on my "Light it up!" t-shirt, a museum promotional item from an old installation called Floodlight. With a nod to presentability, I brushed my short hair and looked in the mirror. For better or worse, the authentic me stared back, a forty-something ChapStick lesbian. Since we were going to the museum, I knew our friend Juniper would get a kick out of the t-shirt. The Floodlight exhibit from last March created a crazy amount of controversy about feral cats and people without homes in Merryville, spurring action from our city council.

Juniper loved her job as a curator at the museum and never missed a chance to use her position to raise consciousness. My choice of outfit made Mitzi smile when I came downstairs.

"Perfect."

I relaxed. Sometimes, I got a lecture on wearing jeans, t-shirts, and flip-flops all the time. What could I say? I was a California native. "Outside is gorgeous. Let's take your convertible."

She opened her hand and dangled the Miata keys. "Great minds."

Even in late November, it was flip-flop weather. We both loved that. Mitzi was from northern California and always said she moved south for the warmer weather. If the truth be known, it was also because it put her four hundred miles away from her mother, whom neither of us trusted. As for me, I was born at Merryville General Hospital and just never left the town. *Why leave when I've already found the perfect place?* People's attitudes about gay couples in Southern California were mainly chill, and we had the beach a few miles away.

Mitzi drove us to the museum, the little car's engine rumbling like a race car. On the way down Main Street, trucks with American flags were everywhere, and we heard much honking. "Wow. This is crazy." Mitzi was taking in what I had seen on TV.

Soon, we arrived at the Merryville Museum. Banners across the museum parking lot entrance announced "This Land is Not Your Land" with a border of stylized feathers around it in green. We both laughed. Did I mention Juniper liked stirring things up? Nice.

The parking lot wasn't exactly packed, probably due to the exhibit nearing the end of its run.

"I feel a tad guilty because we haven't seen the exhibit yet," I said, finger-combing my hair. I had this cow lick that was annoying.

"Speak for yourself," Mitzi said, and gave me the side eye. She then parked the car into a slot near the entrance. I let that comment go; my wife is a free spirit and didn't like having her activities monitored.

"Well, okay," I said with a smile.

A turn-of-the-century Craftsman building, formerly someone's mansion, and two exhibit halls built sometime in the 1960s made up Merryville Museum. Between the Craftsman and the halls was a lovely green space that overlooked the bluff. With the ocean view, locals loved to rent the space for weddings and fundraisers, and Juniper used it for special art exhibits. Flashback. This was the spot where the four of us, Juniper, Valerie, Mitzi, and me, with help from our elven friends, had opened a "dog sun" portal between Merryville and the Hercynian Garden. Now it was an empty, newly mown lawn, and the magical dog sun memory felt like something I'd seen in a movie.

"Ready?" she asked. "We have lunch reservations."

Uh oh. They discussed lunch without me. Curious, I followed her to the table where Juniper and Valerie were already seated in Origins, the museum's meatless café.

Juniper, the more outgoing of our two friends, was chatting with someone standing near the table. They moved on, and she beamed her smile at us. "Yay! Hi Mitzi, hi Panda!" Valerie was seated quietly, and her only movement was her hand stirring what looked like tea. She lifted the other and gave us a wave. I wondered what it must be like for her to be married to such a social creature. Juniper somewhat overshadowed her.

"Come on, come on, sit down! So glad we could do this." In full extravert mode, Juniper adjusted her billowy blouse to better display a bright brass medallion shaped like a stylized sun, with a piece of stone in the middle. "Panda, isn't this pretty? It's one of the Ute pieces."

"It's stunning," I offered. Juniper looked pleased.

Mitzi slid into the booth. "Hi, kids." I silently waved with one hand.

"Darling." Juniper dramatically surveyed us. "Your wife looks like she's going to a dentist appointment." Juniper engulfed me in a seated hug; her perfume was overwhelming. Addressing Mitzi, she asked, "What did you tell her?"

I pulled out a chair and sat. "Am I being ambushed?"

The hostess came by and handed Mitzi and me menus.

"Do you want one of these?" I offered a menu to our friends.

"Keep up." Juniper turned her phone around. "QR Code."

"Oh, of course." Her boisterous energy was even more than usual, and I turned to her wife. "You're so quiet, Val." I tried to get her to look at me directly.

"I'm not good at beating around a bush." Valerie squared her cup on the napkin. Mitzi feigned intense interest in the menu, and Juniper's smile widened. It was apparently killing her to stay quiet.

"We've got the answer," Juniper blurted.

"The answer to what? What?" I looked at Valerie, who looked guilty.

Valerie dropped her spoon, which clattered on the white tabletop. "Juniper, this is not how we were going to do this."

"Do what?" My voice got louder, and I received glances from a nearby table.

Mitzi put her menu down gently. "Hear her out."

Valerie sighed and put her hand on mine. "What our adorable spouses are trying to do, Panda, is help you figure out your Raven magic. Or rather, how my Ute people are going to help you."

We all stopped talking momentarily while the server brought four glasses of water. "What will you be having today?" Like the others working at Origins, the server almost looked like a work of art herself. The multi-colored Origins uniform was wild. She was young and wore a nose ring.

I folded my arms. "Sounds like I'll have whatever they want me to have."

Juniper pulled a face and said to the server, "Please bring us some of those marvelous blue corn onion rings. We, ah, need a minute."

As the young woman retreated, Valerie said, "Dine, Juniper, dine."

"What does dine mean? Is it Ute?" Mitzi loved learning about other cultures.

"Dine is Navajo, and the word means 'the people.' They live at the foot of Ute Mountain in Colorado and have the best blue corn meal in the world."

"And Origins uses this rare corn meal for onion rings?" I raised my eyebrows.

Juniper jumped in. "Panda, we need to teach people about other cultures, and using it for onion rings makes blue meal…" Her hands twisted as if she could pull the word from the air.

"Relatable?" Mitzi offered.

"That works!" Juniper changed the subject. "Did you hear about the Native Patriot idiots at the park?"

"Native California Patriots," I corrected. "I saw them on the television, and we just drove by the park."

"It was mostly over." Mitzi said.

"Don't change the subject, we're talking about onion rings and Doritos," Val said. "You white people do that whenever you feel uncomfortable." Her face broke out in a smile, and I realized she was making a joke.

She went on. "It's got to be about that statue thing. I get that people view Virginia Merry differently now." She shook her head, and her blue-black hair reflected the naked overhead bulb. "I can't believe they're calling themselves Native."

"At least they only claim Native California," I said, trying to be helpful.

She went on. "Anyway, what Juniper meant by *we have the answer* is we have an *idea* that might help you, Panda."

"We're not talking about Doritos anymore?" I asked to be sure.

"Correct. I've talked to the tribal council at our reservation, and you have an official invitation to stay with us for a bit and learn raven magic."

My gut clenched and my face turned red. "With all due respect, the Hercynian Garden already gave it their best shot. I think it'll just happen, but over time." I addressed Mitzi. "I see what you're trying to do here and love you for it, but—"

"Sweetheart, there's no more time." Mitzi got that look she gets when I'm irritating her.

"Has something else happened?" Juniper leaned in and whispered.

The server came back and took our entrée orders. We all paused the conversation. After she left, Mitzi said, "We're leaving in two weeks. I got the tickets ordered today."

"Wow! That's not much time. Panda, what are you doing this weekend?"

"Nothing," My helpful wife offered.

I was speechless. *Were they serious?*

"Remember how my Native American traditions helped Elsa with your healing, Panda? We thought you would be open to this. Our tribe has a history with ravens."

A tear rolled down my cheek, and I wiped it away. My foot tapped, and I looked out the window. "You guys, I don't think anything will help."

Chapter Two

Ute Reservation, Colorado

Valerie's mother, Etsi, lived in a cozy three-bedroom, two-bath adobe house on the reservation. Valerie and I flew to Colorado two days after our lunch at the museum, and brought Twyla, her guardian fairy, with us. Ready or not, it was time to learn how to call upon my ancestors and, hopefully, the ravens. I sat on a leather chair in Etsi's living room with Ahanu, the elder who was to be my trainer. We had barely been introduced and things were already tense. Valerie, Etsi, and Ahanu stared at me, waiting for me to answer a provocative question about my training in the Hercynian Garden. Twyla was curled up in a blanket in the corner with strict orders not to interfere. Faries, in general, and Twyla, in particular, were chatty creatures. My new trainer had been very firm with her in a way that reminded me of Mitzi's father, Ehren. After introductions and a summary from me about my failed training in the Hercynian Garden, Ahanu asked me, without the usual polite niceties, "Why did you let a raven kick your ass?"

"What?" I sputtered. "That's not fair. Raven people are rude." I was tired and sounded whiny. I didn't know this guy and was only here because Mitzi, Valerie, and Juniper had ganged up on me.

"That raven called you dummy." Ahanu had an inscrutable face. He was in his seventies, with gray streaked through his black braids. His features were Native American, but he wore a plaid Pendleton shirt with a bolo tie of a silver eagle, a mixture of indigenous and Western culture.

"She did, but you weren't there." I stared back at him and lifted both arms in explanation. "You have to understand that this was an infrequent meeting between us free creatures and the ravens." I looked at Valerie for help, but since she stayed silent, I continued. "Ahanu, I felt like I was in a state department or meeting representing our side between two nations."

"Are you a dummy?" His dark brown eyes never left my face. He wasn't going to let me off the hook.

Night had fallen, and wind buffeted the house in the pause. "It was a short meeting and too important to make it personal. I'm here now because the raven said I had to call on my ancestors if I wanted their help." He had me on my back foot.

The window was closed against the extreme cold of the high desert night air, and a fire crackled in the grate.

"So you said what in response to her, exactly?" His voice was even.

"Ahanu, I don't know how to speak to a raven. My guardian, a guy named Ekk, warned me they were rude and said to, basically, ignore that."

He didn't blink. "Basically." Ahanu became super still, in a way Valerie did occasionally.

He had me squirming. "I don't know if the raven used those exact words, but that's not the point. Ravens are rude. I couldn't do much. She said other stuff. Why are you stuck on this?" My arms were extended again, palms up in a shrug.

"Uh-huh." His eyes were intense and bore into me. "You ever seen a kid be bullied and just take it?" The fire crackled.

Etsi looked at Ahanu and finally offered, "Panda, her wife, and my daughter have been dragged into this fight. They didn't ask for it."

He said to her, "Doesn't matter. How will she command the ravens if they don't respect her?" The elder shifted in his chair and rubbed his hands together. I noticed they had calluses. This spoke of hard work. "I can't work with a coward." He stood to leave.

"Wait!" I said, and stood also, almost knocking over the heavy chair and hitting my ankle. "Ow. I'm not a coward."

He looked at me some more. "Then tell me why you don't stand up for yourself. And why do you resist me? You sit there and appear calm, but you don't believe I can help you."

He had nailed it. My doubt was confirmed. It was easier to let others take charge. Valerie, Etsi, and even Twyla stared at me, awaiting a response. It was truth time.

"So far, I've heard…that this *Lupus Imperium* is a Roman thing from Europe and that the headquarters for the opposition…us, I guess…is in the Black Forest in Germany."

"So?"

Now, my words rushed out. "I just don't see how a Ute Indian in Colorado will know much about that."

Outside, a wolf howled. We all stopped and listened.

He mimicked me. "How can a coward from California do anything about *Lupus Imperium*? Same dumb observation. Hear that wolf? That's reality. They can kill." He raised his arms, made talons with his fingers, and took a dramatic bite. "Wake up, California girl, this ain't a game."

"The wolf you feed," Valerie said quietly. "It's real, Panda. *Lupus Imperium* means wolf authority. I grew up without wolves but learned stories about them. They are very dangerous."

"Then why does this culture know so much about them if they weren't here? What does this have to do with ravens or our enemy?" I heard the howl again that sounded right in Etsi's yard. I noticed Twyla half-rise from her nest, blanket around her face like a hood, trying to look out the window.

"All the wolves were gone from Colorado by the 1940s. Your government eradicated them because they killed livestock," Ahanu said.

"Well, that sure sounds like a real wolf outside," Twyla said from the corner.

Ahanu unexpectedly laughed. "It is. What we found is that bad wolves killed our livestock, but killing *all* the wolves put nature out of balance. We found we needed the wolf, and your government has helped to reintroduce them to our land."

My head hurt trying to follow. "Why?"

"Yeah, why?" Twyla said. "I thought wolves were bad in this story, but they're like the ravens. Sometimes they do bad and sometimes good." Twyla couldn't help herself from speaking.

"That's right, little girl. We must be careful when we label things good or evil and not forget to live in the now, in balance with nature."

I thought this conversation had drifted too far from the task. "I thought we were here for me to learn to call my ancestors."

"That was your first lesson, Panda. Balance. Your goal is not to kill all the evil, it's to help restore balance." Ahanu finally leaned back in his chair after making this point. "You aren't all-powerful. You just need to play your part."

I sat again and tried to follow his logic. "Wait, what? *Lupus Imperium* needs to go." I thought we were all on the same page on that point.

He laughed again. "If you were successful at killing everyone in *Lupus Imperium* you consider evil, it would be a disaster." His brow furrowed, and he reminded me of every teacher I'd ever had who tried to bring home an important point. "It would also change you."

Etsi and Valerie nodded like this was obvious. Twyla nervously gazed out the window, still distracted by the wolf.

My body sagged. "I'm confused."

Ahanu said, "That's obvious."

This made me mad. "Speaking of rude," I challenged Ahanu. "By the way, I'm glad you know something about wolves. How about European ravens?"

Etsi cackled, and I noticed she was missing a tooth in the back. "Do you think the birds care about fences?" she said. "You came to find out about how to call your ancestors. You need to let go of the construct of time and boundary."

"Okay." I surrendered.

Etsi and Ahanu shared some kind of signal with their eyes. She left and went into her kitchen.

The elder cocked his head, as if listening to something we couldn't hear. "You three settle in." He stretched. "Etsi's going to bring us some hot chocolate. Valerie, you and Panda move your chairs closer. Little girl in the corner, you don't need to worry. That wolf out there's not going to get you. It's story time."

***

Ekk and Elsa Return

The Los Angeles airport, LAX, was only five-point-four square miles. Though it was expanded in the 1980s, it would never be big enough for the job it has to do. Even though it wasn't even in the world's top ten airports for size, the number of travelers made it one of the busiest. All Mitzi knew, by the number of cars, was that driving here was not her favorite thing to do. Getting in and out of LAX was always challenging.

Stop and go. Stop and go. Cars and buses vied for a place on the curb to disgorge or pick up passengers. Mitzi felt like a taxi driver. This was her second trip in two days through lanes choked with cars. The day before, she'd dropped off Panda, Valerie, and Twyla, who traveled to the Colorado reservation for Panda's raven training. Mitzi was also a little nervous about driving Panda's Land Rover that felt like a bus next to her two-seater Miata. She pulled into the cell phone lot and waited for Ekk or Elsa to call and say they were on the curb. As she sat in the sea of cars, it gave her a little time to think.

This was the first time she had been without guardians for a while. Did this mean the threat from *Lupus Imperium* had lessened here in Merryville? Did her dad think she was now an old pro, able to defend herself after having tangled with the enemy a couple of times? He had a history of not telling her everything, and she wondered if he had posted someone else to watch while the Schmidts were away. She looked around at all the cars and didn't see anyone who looked magical, not that a secret guardian would want to be seen. It may be that there were not enough guardians to go around.

Ali Badawi was a magical human who was still in Merryville, but he was running Ralph and Aurora Brown's store where the Winter Stone had been found. The six-foot-four Egyptian was a force to be reckoned with, and she wondered if he would be her brother-in-law someday. Ali and Panda's sister, Puddle, were becoming quite close. Ekk and Elsa were returning after escorting the Browns to the Hercynian Garden for their safety. They were old, and to make that worse Aurora was dealing with both human dementia and a curse, thanks to Gary Smithers. The Garden Healers would work to reverse the spell.

The phone rang. "Fowler's Taxi service." Mitzi was already smiling.

"Cute. Mitzi, we have our bags and are on the curb, ready to go home."

In the background, she heard Elsa say, "Tell her what number we are. It's B5."

"We're at—"

"Gotcha. Column B5. I'm pulling out now. Everything okay?" Even though cell phones were now supposedly secure, Mitzi didn't like to be too specific on the phone. The enemy was crafty and had previously monitored their calls.

"Mission accomplished," Ekk said in a strange, low voice. She wasn't as good as Panda at guessing which movie or character he was playing, but she tried.

"Tom Cruise?"

"*Rambo*, Mitzi, *Rambo*." Honking ahead grabbed her attention.

"Okay, Rambo, I'll be there in a few minutes." Mitzi carefully navigated the stop-start traffic and felt relief roll through her body. She had missed Ekk and Elsa.

***

After ten minutes of bobbing and weaving through traffic from the cell lot, a bus moved, opening a space directly in front of column B5. She whipped in, cutting off a BMW, expecting to find her friends waiting. Except they weren't.

She looked around frantically, and an officer walked toward her car. *Damn*, she thought, as an overhead speaker announced, "The white curb is for loading and unloading only." Where were they?

Instead of waving her on, the officer raised her hand and motioned Mitzi closer to her. When she was at the curb, the woman, who looked familiar, opened the passenger door and hopped in. Recognition finally kicked in.

"Lulu?"

Lulu scanned the area around the car and turned her face to Mitzi. "Quick. Pull out, and I'll explain."

"But I'm here to pick up—"

Lulu cut her off urgently, as her radio crackled.

"Pull out. Look for parking for Terminal Four. Go!"

"Is this a carjacking?"

"No. Trust me, now go!"

While Mitzi looked in her mirrors to see if merging was safe, she noticed a man and woman pushing others out of the way to get to her car. The two were dressed like regular tourists but were leading a parade of shouting young men in soccer shirts. Mitzi was an expert on what tourists looked and acted like, and the couple's behavior was wrong. The woman met her eyes, pointed at her, and yelled something to her partner. Mitzi floored it, narrowly missing a Wally Park bus.

"What's happening?" Her knuckles on the steering wheel were white.

"There'll be time for that later. Right now, do as I say. I need to get you and your little friends somewhere not here."

"I thought you were a Merryville police officer?" Mitzi glanced at the guard wearing a TSA uniform while Lulu looked back at the column area they'd left.

"Still am, sort of. Right now, I'm assigned to the airport."

"But—"

"Later. Look out!" Lulu pointed ahead. The traffic was crazy.

Mitzi stomped hard on the brake and skidded to a stop two inches from the car in front of her.

"The people after those little people you hang around with hijacked a car. See that silver Toyota?" She turned around again. "They're chasing us!"

"Who are they?" Mitzi asked, but Lulu ignored her. She whipped her radio out. "Those two hostiles are on the move. Roll a car."

"Copy that, already on it," came an unidentified voice on the radio.

Mitzi got to the airport return lane, took it a little too fast, and bumped her back tire against the curb. "Panda will kill me if I mess up her car."

"I don't know about that, but, uh, those people back there?" Lulu exhaled. "They might kill you, no matter what you drive. Turn in here."

"But—"Mitzi barely had time to turn.

Lulu pointed at a narrow ramp emphatically and made a comically exasperated face. "*Now.*"

Mitzi made an almost impossible ninety-degree turn into a nearby parking garage, her tires clipping the curb due to her speed and odd angle. The silver Toyota driver was surprised and didn't turn in time. Mitzi caught a glimpse of the woman's angry face as the man driving slamming against another car while trying to get over. They now heard sirens. Mitzi smashed hard on her brakes when she saw Ekk and Elsa huddled under the overpass, each holding onto a bag. She needed no further instructions. She pulled over, and Lulu jumped out to chuck luggage into the car while the elves scrambled to get in. Elsa had trouble with the step, so Lulu tossed her in too. Ekk said, "Thanks, Lulu. Mitzi, want me to drive?"

"It'll take too long to set up your assistive devices." Mitzi looked at Lulu. "I guess we better get going to the house." She adjusted the rearview mirror and asked, "Everybody buckled up?"

Elsa was extraordinarily quiet. In the mirror, Mitzi saw Ekk with his arm around Elsa, who had what would be a good-sized shiner. "Oh, Elsa!"

Lulu's radio squawked. She spoke quietly into it and clipped it back on her belt with a frustrated snap. "They got away."

***

Ute Reservation, Colorado

It was 3:30 a.m., and I lay on one of the twin beds in Etsi's guest room. A full moon still shone through the window and lit the room, one of the reasons I couldn't sleep. The other reason was that Ahanu was picking me up at 4:00 a.m. for "raven training."

With no reason to stay in bed, I got up and dressed warmly. Thankfully, the clothing I packed for Germany was perfect for this weather. Etsi's house was well-insulated and exceptionally energy efficient. Even so, my hands and feet were cold. I walked down the tiled hall into the kitchen with each hand under the opposite armpit. I was surprised to see Etsi was awake and sitting at the table. "Coffee's ready," she said.

Gratitude rushed to my heart. "Thank you."

After pouring a cup, I sat with her in the gray light and enjoyed the warmth of the central heating, which had finally kicked on.

She was a dignified woman and carried herself with pride. I wondered what she saw when she looked at me. Like Valerie, she would have been a good poker player. Thankfully, she told me herself.

"I'm glad my Vava has you for a friend. I've heard about you and Mitzi for years and how you've supported each other."

I smiled at her. "We've had our share of adventures for sure. She and Juniper are our closest friends. I'm glad to finally see where she was raised. This place is a huge part of who she is."

"I don't think it's chance that you met. Tell me, how is she involved in this magic? I see you have a fairy friend. She's a fairy, right?" Etsi sipped her coffee. Her eyes were merry like Juniper's got sometimes around magic.

"Yes, I'm a fairy," Twyla spoke from the kitchen door. Neither of us had heard her coming.

"You might as well join us." Etsi patted the chair next to her.

"Don't give her any coffee." I laughed, remembering she levitated when caffeinated.

Twyla got a glass of water and joined us. "Yes, caffeine is a bit too much for my system."

"So you asked how Valerie was involved with what's happening. A year or so ago, back in Merryville, I think I saw her call on her ancestors. We did a ritual at the Merryville Museum, and a portal opened—"

"Panda," Twyla said, interrupting her. "I don't think you should say everything. Just tell her about Valerie."

"Oh, well, I saw your daughter kind of morph into what I believe is a historical Indigenous person in full Native American garb."

Her mom was still. "It's okay to say Indian. What did she look like?"

I sipped my coffee and tried to recall. "A lot was going on. I could hear drumming," I looked at Twyla, "and other things. I only glimpsed her, but it was like a hologram of a woman with feathers and a fierce face overlaying hers. She also gave off energy."

Etsi pointed at me. "That's what you're going to learn to do."

"Rise and shine, student," Ahanu called from the front porch. I heard the screen door open. "Panda Fowler, your school bus is here."

"Do you want coffee?" Etsi called to him, and again, I wondered about their relationship.

"No. Time to go." Mr. Personality.

Twyla was excited. "Can I come? I should be protecting you."

Ahanu had entered the kitchen and was about to say something when Etsi cut him off and addressed Twyla.

"Stay here and help me milk our cow and get some eggs for breakfast," Etsi said. Her house was truly farm-to-table. "I could use the help."

Twyla looked at me, torn. "Are you okay with that?"

I was relieved. "Yep. This is my journey, Twyla. Make sure Val's mom stays safe." I looked at the analog clock on the wall. "I guess it's time to go." I drained my cup and walked through the living room past the fireplace, where embers from the night before still glowed through the ash. Ahanu was out front again, and the screen door slammed loudly. Etsi, as if reading my mind, said, "His bark is worse than his bite."

Valerie came out from the other bedroom, dressed in a soft, sand-colored leather outfit I'd never seen her wear, and said, "Ready? It's going to be intense."

***

We found Ahanu waiting for us. He held the reins of three horses. He wore a thick plaid Pendleton coat and cowboy hat. I was grateful for my down jacket in the high desert cold and wished I had thought to wear a hat. *Which one of these majestic animals is going to be mine?* None of the three looked particularly friendly as they stamped the red dirt and breathed out clouds of air into the pre-dawn hour. Valerie took one of the reins attached to a sleek black horse and waited. Ahanu handed me another rein attached to a giant, dark brown horse. In an age-defying movement, he grabbed the pommel of his horse's saddle and mounted with ease.

"Where are we going?" I asked my friend, trying to get a boot in the stirrup, and Valerie whispered back, "Tava, the Sun Mountain. Are you okay?"

"Sure," I said, "I got this." Not sure at all. She stayed on the ground and watched me.

"You're riding Major," she said. "She's a solid horse, just follow."

I knew my new trainer was watching and grabbed the horn of my horse's saddle with my left hand, copying Ahanu, put my left boot firmly in the stirrup, and tried to swing my right leg up over the saddle and almost fell on my ass.

Ahanu shook his head and started off. Valerie patted her horse's butt and came to my rescue. I was soon properly seated after Val gave my butt a push on my next try.

"Thanks." I didn't have high hopes for the day.

She mounted her horse gracefully and did that click-click thing with her mouth, falling in line behind my trainer.

I had no experience with horses other than some vacation rentals when our aunt and uncle took us to a ranch in Victorville. Those were good memories, but it had been decades since I rode.

My horse proved to be solid, as promised. Ahanu was well ahead, and Valerie and I had a chance to talk.

"This is Silky," Valerie said. She had her hair pulled back in a ponytail and looked at home atop the shiny black beauty. She pulled a piece of straw out of Silky's mane, and the animal shook her head as if it tickled. "Messy girl."

I looked down at my horse's mane and saw nothing in Major's hair. She seemed muted next to Valerie's ride, and that was fine. She seemed content to plod along behind Silky. I felt comfortable enough to keep one hand on the saddle's horn and use the other to hold the reins. The wind was biting as we climbed the path leading up Tava Mountain.

It was still dark. Our horses followed the narrow trail left then right but always up. We could have talked more, but the purpose of our journey made me quiet. Finally, we reached a place not at the top of the mountain but close enough. There was a flat space with stones arranged in a pattern, somewhat like a labyrinth.

"About time." Ahanu tied his horse to a scraggly bush, moved to me, and held out a muscled arm to help me down. Valerie gracefully dismounted and secured both Silky and Major.

"Sit there. Ravens know this place."

I sat on the cold ground, grateful to be off the horse and out of the wind. My nose ran, and I wiped it on a sleeve. My butt hurt.

Valerie sat cross-legged to the side in what we used to call Indian style. This random thought brought others about her culture unbidden. Tava—the mountain of Valerie's tribe—had once been named Pike's Peak, after some white soldier who'd never even made it to the top. Indian style, what did that even mean? I grew up watching westerns, and Indians were usually portrayed as savages. These thoughts humbled me. I stopped feeling like Ahanu was picking on me and was grateful he wanted to help me at all.

***

The Hercynian Garden

Raph and Aurora Brown had lived in Merryville since the 1980s. For decades they ran Taggart's Emporium together, until Ralph had to run it alone, due to his wife's worsening dementia. He nearly closed the business, but Ali Badawi—a free creature, and Puddle—Panda's sister, took over the day-to-day operations. Ralph was hopeful Aurora would get better in the Garden, where they now lived while Woda and Dr. Mot worked to undo the magical damage inflicted on Aurora by Gary Smithers. Dr. Mot also planned to uncover any critical information Aurora's muddled brain might have about the location of other stones, but only under the supervision of Ralph and Ehren, who believed Smithers must have had a reason for making Aurora's dementia worse.

While Dr. Mot completed his tests, Ralph took some time to relax in the Garden, which had nine provinces, full of rivers, fields, and trees. Ralph felt as free as he had while a boy in Alabama, sitting on a sunny rock with his hook in the water. Today, Shrumm, Ehren's "First Person," joined him.

"Thank you for arranging this." Ralph gestured to the broad stream with his free left hand; he held his reel loosely with his right.

"You don't need to thank me. This is a rare chance to goof off." Shrumm wasn't even pretending to fish, so he leaned back, arms under his head with his eyes closed, basking in the sun.

"Uh, Pumpkin, I mean Popk—"

"Shhhhhh! Don't say it!" Shrumm's left eye opened, and Ralph saw his body tense.

He stopped himself from saying the full name. "Oh, sorry, Shrumm, just want you to know I appreciate all you and your people have done."

He remembered his orientation to the Garden. Ehren said Shrumm's first name was Popkin, but no one called him that unless something was wrong. It was one of many safety rules in the Garden, and using it would trigger a response from security. Shrumm closed his eyes again, and Ralph followed the path of a couple of birds that flew overhead.

Ralph was curious. "So none of this is real?"

At this, Shrumm sat up and held his knees to his chest. There was a dash of black in his white hair, a holdout to aging, but his face didn't look old. Ralph had been told that Shrumm had been the first "forever" person, but this wasn't California, and the rules of aging were different. He sported a pure white Fu Manchu beard but was as limber as a young calf.

The elf's eyes focused on something far away as he mused, "What is real, Ralph?" A light breeze ruffled Shrumm's hair, which reminded Ralph of cotton candy. "You feel the warmth of the sun on your skin, right? Feel this breeze? That's real enough."

Ralph's line went taut, and his face broke out in a delighted expression. "Ha!" Real or not, Ralph's reel bent with the weight of a fish on the line, and the conversation was soon forgotten.

Chapter Three

Meanwhile, Garden experts, both scientific and medical, were studying Ralph's wife Aurora in the infirmary. It was no secret that they were racing against time to find the next powerful stone, rumored to be the Summer Stone. Aurora had a connection to the matter because an aunt had sent what turned out to be a piece of the Winter Stone to her long ago. They were studying the Winter Stone fragment, but so far, they had no answers. Raven intelligence had reported the Stone was somewhere in Tanzania, but they were having trouble pinning down the location. Alaric, the chief technology expert for the Garden, was focused on using machine-aided memory retrieval, which was called transcranial magnetic treatment, on Aurora.

Aurora was at the center of everything. Alaric, trained at MIT, was called upon to see if modern tools could help her remember anything helpful. A rising star, Alaric was invited to join Ehren's council after solving cell and satellite phones security problems for the Garden. He even created a rudimentary social media platform that was very popular among the provinces. Could he improve Aurora's memory and help Ehren's council find the other stone fragments? Not everyone was thrilled about young Alaric's promotion to his position, but so far, magic hadn't given any clues about the Winter Stone. The Director of Magic, Woda, felt uneasy and went to the Hercynian Garden Hospital, where Aurora received some preliminary tests to see if she was strong enough to have her memories probed. She didn't like what she saw or felt when entering the chamber. Alaric's contraption made of metal was right next to a chair in which Aurora sat, its lights blinking. *Was he using his machine on her now?* The elderly woman wore a cap full of electrodes and wires attached to the big metal thing. Lights flickered on and off, but the toggle switches controlling the electrodes were in the off position.

Woda was tall and towered over the woman seated there when Alaric walked in.

"Woda," he said by way of greeting.

"Alaric, what are you doing here?"

"*We're* doing our job. Who are you to question me? Go back to magic."

"Who's this we?" Woda was prone to go into attack mode quickly, earning her a reputation for her sharp tongue. The "go back to magic" set her off. "You may be on Ehren's council, but medical is not your purview." She pointed at a wooden door with frosted glass. The name of Dr. Harold Mot was etched upon it. "Dr. Mot is medical. You're technological. We *all* need to swim in our lanes." Woda took up much space between her size and preferred floor-length purple robes. Her hem brushed against the cabinets. Although she was physically quite intimidating, the younger elf didn't give an inch.

Likewise in new purple robes, Alaric made a pained expression as he leaned back on a stainless-steel table and folded his arms. "My lane?" he snorted. "My lane is anything that affects the kingdom, and I oversee technology now that we can use it. Dr. Mot and I are working hand in hand. The sciences overlap." He emphasized the word science. He had argued at the council that the Garden needed to use what the world had to offer so as not to be left behind by only arcane magic.

Dr. Mot returned to the treatment room from his study and seemed surprised at the new arrival. "Woda," he acknowledged. "What's going on?"

Alaric looked relieved at the doctor's appearance. "As I was about to say to Woda, I was invited. And by the way, I was pre-med before switching to tech. Woda just asked about our use of TMT." His smile showed amusement.

Dr. Mot was part troll and had a human torso paired with oversized arms that seemed destined for a different body. He always combed his hair neatly atop a head about half again as large as one with pure human DNA. Around the hospital, he was often seen in a white coat that fit his body but with the sleeves removed. One hairy hand put his clipboard under his left armpit. "Oh?" He looked questioningly at Woda. "You know about such things, do you?" His facial expression said otherwise.

Woda, put on the spot, said, "I've heard about this, of course, transcranial magnetic treatment. I've also heard that it can damage the brain. We discussed going slowly at the council. Isn't this a bit aggressive? We have other methods that are not so hard on the body."

"Like magic?" Alaric was dismissive. "Feeling a bit obsolete?"

Dr. Mot looked at Alaric, then back at Woda. "I understand this human is particularly important to the mission to retrieve all the Stones. This TMT is state-of-the-art. It's the quickest way to get underneath the dementia to the data in the human's brain, in my opinion. Alaric is the expert."

Woda put her hands on her hips and addressed Alaric and Dr. Mot. "This sort of decision should have involved more than just you two. I've read that any results may be short-lived, and we need to be concerned about the *human*." Her dress made a swishing sound as she turned and walked toward Aurora. "And why is she so out of it?"

"I've administered a calming drug for *Mrs. Brown's* benefit," Dr. Mot said. "Some find these procedures can be anxiety producing."

"Well, her husband should be here for any future treatment," Woda said, then addressed Aurora. "Aurora, are you okay?" When she got no response, she moved within inches of her ear and whispered something. Aurora seemed to awaken a little.

Woda looked satisfied. "Look what old fashioned magic can do."

"You can't deny what we've learned. You haven't even heard it yet." Alaric's eyes glittered.

Mot put the chart on a table and wrote something on it. "Now, if you'll excuse us, we're very busy." He laughed a growly chuckle and seemed to try to lighten the mood, but his words had the opposite effect. "I know some of you magical purists pooh-pooh modern technology, but with all due respect, Ehren put me in charge of the hospital for a reason. Alaric and I will bring our results to the council later today."

It was a standoff. He was technically correct. Each of Ehren's council had a primary area; others were only cross informed in the other's specialty to strengthen the team. Alaric had a right to be there.

Alaric looked smug as he checked the settings on his infernal machine and made notations on a tablet.

Dr. Mot lifted Aurora's limp wrist and checked her pulse. "She's doing fine."

Alaric, officious and ambitious, was forty-seven years old in human time, very young as a member of the inner circle. He walked over to Woda and tried to take her arm to lead her out. "What say we leave the healing to Dr. Mot."

Woda jerked her arm away and left. "We'll see what Ehren says about this! Don't fire that thing up again until the entire council has had its say."

***

Ehren was in his office when a bell rang. This indicated someone had entered the council room outside his study. "Shrumm?" he called, then remembered he had given Shrumm the afternoon off to fish with Ralph while Aurora was evaluated. He hated when his precious "me time" was interrupted. Since becoming human, Ehren found he enjoyed having human hands and loved using his set of writing pens, a gift from Jay. Instead of dictating to others as he had before as a Griffin, he practiced calligraphy with his pens so he could write communications fit for preservation. Jay sometimes handled interruptions when Shrumm was away, but he was working today at the *Wirtschaft.*

The bell rang again. He sighed and put the quill back in the ink well, wiped his hands on a cloth, and strode out of his chambers.

Woda looked exasperated. "It's a good thing the keep's not on fire."

He took a deep breath. Woda, head of spells and strategy, took up almost half a wooden bench; her robes fanned out on the tiled floor. She appeared queenly and was in high dudgeon.

"To what do I owe this pleasure, dear Woda?" He smiled despite his irritation at being interrupted. Her drama was usually entertaining.

"I've just come from the infirmary. Did you know Alaric is working with Doctor Mot? They're already starting treatment."

"All of you need to work together. Isn't there an overlap between Dr. Mot and Alaric's work?" Ehren shot his cuffs and walked to a table that always held his favorite refreshments. "*Kaffee*?" They spoke in German, but coffee transcended language.

Woda adjusted her robes. "Please." She fixed him with violet eyes and bore a hint of a smile. "Cream and sugar."

He raised his eyebrows. The ask was just a nicety, but he had to follow through. *The gall of this woman.* "I thought you were busy creating rituals for Aurora's healing." He regretted letting Shrumm off today as he stirred cream in the coffee. At least it was top-notch, since his partner Jay moved to the Garden from Merryville.

"I would if given half a chance. These two already have her hooked up to a machine for transcranial magnetic treatment and appear to be ready to use it. Didn't we all decide to come together with our evaluations before setting out a course of treatment?"

This got Ehren's attention. "Let's go visit the hospital."

***

Once Mitzi, Lulu, and the elves cleared LAX, they all talked at once. Apparently, a man and a woman had followed Elsa and Ekk. Ekk explained that while retrieving their bags from the conveyor belt in baggage, the couple following them grabbed Elsa, attempting to take her with them. A young man, part of a college school soccer team, yelled, "Hey! They're trying to take that woman!" and his team pounced. Ekk turned around and saw his Elsa amid all that and used his bag to push through the crowd toward her. Two nearby TSA personnel rushed in to stop the melee, but not before fists started flying, and Elsa was hit in the eye.

"I think the attempted snatch was done very badly, right out in the open. They must be desperate." Ekk put his arm around his wife, who leaned into him.

"Who, Ekk? Who must be desperate?" Mitzi asked. She was pumped up from the situation.

"We let our guard down, and I was so glad to see you, Officer Lulu." Elsa leaned forward and patted Lulu on her shoulder, the only place she could reach with her short arms. "Thank you. I should have recognized you from that time you tossed me down the elf hole at Panda's tax office."

Lulu's head swiveled to look at Elsa and gave a "whoop" while slapping her thigh. "It's been a while, but I'll never forget that day." The others jumped when she did that, so she softened her voice. "I can't wait to trade intel. For a while, I thought I was crazy."

They were out of danger for the moment and Mitzi guided the car to an on-ramp leading to the freeway and home. "Were you with the free creatures even back when we had to escape the tax office from the zombie-like karate guys?" Mitzi asked, shooting a quick glance at Lulu.

"Nah. But I got a visit pretty soon after." She shook her head in disbelief. "I got a visit from your friend, Ali. He came to Merryville and kept an eye on you all just like me when I was a security guard. Ali and I are like this." She crossed her index and middle fingers. "When I met him, he ran the Eye of Horus botanica on the other side of town. I guess you know what he's doing now." Lulu kept an eye on the mirrors when she said this, still on the lookout for trouble. "I buy all the stuff for my condo from Taggart's. He's practically family. I know Panda's sister and him are a thing."

"Why wouldn't he tell us?" Mitzi addressed this to the elves.

Ekk answered. "The Garden only reveals itself slowly. Sometimes ordinary humans—"

"Who you calling ordinary?" Lulu belly-laughed.

Even Ekk smiled. "Sometimes extraordinary hero-type humans cross paths with magical people and see things that wouldn't make sense to most. Ehren ensures they are visited and either convinced they didn't see what they thought they saw or sometimes, like with you, Lulu, they are brought into the fold. I hope you know how rare that is."

She turned her broad face to the back seat. "That's me." She did jazz hands. "Super rare." She laughed, and Mitzi's gut eased a bit. It was hard not to feel better around this woman.

"Uh oh." Elsa raised the alarm. "Those people are three cars back."

"Shit!" Mitzi crossed the carpool lane double lines to take advantage of a gap in traffic. Lulu got intense quickly and shouted into her radio.

"Elsa, do your thing!" Mitzi's eyes stayed on the road as she gunned it, knowing the elves had some serious magic that could help.

"She's on it," Ekk said. "What I want to know is who sent these people? How did they find us? Wolfrum was toast after the ravens chased him out of your kitchen." He made sure both his and Elsa's seatbelts were tight.

Mitzi heard Elsa's shaky voice from the back seat. "This is the new leader's work. It has to be. Mitzi, I can hold them off for a bit, but you've got to drive like we're in your little sports car. I'm not sure if home is where we should go—"

"I got you," Lulu interjected, radio in hand. "Get off the freeway, next exit. We've got a place to go." Lulu said into her radio, "I'm getting these people off the freeway. Going radio silent. Officer Tag." She snapped her radio off. To the group she said, "That's going to cause some trouble, but I'm not sure how else they could have caught up with us. Someone back at headquarters ain't on our side."

Mitzi hesitated to turn off the freeway.

"This exit coming up!" Lulu pointed urgently.

"Ekk, you good with that?" Mitzi's voice trembled a little as she glanced at her guardian in the rearview mirror.

"Yes!" His blue eyes were wide.

Mitzi barely made the exit. "Now where?"

"It's okay, Mitzi. Just drive." Ekk was looking out the window. "The port! I thought this might be where we were going."

"Where to?" Mitzi asked as she drove down an asphalt road in the industrial area.

"It's a safe house, or should I say, a safe container." Lulu's eyes were glued to the window. After a few moments, she pulled out a piece of paper.

"What?" Mitzi was confused.

"It's okay," Ekk said.

"Turn right here." Lulu looked up from the paper in her hand and gave directions. Mitzi followed her instructions and found herself in a vast area marked "Do not enter." Shipping containers three high on each side surrounded the Land Rover. "Someone got it wrong."

She started to back up, but Ekk jumped in. "No, Mitzi. This is probably right. I heard we had a safe house at the port but hoped we would never have to use it."

Lulu leaned forward and checked her little piece of paper again. "Go right and count seven big boxes. Then stop."

Mitzi was thinking that, if not for the chase, they would be arriving home right now and having a bite to eat. Instead, she was lost in a forest of shipping containers with Lulu and the elves. "How do we—"

"There," Elsa said. "It's this one."

"Are you sure? They all look alike." Lulu scratched her head.

"See that little octopus on the outside?" She pointed to what looked like a logo fading under rust.

Mitzi stopped and decided she simply needed to trust. Elsa had never led her astray before. This was magic-folk business.

Ekk jumped out of the car as soon as it stopped, as did Lulu. Together, they opened the back of the container and motioned for Mitzi to drive in.

"No drive-through magic portal?" This was not like Mitzi's experience in the Black Forest where the entrance to the Hercynian Garden was an illusion.

"No. This spot is only rarely used. Best not to keep a magic signature on it," Elsa said. She had brightened considerably.

Mitzi drove inside the big shipping box with a leap of faith, wishing Panda was with her.

"It's okay, Mitzi," Elsa reassured, as Lulu and Ekk followed their SUV inside and closed the big metal doors behind them. The darkness was complete.

Ekk took charge. "We need light. Doesn't Panda keep camping gear in the car?"

Mitzi got out and felt her way to the back of the Rover. She opened the hatch, found a battery lantern, and turned it on. Everyone gathered around the light and talked quietly. "Talk to us, Lulu," Mitzi said. She leaned in the open hatch, pulled out the waters, and passed them around. "Where did you get those instructions?"

Lulu loosened her collar, exhaled, and sat on the open back of the Rover. "Give me a minute." She guzzled some water and wiped her brow. "It's warm in here, and I'm slightly claustrophobic."

"That's why you didn't want to go down that elf hole." Mitzi referred to a similar emergency months ago when Lulu said she would stay and protect them rather than jump into "some magical elf hole."

Elsa fanned herself. "It is warm. Ekk, shouldn't there be some magical source to support life?"

Ekk took out his smartphone and, using the flashlight app, studied the container's interior. "You would think, but this one is pretty empty. We were briefed about various safe houses, but it's been a while."

Lulu's face showed concern. "You're sure this is the right container?"

"It had the octopus on it," Elsa responded.

Ekk's face drained. "Who told you about this place, Lulu?"

"My handler gave me this map."

Ekk and Elsa said almost in unison, "Ali?"

Ekk moved his arm in a circular motion, anxious for the response.

"No. It wasn't a guy." Lulu looked at Mitzi, who stared at her like she had two heads. "It's a friend of yours from the garden club, Mitzi. One of the gals that was at the press conference."

"There were a few. Describe her." Mitzi was incredulous to think that one of the Merryville Horticultural Society mavens could be involved in any way. "Was it a tall British woman?"

Lulu shook her head. "I was coming out of the press conference—by the way, you were amazing, Mitzi—where I got my medal for helping to catch Gary Smithers." She furrowed her brow. "I was kind of on a high from that. I got in my car, and this woman in, like, a little cowgirl outfit tapped on my window."

Mitzi repeated, "A cowgirl outfit."

"Well, wearing jeans and a shirt with piping and pearl buttons. No hat, but I think she had on cowboy boots. She was blond."

"Did she give you a name?"

Ekk and Elsa watched Mitzi closely since she was being so specific.

"No—"

"It's Sally Johnson," Mitzi blurted. "Oh. My. God. No one would have suspected her."

"I think I know which one that is, but don't jump to conclusions." Elsa sought to comfort her. "Maybe she's one of us."

"She seemed nice and, uh, harmless." Lulu's face reddened, and she had her arms in front of her in explanation. "Look, after what I've seen, it made sense as much as anything else has. First, you guys all jumped in an elf hole, then Gary Smithers shot up Merry Hearts." She started walking in circles, overwhelmed. "I saw you with wings, Mitzi." She pointed to Mitzi's shoulders.

"Calm down," Ekk said in a firm voice. It had an effect as Lulu stopped pacing. She took a deep breath.

"It never occurred to me the lady might not be on the right team, whatever that is. I still don't know the whole deal." Lulu adopted a thinking pose, talking to herself. "She said not to talk to anyone and told me there might be trouble and she would call. I needed to keep you all safe. She called my cell phone today and told me you were coming in from Germany," she pointed to the elves, "and might be in danger at the airport and to keep an eye out."

"And we were." Ekk turned his cell flashlight on Elsa's shiner.

"I don't blame you, Lulu. We just need to know everything." Mitzi's voice was calm. "So what do we do now? Maybe we should go back to the house."

"I'm calling the Garden first." Ekk pulled out his dagger, which was also his communication device, to call the Hercynian Garden. Ekk held the dagger high and walked around, as if trying to catch a wireless signal. He commented idly, "I suppose keeping the magic flowing all the time on all the spots in the world would drain the Garden's resources. Don't panic yet."

"It's only a steel container," Elsa said. "That won't stop us from communicating." She gave off a faint lavender scent, which helped Mitzi relax a little.

They all waited and watched Ekk hold his little arm in the air as he walked to every corner of the steel box they were in. He even shook it, fiddled with the ruby button on the dagger, and tried it again.

"This is bad," he said. "It's almost as if we are being blocked by dark magic."

Mitzi sat down hard on the bumper. "Sally Johnson is part of *Lupus Imperium*?"

"Wait. Let's not panic." Elsa put her arm around Mitzi. "It's possible that she just wasn't on our radar. Remember, we didn't know Ali was running the Eye of Horus only a few blocks away from your house. The Garden sometimes doesn't reveal everything to keep everyone safe."

"She did seem kind of otherworldly. I thought she was just spacey." Mitzi turned to Lulu, who seemed to be getting upset again. "Let's wait for more information, okay?"

"Oh man, cowgirl said she was here to protect you guys and not to tell anyone for that same reason. She called me and told me to go to the airport. I know people there, and she knew that." Lulu shook her head. "What now?"

They heard the sound of a motor coming from all around them.

"I say we get out of here." Mitzi went to the doors, but the handle inside the container wouldn't budge. "Help me, Lulu." Before Lulu could reach the door, the container started to move, tilting a tiny bit to one side. Lulu widened her stance to keep from falling.

"Mitzi, make sure the parking brake is on!" Ekk finally looked alarmed.

"I think it's time to panic," Lulu said, as the container left the ground.

Chapter Four

Ute Reservation, Colorado

Tava Mountain was otherworldly, and I wondered if that wasn't why Ahanu picked it for my training. I looked down in the predawn hour; only lights in native homes broke the vast darkness of the desert. My exhalation came out as fog in the crisp, early morning air. We had been busy traveling and talking, and I'd been too full of my fears and thoughts to fully appreciate where we were until now. The physicality of moving my body to dismount in this space put me in another mode. I wondered if this sacred ground held the well of stillness Valerie drew on when she was back in Merryville. My resentment at Ahanu had faded as we plodded along the dark dirt roads. I patted Major and looked at Valerie and Ahanu, wondering what was next.

The elder took a swig from a thermos in his saddlebag. The realization that he and Valerie were taking their time to teach me to call my ancestors humbled me. I said quietly, "Whatever happens, thank you both." Valerie's empathetic eyes found me. Ahanu quietly tucked the thermos away and pulled out a bundle of white sage that he waved over me and the area. The smell was wonderful and helped me relax. His voice that had seemed so harsh was simply that of an older man. I resolved to stop acting like a child. The desert was cleansing.

Perhaps I'd been confusing his voice with my inner critical parent.

It was quiet as we arranged ourselves in an area marked by stones. Ahanu seemed ready, and I tried my best not to disturb the vibe.

"Panda, it is time to let go of all the noise—busy thoughts, thinking of home, of the past or future. Feel where your body sits, the temperature, the smell of this sage." He touched the crown of my head. "Be here now."

I felt the cold through my thick jacket, although being out of the wind helped. The burning sage smelled wonderful. We sat in the quiet, only hearing the wind and the creak of leather saddles. I felt a pebble under my left butt cheek and fixed that. His spoke again.

"You are a link in a chain. Close your eyes and see. There are thousands of years of people behind you, and they are a part of you. You must find your place, make the connection."

My eyes were closed, and I didn't know what to expect. I sincerely tried not to fight his words. I breathed deeply and became very still.

"This is bigger than you, Panda Fowler, and you are in a special place that will help you see without your eyes. Thousands of years, lots of changes. You have been women. You have been men. Your ancestors' genes flow through you, an unbreakable code."

Valerie started to sing quietly. It was a song without English words and was like what she sang when I was going through a sweat in Merryville after almost dying from an injury.

"When we are born, our memories are erased until we find our way to the thread. It is time for you to find your way." Ahanu walked slowly in a circle around us. How did I know this?

That's when things shifted. I "saw" in my mind an endless line of chairs behind me from one up near and clear into a vanishing point. The background was indistinct, and I wondered if I was making it up because I wanted to please Ahanu and Valerie. Something was happening.

"Deeper. Deeper, Panda, don't fight it." Ahanu's voice sounded like it was coming from far away and getting quieter.

The images in my vision sharpened so that I saw the faces of mostly older people. Then I saw myself sitting on the ground and hundreds of females sitting on chairs. I saw Grandma. She wore an apron and wire-framed glasses with a cloud of white hair framing her face. I missed her with all my heart. She was a staunch Southern Baptist, and although she'd disapproved of my parent's hippie lifestyle, she'd loved me fiercely. I could almost smell her kitchen, which always hinted at her favorite spices. She died when I was twenty.

I saw Aunt Delia, who raised me, seated primly in a pantsuit. She was a good provider but not a hugger and had a solemn face. Not ready to take on her sister's children. I felt her resentment. It was startling that these people could see me, too, and possibly knew my feelings. Realizing that gave me a jolt, and I almost lost the vision. I inwardly knew they could see more than my physical self but also my life. Their faces were mostly not welcoming, and my soul withered as I realized it was because I was a lesbian. This was like having a bucket of freezing water poured over my head, waking me up. I was sitting on the cold ground again and shook my head. I wanted to push the vision away. Tears leaked from my eyes.

"Panda, Panda, are you okay?" Valerie was at my side.

Ahanu stood, arms folded. "She broke through. We'll do more tomorrow." He walked toward his horse and made to leave.

I was dizzy and let my friend help me up on Major. I tried to speak. "Val, I saw—"

"I know. We saw too. Let's go get you warm."

I barely remembered the ride back, focusing on the squeak of leather. When we returned to Etsi's house, Etsi helped me down from the horse, and Valerie led hers and mine to the barn. Twyla and Etsi had a spot in front of the fireplace ready. I was given some kind of tea and wrapped in a blanket. I felt hollowed out and soon fell asleep.

***

The Garden

Ralph and Shrumm were laughing as they entered the back of the kitchen after fishing. Inside the back door, various kitchen staff had lockers, and Shrumm showed Ralph where the fishing rods went.

"You got a lot of gear."

"Charlie Potts is the real fisherman. Most of this is his, and he doesn't mind us using it. I hadn't ever tried it until he came."

"Charlie Potts? The detective?"

"Yes, but retired now. He's married to Alexandra, who works for the Garden. She's on the council."

Ralph laughed. "Seems you can't get too far without a lawyer these days. Even in a magic garden."

Shrumm dusted his hands off against each other, then held up an index finger like he was having a brainstorm. "I think we need a snack."

"Won't get an argument from me." Ralph followed him into the kitchen and chose a stool around a wooden chopping block table. As he watched his friend, he did that little drumming thing people do on the worn surface of the block. "After our snack, I'll go check on my bride. She's getting some sort of medical test today. I sure hope that doctor knows what he's doing."

Shrumm put an apron over his head and tied it in the back. "Don't worry. Dr. Mot is really good. He went to medical school in New York."

"New York!" Ralph shook his head. "I can't get over how y'all come and go between this world and that."

Shrumm's head was hidden for a moment when he opened the refrigeration unit. "You want a fish sandwich?"

This got a laugh out of Ralph. "It'll be the only one we caught today."

"Maybe some turkey."

While Shrumm fiddled in the fridge, Ralph studied the walls and asked, "Could you show me the workshop where they make all this green stuff y'all build everything with?"

"Yes. We call it *grunzwieg*, and sure, but it'll have to be later...Aha! Would you rather have Quark or Butterkase cheese?"

"Quark? My Aurora used to call cottage cheese that. Maybe the other butter one." He ran his hands over the wooden chopping block. "I love how this thing was put together. It feels really old with the grooves and all." Ehren and Woda stormed past the kitchen door and caught his attention. "Uh, Shrumm, isn't the hospital down thataway?"

Shrumm's head reappeared from the fridge to see where Ralph was pointing. Frowning, he bumped the fridge door closed with a hip, his hands busy balancing a tower of bread and lettuce atop some sort of container. "The hospital's that way, why?"

"Cause Ehren ran that way just now. Should I be worried?" Ralph got up from his stool. "That lady from the council was with him. The big one in purple."

"Everyone on the council wears purple. Was it Ehren and Woda?" Shrumm set down the food so fast a roll fell on the floor. "Come on. Something's up."

Snack forgotten, Ralph followed Shrumm out of the kitchen as best he could. He was still recovering from a hip injury he suffered when he slipped on ice in Merryville. He limped as they hurried toward the hospital. Shrumm was faster, his apron flapping as he said, "Ehren, Woda!" They were too far down the hall to hear.

When Ralph reached the door to a large, green-tiled room, he heard raised voices. The hospital lab was full. If Ehren and Woda were cats, their hair would have been standing up. That little feller, Alaric, jaw jutted out, was in defensive mode.

Aurora, glassy-eyed, was sitting on a chair in the middle of the lab with a metal band around her head. Wires were connected, leading to some machine. Ralph immediately went to her. "What in the Sam Hill is going on?" Ralph was upset and reached out to remove the electrodes from his wife's head.

Dr. Mot moved toward him and Aurora. "Please don't touch those wires, Mr. Brown! You could hurt her. Wait, please."

Ehren walked to the machine and looked at the setup. "Mrs. Brown was supposed to be getting tests to see if she was strong enough to proceed. Looks like you're already treating her."

"Yes. Tell us all what's going on," Woda said and folded her arms. She stood side by side with Ehren.

"Ehren, it's all *fine*," Alaric said. He motioned to the machine. "The TCM has been used all over the states and is cutting edge. I'm trained in it. This is how we're going to find the Summer Stone. Aur—Mrs. Brown has already shown—"

Ehren's face practically turned purple as he loomed over the shorter Alaric, stopping his words cold. "Already shown...what? Have you mined information from her brain? I'll tell you when it's fine, and right now, this is not. We discussed mechanical memory search, but the council has not decided if the risks are worth it." Ehren motioned to the machine with lights blinking and a soft whirring sound.

"And her husband should have a word about that too," Ralph said. "If you hurt her..." He took an aggressive step toward Alaric.

Woda could stay silent no longer. "Dr. Mot? Why did you allow this?"

Ehren gave her a warning look. He was in charge.

Ralph pointed at Aurora, then wagged his finger at Alaric and Dr. Mot. "She's my wife. Nobody asked me if she could be hooked up to a machine like this."

Dr. Mot cleared his throat and threw Alaric under the bus. "Your council member said we should go ahead."

All heads turned to Alaric, who began, "No, no, no." Hand gestures accompanied this. "I actually said we need to do this to test the equipment."

"On my wife?" Ralph was steamed. "She's not a lab rat!"

Alaric quickly responded, "We already learned the stone isn't in Tanzania."

"What?" Ehren and Woda said this in unison. Mitzi would be on her way there soon.

Aurora reached for Ralph's hand. "Ralph, I want to go home."

Woda, knowing whose decision it was, simply said, "Ehren?"

Ehren scratched the back of his head. "Shut it down. Ralph, take Aurora back to your room after they...disconnect her. I want the whole council in our meeting room in two minutes."

***

Trapped

Amid the sounds of a hydraulic lift, Mitzi almost lost her balance when the cargo box they were in tilted wildly. She widened her stance and put her arms out like she was surfing, feeling the vibration of movement through her feet. "Oh my god, we're moving."

"Hang on!" Lulu yelled and grabbed the bumper of the Land Rover. The lantern hanging from a hook on the opened hatchback swung crazily.

Mitzi panicked, thinking the heavy vehicle might crush them all if the parking brake didn't hold, but the floor quickly leveled out, although it still vibrated mightily. Panda had taken her to a fun house years ago where the floor tilted, but that had been fun. Panda! Would she ever see her again? Being in a dark metal container with no windows and tilting, she felt helpless. She looked at Ekk, his head swiveling this way and that, no doubt trying to suss out what was happening. Elsa sat with her back against the steel wall, her eyes closed. Her lips moved. She must be casting a spell. The fragrance of lavender soon filled the space again, and Mitzi felt herself calm by a few degrees. She realized there was nothing anyone could do until whatever was happening played itself out. "This could only be the work of

Lupus Imperium," Mitzi yelled to Lulu over the noise, "Anything else you need to tell us?"

Lulu's eyes were wide. "That blond lady, she said she was on your side. I'm so, so sorry!" Lulu fished out a necklace from beneath her uniform shirt and clutched at it with one hand as she hung onto the car's luggage rack with the other.

"I wasn't around her much but didn't feel any bad vibes," Elsa said. She had opened her eyes and looked ready to cry. She was so pitiful with her blackening eye. "Don't feel bad, Lulu."

"She fooled me too," Mitzi said. She wasn't ready to blame Lulu, who was guileless. *Evil comes in all shapes and sizes*, she thought. No one suspected Sally Johnson from the Garden Club! She would have guessed Hortense Miller if anyone would be on the evil team. Her brain spun, thinking about who else they knew might be with *Lupus Imperium*.

"No one saw this coming," Ekk said, his voice steady. "Just hang on. Mitzi, do you have your pendant?"

Mitzi smacked her head with her hand and pulled the medallion out from under her blouse. Lulu getting her lucky talisman, or whatever it was, out and hanging onto it for dear life must have made Ekk remember. She sure hadn't. *The octopus pictured on the container!* The pendant, with an octopus on it, had been given to her as a baby for protection. She was so used to it that she treated it like regular jewelry.

She tightly wrapped her hand around the plastic round bubble over the octopus, hoping whatever magic had never shown itself before was still present to help them. Her thoughts then turned to Panda, who, if here, would not have been able to do anything either. Even knowing it was futile, Mitzi pulled out her phone and tried to call, but there was no service. She was glad Panda was out of danger but sad as images of them saying goodbye at the airport the day before filled her mind. Panda had been in a "twizzle," having had to pack for the Ute reservation quickly. Juniper dropped off Twyla and Valerie at the same time, so goodbyes among everyone were chaotic and rushed. Was this it, after everything they had been through?

Mitzi had been sure they would see each other in a few days, once Panda returned from Colorado. Honestly, she'd been a little irritated with Panda for dragging her feet on the raven issue. Mitzi sincerely hoped this wouldn't be an end to their story together. Panda might never even find out what happened to her. Tears stung her eyes.

The metal container groaned and brought her back to the immediate moment. Thankfully, the Land Rover stayed put as they kept moving.

"We're going up. Do you feel it?" Ekk was now wedged in a corner for stability, back to the wall, and said this to Elsa, who opened her eyes and nodded in agreement.

The octopus pendant she held made Mitzi remember she was half-griffin. It had been so long since her wings had deployed that she had almost forgotten she had this option. The mind was an amazing thing, always trying to rationalize the impossible. So where were her wings? Not that they would do them any good while inside this metal shipping container. The cargo box they were in juddered, and she heard human shouts, along with a grinding, groaning noise.

Lulu yelled, "Hey! Help!" and Ekk immediately shushed her.

"We don't know who's out there."

Lulu stopped yelling and hung on to the Rover's bumper with all her might. Her eyes were wide. They were all frozen in place.

Soon, their cargo box stopped moving. It was hot, and Ekk looked grim. Mitzi asked, "What?" Lulu looked about to faint and now crossed herself. Elsa moved over to Ekk and stood next to him. They were all silent as they heard the bar lock being manipulated.

Chapter Five

Ute Reservation, Colorado

The fire in Etsi's house crackled as Valerie put another log on it. "Are you ready to tell us about your vision?"

Etsi was wrapped in a multi-colored knitted blanket in a stuffed chair. I noticed how thin she was. "Half the day is gone."

"How long was I out?"

"A couple of hours. Ahanu will be back soon."

"No wonder I'm starving." I stretched and put my feet on the floor. "Where's Twyla?"

Etsi and Valerie shared a look. "My mom showed her a place where there is purple glass. Some bottles have been sitting in the desert sun for eighty years. She's fascinated." Just then, I heard the back screen door slam.

"Guys! Wait 'til you see what I collected!" Twyla burst into the room. The low wooden table had a mat, and Twyla placed her treasures on it. "Hi, Panda. Did I miss anything?"

"Nope, just woke up."

Etsi headed for the kitchen, and Valerie followed. "Mom, let me help with lunch."

"I need to call Mitzi." I started to get up but still felt tired.

Twyla vibrated, something she did when nervous or excited, usually a precursor to lift off. "Don't make us wait! Did you call the ravens?"

"Mitzi first." As I left the room to find my cell phone, I said, "Twyla, let's wait 'til Val and Etsi are in the room. I don't want to do this twice." *Why am I always so grumpy?*

The phone was on the bedside table, and I'd missed two calls. The cheerful sounds of my friend and her mother in the kitchen were reassuring, as was the general warmth in the house. The first message was from Babs at my tax office, asking where I'd put the tax return for a particular client. She also reminded me that her vacation was coming up and hoped I was having a good time. It made me wonder if she resented my trip. She held down Fowler Tax Services while I'd been to Germany, Peru, Germany again, and now in Colorado at a reservation. Without knowing the whole story, she must feel taken advantage of with me galloping around the world and her working so hard. I made a mental note to talk to Ekk and Elsa about that. They might have some ideas about how to bring her into our missions, if only a little. The second message was from Mitzi. "I'm missing you already. About to leave and pick up our little friends at LAX. Hope your training is going well. Love you."

Bursting with news and missing her, I called back, but the phone went to voicemail. It was an hour earlier in California, but that would have made it eleven a.m. I tried Ekk's phone, which also went directly to voicemail, and Elsa's too. When I walked back into the living room, Etsi, Valerie, and Twyla looked at me with eager faces. "Finally!" Twyla said. "The hot chocolate is fabulous."

Etsi looked amused. "She's on her third. Does sugar affect you like caffeine?"

"It might." Twyla put down her drink and made a face. "Thanks for the warning."

Etsi put a plate for me in front of the chair I had previously inhabited, as everyone else had eaten lunch already. I sat down. "Thank you, Etsi, so much."

Valerie said, "Eat, then tell. I've already told them my impressions. Your training is going well."

"We haven't seen one raven, Val," I said around a forkful of egg and cheese.

"This training is about opening whatever is blocking your magic," Val said. "The ravens will be a piece of cake when we figure that out."

I finished my plate, as we were all entertained by Twyla's explanations for each of the treasures she'd brought back. I was sure Mitzi would call me back soon.

***

Ehren's Council

The council had devolved into a shouting match again. Ehren, Shrumm, Woda, Alaric, and Dr. Mot, called to discuss the hospital testing of Aurora, surrounded the heavy wooden table. Alexandra Stephanovsky and historian Karla were not available to join on such quick notice. Heloisa, muscled and cleaning her nails with a small knife, leaned against the wall. Heloisa was automatically a council member, although she was often away. Ehren happened to run into her on the way back from the incident.

"One at a time," Shrumm said. "I've had about enough of this. Alaric, you keep alluding to what you have already learned. It's time to tell us." Shrumm was nominally in charge of the chaos, allowing Ehren to focus on decision-making.

"First, since there's been so much pushback, let's set the record straight. My team is the only one that has found valuable information." Alaric was smug, looking at the faces around the table. "I felt that needed to be said. It's science, not magic," he looked at Woda, "or threats of violence." He looked at Heloisa.

"You little shit." Heloisa's hand was on her sword. She looked ready to behead him.

Ehren put up an arm, and she stayed put, wisely swallowing whatever she would say next.

"If Woda wouldn't have burst in as she did..." Alaric was blame-shifting.

"Excuse me? You're blaming me? I'm the one who saw you treating Aurora without authority!"

"We were testing, not treating!" Alaric was red in the face. "Stand down."

"You need to learn your manners, elf," Heloisa growled from the corner. She wasn't a fan of the scientist.

"As do you! A sword in chambers—really?" Alaric stood his ground.

Woda pointed dramatically at Alaric but directed her comment at Ehren and Shrumm. "Setting aside the out-of-order rudeness," she glared at Alaric and Heloisa, "by everybody, we haven't yet resolved the issue of how he got that information! Shouldn't that be first?"

"You sound like children squabbling." Ehren was firm. "You are my council. Act like it. We're here to talk about what happened in the Keep hospital. Honestly, Alaric, I'm stunned you would act with a fragile old woman alone and without her husband present. I must remind you the Browns are here at my invitation and under my protection."

Shrumm, standing by to assist the council, added, "Sir, Ralph Brown said he wants to take Aurora back to Merryville."

"Good luck getting there without magical help." Alaric was unapologetic.

"Oh, now you recognize magic."

"Stop it!" Ehren fixed his eyes on each of them. "No more of this. Do you forget the big picture? With the Stones out there and *Lupus Imperium* searching, too, it's a race to find weaponized magic. Many could perish." Ehren, looking tired, leaned forward and said with a softer voice, "We might as well assess what we know now. Although, Alaric, you will do no more work with Aurora without Ralph present. Is that clear?"

Alaric looked triumphant. "Clear."

"Dr. Mot?" Ehren wasn't letting him off the hook.

"Fine." He shook his big head and put his hands up in mock surrender, always acting as if he were above the rest.

Alaric clicked what looked like a pen in his hand, and a hologram of Aurora sitting in a chair next to the transcranial magnetic treatment machine appeared, floating above the center of the table and eliciting a groan from Woda. "Poor duck." Electrodes were attached to a cap on her head, and she looked sedated.

"Here is the part you need to hear."

Aurora spoke softly, but a microphone attached to her chair captured her breathing and anything she said.

"My Oma sent me the box with a letter. 'Don't open it, Aurora. Forget it's here. Not safe.'"

She then muttered something unintelligible. They could hear Alaric's voice coaxing more out of her. "Okay...your Oma, your grandmother, sent you a box. Where did you put it?"

Unexpectedly, she laughed. "Ralph said," she mimicked a man's voice, "'I bet they couldn't find Jimmy Hoffa in there.'" Her blue eyes moved as if she was back in that memory.

Woda said, "All that risk? For what? And who is Jimmy Hoffa?" Everyone ignored her, riveted, as Aurora said more.

"Like the purloined letter." Aurora closed her eyes, and they could hear Dr. Mot in the background.

"So, Aurora, do you know where the other Stones are?"

Alaric looked irritated in the hologram as he lifted his head to respond to Dr. Mot. "We need to go slow—"

"Namibia," Aurora said. "Diamond, Kolmanskop, not just a diamond, but forget it. My head hurts. Ralph? Where is Ralph?" She lifted her head and looked anxious.

At first, it was hard to tell what Ehren thought. He only asked, "Were there any other revelations?"

"Not yet. Right after this clip, the session ended." In the hologram, Alaric walked off-screen, which faded to black, the last image being Aurora in the chair alone. She looked like she was crying. Alaric was immune to her distress. "Germany was building a railroad through this desert—"

"—and discovered a diamond. I know our history, Alaric. It's a ghost town now." Ehren was testy.

"I'm so close. Clearly, because of my work, we need to change the mission."

"*I'm* so close, *my* work?" Woda shook her head.

"You are not running this show and, may I remind you, you are new on this council." Ehren's voice was fierce. "I am still concerned about you moving forward without permission. Do I need to put Aurora Brown under guard? Alaric. Mot. You are not to so much as say hello to her without my permission." There was silence in the room. "Also, do I need to remind you this is confidential information?"

"But…" Alaric sputtered. "You can see, we have a location. Probably only one more session and we—"

"Alaric. You're very smart. We all know that. That's why you were invited to my council at such a young age, to bring state of the art technology to the. Garden." Ehren stood and leaned over the table. His knuckles were white, supporting his weight. "What you have missed…" He took a deep breath. "What you have missed is that we are the good, not evil. They use people; we don't. Above all, we value the lives of all free creatures. Aurora is a free creature. If any further work is done, it will be done with Ralph and myself present."

"And me." Woda jumped on the bandwagon.

"No. Woda, continue working on your magic. And do I need to say this? Alaric, you live in a magical Garden. Our skies and all the beauty we enjoy are either created or enhanced by magic. You seem to have forgotten that to us, magic is equally, if not more important than technology. We all need to stay focused on what was assigned." Ehren's orders were clear. Woda looked placated.

"Alaric, you and Dr. Mot are dismissed." He turned to his first person. "Shrumm, get me logistics. We were about to look in the wrong place. We must call my daughter and tell her plans have changed."

Dr. Mot left quickly. Alaric loitered at the door. "Ehren, you do recognize, then, the value of the intelligence I found."

Ehren stared at Alaric and simply said, "Yes. I do." His words were clipped, and his nostrils flared. "You and I will have a word later."

Alaric turned and left.

Chapter Six

Still Trapped

They were frozen. Lulu, gun in her hand, focused on the sound of the door opening. "Get behind me."

Elsa was shocked when she saw the gun. "Put that away!" Lulu lowered her arm but didn't re-holster it.

After prolonged darkness, sunlight flooded through once the heavy metal door was swung open, making them blink. It blinded Mitzi. A clean-shaven man in his fifties, wearing jeans and a peacoat, stood at the open door. Mitzi's eyes began to adjust. "Jack! That's Jack Johnson, Sally's husband!" Mitzi wasn't sure if she should be relieved or not.

He put his finger in front of his lips in a "shh" motion and beckoned them to follow. Mitzi was first out of the box.

"What's going on?" she asked, and as if on cue, a seagull screeched overhead and dropped its white missile, which splattered at Mitzi's feet. "Great." With her first chance to look around, Mitzi saw their container was next to an almost identical row of containers. He put his index finger in front of his lips again.

"Jack, what's happening?" she whispered.

"We need to be safe first," he commanded in a low voice. "You must follow me quickly before the crew comes back. The ship is ready to pull away from the dock and will be swarming with personnel who don't expect to see civilians popping out of a shipping container. Take what you need from your car, but..." He looked left and right over his shoulder.

"I know, we heard ya. Hurry." Lulu put her firearm away. "Can I bring the luggage?"

Jack nodded and put out his arms to receive a bag or two. Elsa came out with her purse, blinking.

"Your eye." Jack shook his head. "I'm so sorry."

Elsa smiled but stayed quiet.

Less than five minutes later, they held all their belongings from the car and secured the door to the container again. They could hear voices coming their way as the ship's horn blew three times. The little group followed Jack down the corridor of shipping containers to an unobtrusive square opening in the deck with the hatch already open. "Down here."

"Oh no," Lulu said. "This is a trick." She looked green.

"I'm not sensing anything dangerous from the hatch. We need to trust him," Elsa pleaded. Lulu had her arms crossed and shook her head no.

"I'll go first." Ekk handed Jack his bag and descended a metal ladder to a deck below. "It's fine." Jack handed Ekk his bag back, and soon Elsa followed, her bag lowered too. Mitzi was the next to go. "Come on, Lulu, this could be life or death. Don't you feel it?" Mitzi's hair prickled on the back of her neck, a sure sign the energy was shifting.

Lulu looked like she was going to be sick. "All I feel is you want me to go in that tiny hole. What is it with you people? I'm claustrophobic."

A loud horn blew again, and the crewmen's voices sounded closer.

Jack had dark, intense eyes. He faced Lulu and put a hand on her shoulder to ensure she was listening. "Lulu, any second, we'll be discovered, and all of this will be for nothing. For the sake of these people that you want to protect, now's the perfect time to push through your fear." The scent of lavender drifted up from the hatch.

"It's not a *fear*," Lulu grumbled.

Jack pointed emphatically twice at the hole in the deck.

To her credit, Lulu moved to the rectangle and started down the metal ladder. Jack deftly followed, closing the hatch behind him just in time as they could hear men's voices above. When the five were on the deck below, Jack again silently motioned for them to follow. He led them down corridors lit with dim oval lights, protected by thick glass in heavy metal frames. A groaning sound that seemed to come from everywhere accompanied a final blow of the ship's horn, and Mitzi staggered as the big ship moved. Jack walked quickly, and Mitzi, Ekk, Elsa, and Lulu followed closely behind him in the narrow metal corridor, having no choice but to trust him. They walked down more stairs and hallways, the smell of oil and diesel faintly in the air. They went this way and that, finally stopping in front of a gray metal door marked with a faded and scratched "Authorized Personnel Only" sign, painted in red stencil letters. He held the door open and motioned them in. It took more coaxing, but Lulu finally entered and sat on the single bed. "Why are you here, and are you with that blond lady?" she asked.

He exhaled. "I'm with the Garden. Both me and Sally." Jack stood by the door because there was nowhere else to be in the single-bunk cabin. Aside from the narrow bunk, a miniature sink, mirror, narrow closet, and a pull-down desk big enough for a tiny person to write on filled the cabin. The room smelled vaguely of wet boat.

Lulu looked about, ready to explode. "Okay, I've been a good sport and all, but this is way too small for all of us. I must also return to Merryville PD by Friday oh-seven-hundred." She used her hands to punctuate her words. "I'm a cop. If I don't go back, it's a big deal."

Elsa spoke up. "This is our size, but it would even be crowded for Ekk and me to stay. How long do you expect us to be here?" Elsa sat down beside Lulu, who patted her, obviously sensing an ally.

"Ain't no way I can stay in this with all of y'all." She pointed at her friends. "No offense. It's not the company. I couldn't even stay in here with Jason Momoa."

This made Mitzi laugh. "So, next?"

Ekk motioned to Lulu to be patient and addressed Jack. "I've seen you a few times before around the flower group. You own Johnson Roofing, right? Your golf carts are all over the garden project in Merryville."

Jack exhaled again and ruffled his dark black hair with a lean hand. "Among other businesses. Things happened fast. Sally got the message to Officer Tag, um..."

"Lulu's fine," she said. "Everyone messes up my last name." Lulu's arms were folded, and she was frowning. "This is a trap, isn't it?"

Jack cleared his throat. "It's not a trap. The two agents after you were assassins. They meant business. They were at the airport to take Ekk and Elsa out, permanently. Sally and I only got word from the Hercynian Garden yesterday that something like that might happen. That Shrumm fellow told us about the container being safe for you. Sally and I hadn't been activated in some time, but they knew about my connection here at the port."

Ekk was practical. "Now that we're on this ship, how do we get off?"

Jack looked at his shoes. "I can take Mitzi and only one of you on a helicopter before dawn. It's all I could arrange on very short notice." He pulled a face. "Mitzi is vital to the next part of the mission. I'm afraid it will be at least twenty days before this ship hits the African coast."

Mitzi felt her stomach drop. "I take it Panda's Land Rover isn't leaving in a helicopter before dawn?"

"No, I'm afraid her car is going to Africa."

Despite the threat to them all, Mitzi blurted, "Panda's going to freak out. She loves that car."

"Excuse me." Lulu stood and said with heat, "You're worried about a damn car? If you all think I'm gonna stay in this tiny bunk room for twenty days, you've got another thing coming. I'll swim back to Merryville first."

Jack was nonplused. "That's not what I'm saying." He cleared his throat and started over. "Look, you and either Ekk or Elsa will be leaving too in a couple of days. Coordinating a pick-up mid-journey isn't easy. These people on board have no idea what's at stake or why you are here. We must keep it that way. I have yet to fully explain why I jumped on board."

They all started talking at once until Jack put up his hands in a stop motion. "This is the best I could do under the circumstances." A light flickered on beyond the door. Jack tensed. "Please be quiet." He quickly left and hailed someone loudly. Their steps receded.

"I gotta get out of here," Lulu said. She didn't look good. She stood up, but there was no place for her to go.

Ekk moved out of her way, and Mitzi looked at Elsa.

"Let's all take a moment and breathe." Elsa was being her typical healing self, and lavender energy emanated from her. "We could have been killed back at LAX, but we're here now. We're alive, and Jack said we won't be here long. The decisions we make next will not be helped with panic."

Lulu sat again, closed off, arms tightly crossed.

Mitzi leaned against the tiny sink, tired of standing. "Okay, to recap. We were to pick you up,"—she motioned to Ekk and Elsa— "Panda would come home, and she and I would fly to Africa together. I've only just gotten information about Nairobi. That tour starts in six days."

"We didn't have time to brief you," Ekk said and moved his hand around in a circle, "because of everything that's been happening. This is our first opportunity to talk, so let us bring you up to speed. We got Aurora and Ralph to the Garden and were briefed on the progress of the Winter Stone piece we brought back. The council has been working around the clock to find out where the Summer Stone might be by working with Aurora."

"What's the Winter Stone?" Lulu looked marginally less grumpy. "I know Aurora. She's the lady from Merry Hearts Memory Care, right?"

"Yes, that's her, but I'm afraid the Winter Stone intel is need-to-know only," Ekk said.

"Well, I need to know," Lulu said stubbornly, arms crossed.

Both Elsa and Mitzi reacted. Mitzi got the first word in.

"Ekk," Mitzi said. "Lulu's put her life on the line and deserves to know what's going on." Mitzi was firm. "If you recall, she helped us before when we were under attack at the tax office and never told a soul."

His shoulders relaxed. "Okay, I need to bring you up to speed anyway, Mitzi." Ekk settled in. "Long ago, there was an intact Circle of Stones like Stonehenge, except with only four stones— one for each season. We still don't know who made them or placed them in Cornwall. The scribes and researchers at the Hercynian Garden are working around the clock to find out. Unlike Stonehenge, this stone circle was imbued with almost unimaginable power. You've heard of Atlantis?" The ship creaked right on cue. Mitzi was learning along with Lulu, and both women gave Ekk their rapt attention.

"Atlantis...go on." Lulu was not going to let him rest until he got it all out.

"Wars have happened between tribes since before recorded history. Not all tribes believe the other must be destroyed for them to thrive. Other tribes had horrible weapons of war that sank Atlantis. It was so shocking, the worst weapons were separated from each other and turned to stone in a brief moment of shared horror. The stone circle was public at first, a symbol of the balance between the tribes, reminding everyone they must coexist for any to survive. This 'truce' lasted for only a few hundred years, then those who didn't remember or care about the hideous power contained in the stones desired them for themselves. From what we learned in the Garden recently, ancient wise creatures knew that the circle was far too dangerous to be captured. So..."

"So what?" Now it was Mitzi moving him along.

"After a gathering of leading tribes, the stones were destroyed, and the pieces thrown into the ocean, the desert and other places. The four stable tribes—elf, griffin, fairy, and dwarf—were given a stone to destroy, except we now know some smaller pieces were kept."

"Tribe? This is the first I've heard of tribes." Mitzi leaned in.

"Yes, in the Garden, we have nine provinces, and each one corresponds to a tribe. The tribal distinctions are not as important now as they used to be. We do a pretty good job of working together. There were other tribes, but they went rogue and didn't join us. The current thinking is that they went extinct for some reason or became isolated somewhere we don't know. It's possible they found pieces of the larger stones, which we all thought were destroyed. Now we have the Winter Stone locked away but need to find any other pieces before *Lupus Imperium* does."

"How do you know they still exist? Maybe this was the only remaining remnant," Mitzi asked.

"Again, ancient lore says that it's all for one and one for all. If the other stones didn't exist, then the Winter Stone wouldn't have been able to be switched on."

Lulu looked thoughtful. "Ah. I see."

Elsa looked at her husband. "Are you thinking what I'm thinking?"

Ekk did that thing with his tongue over his teeth, then spoke. "Yes." Turning to Lulu, he said, "You will go with Mitzi. Elsa and I will wait for the next opportunity."

Now Lulu looked guilty. "Are you sure? I mean, will you be safe?"

Mitzi, Elsa, and Ekk laughed.

"These two are incredibly capable," Mitzi said, fully aware of their exceptional abilities.

"It will also give us time to rest for a minute," Elsa said modestly. "We just got back from a trans-Atlantic flight. And besides," she looked around the cabin in an exaggerated manner, "it's our size."

"You always wanted me to take you on a cruise," Ekk said.

The door opened, and their "host" returned.

"Okay, it's all set. Who's going with me and Mitzi?"

Lulu raised her hand.

"Fine, lift off is 4:00 a.m. There's another bunk room down the hall that's empty. We can stay there. I told the crew to leave me alone, and they will. Their livelihoods depend on this eccentric billionaire." He jerked a thumb at his chest and opened the door. "Follow me."

"Billionaire?" He now had Lulu's full attention.

As he led everyone a few doors down, Jack said, "Family business." The usually serious man laughed and opened another oval metal door with a key. "They think it's totally in character for me to show up unexpectedly and commandeer the humblest rooms on the ship. I told them that Elon Musk and I had a competition for unique lodgings."

This room had bunk beds on each wall, enough to fit at least six comfortably. The bathroom had a closed door, and there was a table with stools bolted to the floor in the middle. The air was stale, but Lulu appeared relieved she wasn't so closed in and stretched her arms out. Mitzi put her bag on one of the bunks and sat at the table. "So Sally's an agent of the Hercynian Garden."

At this, Jack's smile widened. "She is, by marriage. Sally and I do everything together, and the Johnson family has worked with the Hercynian Garden for at least eighty years." He went to a slit in the wall, unscrewed wing nuts, and fresh air blew in. "It's cold but fresh."

Lulu walked to it and stared out at the rapidly diminishing shoreline.

Jack took a seat at the table across from Mitzi. "My grandfather was Captain Theo Johnson, who was once pressed into service as the, well. 'Navy' of the Hercynian Forest. His ship was in the Baltic Sea." Ekk quietly joined them while Elsa rummaged in her bag and pulled out a handful of German granola bars.

Lulu eyed the bars. "Now it's a party."

Mitzi studied Elsa. "Your eye is really turning black now. Does it hurt?"

"Only when I smile. Eat. We need to settle down right now, and this will help."

Mitzi tried to engage their rescuer. "So, Jack, was it a magic Navy?"

"Not *per se*, but we did have one very special crew member." He checked his watch. "We need to turn in after this. Tomorrow will come early."

"Mitzi, I brought these for Panda. She's always hungry." Elsa put what looked like granola bars, labeled Granade, on the table before zipping up her bag.

"I want one." Lulu grabbed a bar from the pile and unwrapped it. "Will this grenade explode?" She took a bite.

"The brand is called Granade." Elsa said. "It's the German version of a Lara bar. We do need to get in touch with Panda. Tell her not to worry."

"Your cell service will probably be gone now as we are at sea, but you can try. I guess they'll think it's me making a call." Jack finally grabbed a bar and joined in.

"Who's they?" Mitzi asked. She jumped up and stood by the open slit of a window and listened to her message from Panda. "Panda said the training is going well. What do I tell her now?"

"Nothing." This was from Ekk, who had been uncharacteristically quiet. His face was serious. "This is a mission, Mitzi. You can call her when you get home tomorrow. Look. The fact that *Lupus Imperium* sent agents to attack us at the airport tells me this is not a time to risk being discovered. We must get somewhere safe and find out what's happening."

Ekk's words took whatever levity was left out of their little party as each sat chewing and thinking about the situation.

"Frederick Winter was one of his crew." Jack broke the silence.

This drew Mitzi back to the table. "Oh my god. He was one of my dads. I never got to meet him." Mitzi sat on a stool, a bit overwhelmed by the mention of her father, Ehren's former partner, who died in battle.

"Frederick was very brave and a good warrior," Jack said. "He was young when he signed up on our ship."

"I'm still trying to get my head around the Hercynian Garden having a Navy," Mitzi said. She fingered her necklace. "I'm tired of learning this all piece by piece."

Jack sat beside her. "No, they don't exactly have a Navy, but they partner with whoever they can to do what needs to be done. Back in the 1920s, when *Lupus Imperium* was still called Wolf Raven, they whipped up the monsters in the Baltic." He used his arms expressively to describe them. "Giant octopus and other creatures that don't even have names were sinking ships with free creatures on them. The Garden started to embed magical guardian folk on the ships for protection." He pointed to her neck. "Frederick was the one who made sure you got the octopus amulet, Mitzi, his personal magic is in there."

She cupped her octopus pendant with both hands. "I don't even know where to start. How did this get to me?"

"Family legend has it that before he died, he told my grandfather to give it to you once you were born. Maybe he had a premonition. Frederick loved the sea and wore the octopus medallion all the time. He was excited about your birth and giving it to you was all he could do to protect you."

"That can't be right." She looked into space. This new information was a lot to take in. "My mother said a gypsy-type woman or a witch gave it to her when she left the Hercynian Garden. And why would Frederick leave anyway if he and Ehrenhardt were having a baby?"

Now Ekk jumped in. "It's been a long time since the gift was given. I'm guessing Theo Johnson gave it to someone he trusted. His job was at sea, not in the Black Forest."

Jack tried to answer Mitzi's question. "Apparently, Frederick and your biological mother didn't hit it off. She was getting ideas about her role as the surrogate and wanted to keep you. It caused fights. He wanted to be away until Susan, that's your mother's name, right? Was gone."

"Makes sense." Tears sprang from Mitzi's eyes, and Elsa sat on the other side of her and put her arm around her. "I understand the wanting to stay away from Susan part."

While they talked, Lulu walked around the bunk room, touching the walls. "This room felt big at first next to that other one. Now the walls are closing in."

"Breathe," Elsa said. "Or lay down and close your eyes." Lulu groaned in frustration.

"Okay, so what's the plan?" Mitzi turned her eyes toward her anxious friend. "Lulu does need to go back to port. What's your role with this ship? Why did you need to hide us?" Mitzi needed to regain control of her life.

"I'll answer those questions, but"—Jack checked a message on his expensive watch—"this crew is not known to me. I've got to meet with the first mate again." He pressed something on the watch dial and moved to the exit. Lulu flung herself forward and grabbed his sleeve. "Oh no, you don't! I saw this movie. You're going to lock us all in here, and we're gonna die."

Jack looked alarmed. "There's no time for this." He looked to the elves for help.

Elsa simply said, "Trust him."

Mitzi added her two cents. "In for a penny..."

Jack nodded and walked through the hatch. They all heard the lock click into place.

"I hope you're right," Lulu said, her hands on her hips.

Chapter Seven

Breakthrough

Ahanu seemed less mean to me this morning. He showed up with the horses and stood to the side, laughing softly with Etsi and drinking coffee before we left. His face was different around her, less scowly and even with a hint of a smile. Valerie didn't need to help me today, and I mounted Major like a boss. The routine was the same: dark thirty, coffee, horses, and plodding up Tava Mountain, but it was no longer brand new. My thoughts were more settled after a good night's sleep, and instead of negative thoughts, I was resigned that either it would work or not. Either way, I was going home today. We reached our "raven calling/ancestor whatever spot," and I sat in the maze's center. Whoa. Almost at once, I ceased to feel the little pebbles under my butt or the cold. As soon as I closed my eyes, I felt a massive shift in energy. Upon opening them, instead of pre-dawn darkness, a bright light surrounded me and a soft wind blew. My ancestors, male and female, were there. I heard music of some kind just far enough away so as not to be able to identify it. I stood, my overweight, messy-haired self. But I had ridden a horse, run a tax business, and was in a long-term happy relationship with my wife. I had stared down Wolfrum and almost died because of it, and now, I was here. The women stood with me. All those women seated on hard wooden chairs were now milling around. My badass litany of successes melted, and tears sprang in my eyes when I saw her. "Grandma!"

She opened her arms, and without words, the shade, for she was not corporeal, hugged me tight and whispered in my ear, "You have everything you need."

"Is this heaven? I've missed you so much." My grandfather walked up behind her, reminding me of Ahanu with his rugged face. We paused as we looked at each other. The wind blew harder as the sky darkened. The flapping of wings was deafening. My grandfather touched my shoulder and walked back into the nothingness.

Without me moving my lips, my voice said, "Leave me for now. I will see you in Africa." What? This would take some time to figure out. For now, the loss was heartbreaking as my people dissolved into a swirl of energy around me. I reached after my ancestors as Grandma melted into me and kind of "landed."

I stood alone on the top of the mountain, chest heaving, racing heart, and a broken maze at my feet. *Did I do that?* The wind was a typical predawn cold breeze. The rocks were scattered here and there, and Ahanu even had his mouth hanging open. Valerie petted her horse and stared. I felt different, whole. I knew the darkness in that other sphere was an uncountable number of ravens that had blotted out the sun. I wondered, *Were these confident words mine? Were my ancestors inside of me? Where did they go?*

"Wow." Valerie hugged me. I had no words, as I assumed they saw what I did.

Ahanu grunted, but it was more like a "huh" than a growly disapproval. I hid my smile, untying my horse. After a couple of days, I figured I'd be able to interpret this man's noises.

Taking control, he cleared his throat and said, "Let's go. We're finished here."

***

I jumped down from Major and ran into Etsi's house. Valerie called after me, "No problem. I'll take care of your horse."

"Thanks!" I called back over my shoulder. She couldn't see my sheepish apologetic smile as I raced to the guest room. I couldn't wait to tell Mitzi about the breakthrough. Twyla was waiting in the living room and said, "Panda!"

"Sorry, just give me a minute," I breathlessly said as I ran by them. Etsi went toward the front door, probably to find out what happened on the mountain from Valerie and Ahanu. "Somebody had a good day," she said to Twyla.

"Either that or she had to pee," Twyla said.

My phone was near my backpack, and I scooped it up after a quick wee. No messages. The one from my dentist's office didn't count. Why hadn't she called me back? I used voice control. "Call wife." I sat on the bed and waited for the connection, thinking that it wouldn't take long to pack. A recorded voice said, "You have reached Mitzi's guided travel. Please leave a message."

I punched in the numbers for Ekk. Then Elsa. Then Mitzi again. All I got were the recorded messages. Frustrated, I packed, shoving in clothes a bit more forcefully than what was needed. Twyla appeared at the door. "Panda."

"What?" I turned toward her and exhaled. No need to take it out on her.

"We need to call the Garden." Her face was pale.

***

After receiving news of my wife's predicament, Valerie drove Twyla and me to the airport. "Please stay safe. I've decided to stay a couple more days with Mom to ensure she knows what we are up against."

"That's wise. And tell her again how grateful I am to her and Ahanu for everything."

"You will let me know the second you find out about Mitzi?"

That made me start to cry. I searched in my pocket for a tissue.

"It's going to be okay, Panda," Twyla said. "You wouldn't have had the breakthrough you did unless you were on the right path."

"Yay for me, but what about Mitzi?" We bumped along the road, and I said, "Ow," when my head hit the B-pillar on the passenger side. My right hand found the "Jesus" strap attached to the roof above the window. "This is rougher than the road to get to your mom's house."

"It's quicker." Valerie slowed a bit. "Sorry."

"You don't need to apologize. I'm just sick with worry. Mitzi and the elves are on an ocean liner? This is crazy." I shook my head. "And who would have seen Sally and Jack Johnson as part of the resistance?"

"That's part of being an agent of the Garden. You're only effective if no one knows," Twyla said. "Oof." I was afraid Twyla might bounce out of the truck bed as we went over a dip in the road.

"It's a lot." Valerie drove with purpose.

"Mitzi's not going to be there long, Panda. Elsa and that guard they picked up at the airport will leave separately." Twyla had gotten the call and was quite chuffed about being the one with all the news. "He also said they had new intel about where you're going."

I was still obsessing about the strange turn of events. "Lulu is with them. This is so crazy." I looked out over the desert, now bright in the pre-noon heat. "She was the guard at my tax office. It seems like a thousand years ago."

"A lot has happened, to be sure." Valerie turned back onto a main road. "The fact that the elves were attacked in the baggage claim at the airport is a big escalation in the conflict. So public!"

Twyla reached through the window from the back of the truck to smooth my hair. "Don't worry, Panda. We'll figure it all out." She was proving to be part of our little family, but this was weird.

"What are you doing?"

"You pet Brutus. I'm petting you."

I laughed. "Why?"

She retracted her hand, and after a pause, she said, "Sometimes, I don't know how to help you."

"Join the club."

Valerie smiled and used her right hand to jostle my leg.

The airport was now in sight. "Help me what?"

"Help you get over yourself." Twyla was always straightforward and sometimes even answered rhetorical questions. "I've watched you since coming to Merryville. You need more joy." At my baffled expression, she squealed with laughter. "Petting works with Brutus."

"Brutus is a cat," I snapped. "Can't you see? I don't know where my wife is, so excuse me if I don't seem cheerful."

Valerie stayed quiet, and tension filled the car.

Twyla's face reddened. "I'm sorry, Panda. I just want you to be happy. You have such a good partner in Mitzi, and a nice house, and you live in the sunshine with friends. I would love that."

I squinted at the airport for almost a minute and tried to hide my watery eyes. Twyla's words hit home. Was my mountain experience enabling me to clear out my ears and listen to what people were saying? How selfish I could be! My life looked pretty good from the outside, yet I often insisted on finding the fly in the soup to complain about.

I turned to her. "Twyla, I'll think about what you said." She looked pleased.

As Valerie navigated the crazy airport signage and pulled up in front of our white zone, I said, attempting humor, "Things should be different now that Ahanu and Valerie took me to the mountain. I'm the caller of ravens now." Seconds after Val pulled to the curb, Twyla hopped out of the truck bed, opened my door, and bowed.

"Raven caller." She burst into laughter. Even with the present circumstances, I had to smile.

Valerie went to get the bags out of the back, and we rushed to help her. We hugged. "Valerie, see you in a few days. Please thank your mom and Ahanu for me."

"I will, and this time will be good for Mom so she can process what she now knows. Call me when you know something."

As she hugged me back, Twyla hugged both of us, almost knocking us over. Despite the worries about Mitzi and the elves, my heart was filled with their support.

The flight home was only a couple of hours. I worried about danger at LAX. Didn't the elves just get attacked there? I let Twyla have the window seat, and she stared at the clouds. Once on the ground, Juniper met us at the curb by baggage. We jumped in her car quickly.

Twyla sat in the back with the Gooden's beloved dog, Layla, and had a love fest while I caught up with Valerie's wife. "So that's all I know. We're going to use Twyla's dagger to contact the Garden when we get home. With any luck, Mitzi will be back by tonight."

"You need protecting, Juniper, but so do you, Panda. Maybe we all need to stay at your house 'til Mitzi gets back." Twyla's face was suddenly between us, hovering over the console.

Juniper maneuvered her Citroen through traffic. "Oooh. That's not going to be easy. I'm negotiating our next exhibit, and I have to be at the museum pretty soon. I've arranged for Twyla to be present as an intern."

She addressed Twyla. "Do you think you can be an intern without calling attention to your fairy-ness?" Juniper nailed her with a look in the rearview mirror.

"Oh yes! Let's call the Garden, then off to the museum. I won't leave your side for a *second*." Twyla looked positively elated. She didn't catch the look that passed between Juniper and me, and I had to turn to look out the window to hide my smile. The knowledge that I would see my wife soon and leave for Africa consumed my thoughts for the rest of the ride.

I unlocked the house, and Twyla insisted on doing a check of each room before we went inside. Juniper and I sat on the couch and waited. She entered each room like a TV FBI agent.

"She's been watching police procedurals," Juniper explained. I was patient and petted Brutus, remembering how Twyla petted me in the truck. In each room, she called out loudly, "Clear!" and we giggled every time.

"Let me check the treehouse." Twyla went out the back sliding glass door to check Ekk and Elsa's home.

"Hurry up, Twyla. I want to call the Garden," I called after her.

We heard one last loud, "clear," and she joined us in the living room. I knew Twyla as not particularly lethal, more like a court jester, so I asked a question. "So, Twyla, if you had encountered a hostile person or thing, what weapons do fairies actually have?"

Juniper laughed aloud at that, and I joined her until we cried. Twyla looked hurt. She stood up, went out the front door, and returned with a pile of old newspapers she brought in from the porch. She was small, and the papers almost covered her eyes. She held a stick from the front yard in her hand, still with a leaf on it. I thought she looked so adorable. It was no wonder people sold glass tchotchkes of elves and fairies.

"Panda, do you need these?"

"Mm, not really." I turned to Juniper as she placed them in the fireplace. "I always say I'm going to catch up and read them all but..."

I didn't finish my sentence due to shock as Twyla incinerated the papers by pointing the crooked little stick at them. The newspapers not only burned but vaporized in a green flash, leaving a fine gray ash.

"Oh." That was all I managed. Juniper was frozen as if she couldn't believe her eyes.

"Well, now. I must say, I do feel safer," Juniper managed.

"Basic tree fairy stuff." She smiled and looked as innocent as a two-year-old. Juniper and I shared looks that reflected our astonishment as our silly, but lethal, fairy friend put her dagger on the living room table. "Now, let's call Germany."

***

At Sea

Despite the circumstances, Elsa, Ekk, Lulu, and Mitzi could sleep. In fact, Lulu was snoring loudly. Mitzi wondered if Elsa had something to do with that, but they were all very tired anyway after the adrenaline rush from the car chase wore off. Racing from the airport with *Lupus Imperium* chasing you, and then being trapped inside a shipping container, were heart-pounding experiences. She couldn't wait to get off the ship and call Panda. Her watch woke her with a strong vibration shortly before 3:30 a.m. Jack had left to ensure all was in place for their helicopter departure and would return to get her and Lulu soon.

Ekk was sleepy but sat up and yawned. Moving to her bunk, he sat. "Are you ready? The first thing you need to do is call the Garden and make sure they know what happened. We've been out of contact for too long. I'm sure everyone there is worried."

"Of course. Right after I call Panda. You know how she gets."

She could see him smile in the semi-darkness. "I do. Okay, after that. I think Jack is arranging for one of the lifeboats to take us back to the Merryville port. Ships are equipped with speed boats now. We should be home before too long."

Elsa, who had been sleeping quietly, stirred, suddenly awake. "Do you hear that?"

"All I can hear is Lulu snoring," Ekk said.

"Make her stop." Elsa was wide awake now.

Mitzi moved to Lulu, never questioning Elsa's instincts. One gentle shake and the woman was awake and already in attack mode. "What? Where?" Then she slumped a bit. "Oh, we're still here."

"Elsa says we have to be quiet. Your snoring is loud." Lulu looked ready to argue or comment on that when they all heard a noise in the corridor. Mitzi put her backpack on and said, "Our helicopter must be here. As soon as I'm in the air, I'll contact the Garden."

The sound was not as stealthy as they would have expected with Jack returning. As it came closer, Lulu said, "That sounds like an army marching on the metal grating."

"Oh dear," Elsa said and looked so vulnerable with her now very black eye.

Before they could talk more, the metal hatch door wheel spun and opened. Jack was thrust in. His clothing was disheveled, and he had a swollen face. They were stunned for a millisecond as he said through bloody teeth, "I'm so sorry."

Two soldier types in olive drab green uniforms stepped in, their pants tucked into army boots, ready for action. Both carried some kind of automatic rifle held at the ready, and both men wore hard facial expressions.

Jack joined his motley crew, and as if by agreement, they were all silent while whatever this was played out.

Behind the soldiers, a man in fatigues with medals on his chest and stars on his collar marched in, smiling as he surveyed them. His blondish hair was in a fade, and cold blue eyes framed his tanned face. "Good morning. My name is Viktor Volkov, and you are my prisoners." To his armed men, he said, "Search them, then take our *billionaire* to the brig." Several more soldiers entered the room behind their commander, and they patted each of Jack's party down in turn, looking for weapons and communication devices. Lulu was soon relieved of her gun and Ekk his dagger. An officer they called Sergei crushed each of their cell phones with one stomp of a boot. They were screwed. "It was an ambush," Jack said to Mitzi through swollen lips. "The helicopter arrived—"

"Stop talking." The beating Jack had taken must have been brutal because he shut his mouth without making another sound. Viktor walked over to Mitzi, finishing the explanation. "He was going to say that your helicopter arrived, but my men and I were on it. Oh, and I'm afraid there's been a change in your itinerary."

"Where are you taking us?" Ekk may be somewhat small, but his voice was strong and challenging.

As if noticing Ekk for the first time, Viktor Volkov commanded, "Take him to the brig too. Our lab needs creatures like him to study."

Elsa made a strangled "meep" sound and looked ready to crumple.

To the group, he said sarcastically, "I'm sorry I can't join you for your ocean journey, but there's a search on for the Summer Stone right now, and I'm coordinating efforts worldwide." He appeared to enjoy his cruelty.

At a gasp from Mitzi, he said, "Oh yes, you have no secrets." Viktor sneered. "You all run around, thinking you're so smart and righteous." He looked at his men, who laughed on cue. "Your efforts were entertaining but have become a nuisance. Once we are far enough out, Davey Jones will have a word." He laughed at his reference to the oceanic abyss, then crisply turned and walked to the door.

Lulu yelled, "Hey. Those were your agents at the airport? They were pretty lame. A soccer team in baggage took them out."

Mitzi's eyes widened. The part-time cop had just sassed the leader of *Lupus Imperium*.

Victor's jaw tightened, and he addressed her. "You should have stayed a," he moved his arm in a circular motion, "what do you Americans call it, a mall cop." As he walked out the door, he ordered, "Sergei, the fat one goes first when we dispatch them."

Elsa moved toward Ekk as he was taken by two soldiers, one on each side. Jack was in such bad shape that it only took one soldier, holding an arm, to steer him out to the corridor.

They closed the door, and Mitzi watched the security wheel spin. Elsa, Lulu, and Mitzi stared at each other.

"He doesn't think women are a threat," Elsa said. She had a glint in her eye that hinted otherwise. She walked to the slitted window and looked through it with a thousand-yard stare. "That was his second mistake."

"What was the first?" Lulu asked.

"Underestimating Ekk."

Chapter Eight

The Fowlers' Living Room

I stared at Twyla's dagger as it spun. "Come on, come on."

Ehren appeared holographically, seated at a table next to Heloisa, his right-hand security. Both looked grim.

"Panda." His face was like stone.

"Ehren, we just got home. Mitzi's not here." He was scaring me. "Has anything happened?"

"Sorry, Panda. It's Twyla reporting in, sir." The fairy tilted her head in front of my face with a big smile. Could she not read the room?

"Panda can call the ravens now." She paused. "Or at least is mostly on her way to calling them. You see—"

I pushed her out of the way. "Twyla! Not now!"

Ehren exhaled. "We just finished a security briefing. There is much to tell you." I heard Heloisa's heavy chair scrape as she pushed it back and stood. Ehren got up also and addressed her. "Go now. You know what to do."

Through the hologram, Heloisa saluted us and marched out the door. This magical communication always impressed me.

After the sound of a door closing, Ehren appeared to be alone. "Panda, Mitzi won't be coming home tonight."

Blood drained from my face, and I almost fainted at his words. Our magical lives had already put us in danger too many times. "Is she alive?"

"All indications are yes, but—"

"What happened?" My voice was flat. All indications. Juniper leaned forward with wide eyes. Nobody cut Ehren off.

"Ekk, Elsa, your old security guard, and my daughter are all captive aboard a ship headed to Africa."

"My wife? Lulu? Captive?"

"Yes, Panda. Taken captive by no less than the new leader of *Lupus Imperium*."

"How could this happen? Mitzi was only going to the airport to pick up Ekk and Elsa. There must be some mistake. How are they on a ship? What kind of ship? This makes no sense." I was babbling aloud.

Juniper looked for paper and a pen.

"No time for further explanations right now. You're going to get a new airline ticket shortly. You will board a plane and fly to Namibia tomorrow to meet your tour bus. You will have a new name and—"

I shook my head vigorously. "No!" More head shaking. "No, I'm not going anywhere until we get Mitzi back!" I stood in my living room in Merryville, staring down the leader of all free creatures in the Hercynian Forest, but I didn't care. "Tell me how she's going to be rescued."

Juniper turned around a piece of paper that had one word on it.

After a breath, I added that word. "Please."

Tension was high. Both Juniper and Twyla stayed silent. Juniper usually relished these communications with the Garden, but her face was solemn at the news that something had happened to Mitzi and our guardians.

Ehren looked fit to be tied but said, "Viktor Volkov has emerged as the new leader of *Lupus Imperium*. This is unwelcome news, as he is a skilled military man. Somehow, they learned of our safe house container in your port."

Juniper mouthed to me, "Safe house? Port?"

I asked, "Why did they need a safe house?"

He sighed, clearly frustrated. "They were being chased from the airport by agents. Now, can I go on..." he asked, "please?"

I nodded, realizing my runaway mouth wasn't helping.

"A member of a Merryville cell, Jack Johnson, does considerable business with the shipping line they are on," Ehren said. "He'd arranged to fly Mitzi out this morning when Volkov and his men ambushed them. That's all we know."

This time, Juniper wrote, "Jack Johnson? Like Sally and Jack?" on her paper.

I ignored her. "How do you even know that?"

"Jack did get through, Panda. That's how we know who did this. But the call was cut off. The ravens told us the rest. This is why I insisted you learn to call the ravens. They're our eyes in the skies." He adjusted his view. "Twyla, thank you for the good news that Panda now controls them. It could not have come at a better time."

Twyla no longer smiled. "I think I should clarify—"

This time I silenced her. "No." For a split second, I panicked. Yes, progress was made on Tava Mountain, but calling the ravens at will? I looked at the couch where I'd wasted so much time and felt a deep regret.

"Panda?" Ehren's brow was furrowed.

I snapped out of it. "Tell me what we need to do." I resolved internally that no matter what, no matter how, I would make whatever was needed happen.

"Here is the plan..." Ehren began.

***

Captured

Aboard the ship, Elsa and Mitzi were busy making their own plans. Lulu was again studying the walls, looking for any weakness they could exploit. She had the grate covering the air duct unscrewed and leaned against the metal wall. She motioned with a dime she'd been using as an ad hoc screwdriver between two fingers, Lulu said, "All those spy movies are bullshit."

"What?" Mitzi lifted her head.

"They all got Tom Cruz and Sigourney Weaver crawling through these things to get to somewhere else. I don't even think Elsa could fit in there."

"We're not sure where it goes anyway," Elsa said, and looked through her bag.

Lulu dusted her hands off. "All I could see was a lot of rat poop."

"Maybe we're looking at this all wrong," Mitzi said. "Panda took me to one of those escape rooms once. I mean, if the ship were sinking, the owners of the ship wouldn't want all their crew people to drown, right?" Mitzi was trying to think her way out of the situation.

"Yes, but they also wouldn't lock each other in like this." Elsa stopped rummaging. "There must be a way to open that door."

"I already tried! There is no way to open the wheel thing from this side." Lulu went back to it again, energy renewed. "They must have put a bar to wedge it on the other side like a Lo-Jack on a car."

For a few seconds, all they heard was the sound of the ship's engines taking them further out to sea.

"I feel so helpless." Mitzi put her face in both her hands, elbows on the table. "We're going to die on this ship, and no one will know."

Elsa moved in front of her, a hand on each hip. "You are one-half griffin, Mitzi Fowler. Don't ever forget that."

Motioning with her hand around the steel room, Mitzi responded. "In case you haven't noticed, there's not much room to fly out of here. My foot is about the only body part that could get through the window slit." They could hear the wake and smell the ocean air through the tiny slit, which was only put in the room for ventilation.

"How's your eye? It looks painful," Lulu asked, changing the subject.

"I should meditate, but first, there must be something we can use." Elsa went back to her bunk and searched in her bag again. Then, throwing her short arms in the air, she announced, "Nothing." Elsa joined Mitzi at the table and started to meditate.

After a minute she opened her eyes wide. "Of course. Griffins fly, but they also have great strength. I think you should try the door, Mitzi."

"Seriously?" Mitzi was slight and wasn't feeling particularly powerful. She had dressed for the airport, not to fight *Lupus Imperium*. She motioned to her shorts, summer top, and Sketchers. "My shoulders aren't even making those nodules that happen before my wings sprout." With Lulu and Elsa staring at her, she went to the door and grabbed the opening wheel at ten and two, like they taught you in driver's ed. "But I will try." She widened her stance and gave it a mighty pull. The metal beneath her hands was heavily painted and felt rough and cold. Her yoga-toned muscles strained and...the thing wouldn't budge.

"Let me help." Lulu went to her and, using their combined strength, the women again tried to turn the wheel that would open the door. It seemed to be frozen in place.

"It's no use." Mitzi shook her head.

"I have another idea. The octopus medallion." Elsa pointed at Mitzi's chest. "Sometimes you can boost a magical ability with a magical item."

"Honestly? Sometimes I wonder if Ekk didn't get the wrong medallion. I've worn it off and on most of my life. To me, it's a cool piece of plastic with an octopus image underneath." She sat again, deflated. "How would I even activate it?"

"Mitzi Fowler! How can you doubt the stories? Especially now that Jack Johnson told you it was your father's! And don't you dare give up! Either of you. They may be torturing my husband and Jack right now while you sit here and mope."

"But," Mitzi felt a rush of embarrassment and cried. "I'm so sorry, Elsa. You're right." She walked to the little window, took the pendant in her hand, and looked out at the sea. She said a little prayer for Ekk and Jack Johnson, called on her father, and even said "octopus, octopus" many times silently to no effect. She returned to the table and sat. All three women were silent.

"*Gott in Himmel.*" Elsa's eyes were wide again.

Lulu perked up and looked at Mitzi, pointing. "That necklace."

Mitzi pulled it from her blouse and stared at it. For the first time ever, a soft glow emanated from it.

"Now try the door!" suggested Elsa. All three scrambled off their stools and ran to the door. "One, two, three!" They tugged in unison. Nothing.

"Again," shouted Elsa.

"One, two..."

This time, Mitzi threw her emotions into it. Images of Ekk being tortured, Jack's bloody teeth, Panda almost dying, ice covering Merryville, and then...a giant octopus tentacle rising out of the ocean. With a yell, Mitzi shook the wheel back and forth with great griffin strength. Lulu stepped back as the wheel turned, and they heard a metallic thunk on the grating outside the door.

"Whatever they barred the door with fell." Elsa was already getting her bag and quickly returned back to them. "Let's go."

***

Panda to the Rescue

Juniper drove to the port with me in the front seat and Twyla in the back. "What do you expect to find, Panda?"

"I don't know." I had an idea, but it was too outrageous to put into words.

"Shouldn't we wait at the house?"

"Juniper, if there's a rescue, I'm in on it. You heard what I said to Ehren."

Twyla popped up from the back. "Turn here. The helicopter pad is that way." Juniper turned sharply, and her Citroen tires squealed a bit as we all jerked to the left.

"Um, a little more advance notice would be helpful, Twyla." Juniper was nervous.

"Sorry. The helicopter spot is—"

"There!" I could see the helipad was empty. "Pull over and let me out."

"But." One look at me, and she said nothing more. Juniper parked her car illegally on the tarmac.

Right away, a voice came over the loudspeaker. "This is a restricted area. Move the vehicle off the tarmac."

"Go. Wait for me at the end of the road." I felt a deep calm.

"For the record, I don't think this is a good idea." Juniper looked around and said, "Uh oh."

"Let me go, Panda. I'm the guardian!" Twyla looked worried. "At least I can fly, I mean sometimes, and not that far...it's more like levitation..." Her words faded as I slammed the door. A black Tahoe that said Port Security on the side started toward the Citroen as Juniper turned the car around. Instead of following her, however, they tracked me as I walked resolutely to the center of the helipad. The voice on the loudspeaker was practically yelling now. "Get off the helipad now or be subject to arrest. This is not safe, we have incoming."

***

Juniper drove down the road and out of the air traffic area, parking where she and Twyla could see what was happening. Nothing could have prepared her.

First, she saw a spot on the horizon. Then she and Twyla watched as a large helicopter with AIRBUS on the side got bigger until it was poised to land. Panda stood in the center of the painted landing area, directly below, hands raised to the sky.

"She's lost her mind," said Juniper.

"I think she's trying to call the ravens," said Twyla.

"Is that what she's doing? Looks like suicide to me." Juniper watched in horror as the big helicopter got closer. The black Tahoe was idling at the edge of the painted circle, waiting. When the copter got close enough to land, it hovered instead of landing, Panda preventing the inevitable. Finally, two men with guns got out of the Tahoe and approached Panda, who stood, wind blowing her short hair, hands raised as if frozen.

"She's going to get arrested or shot," Juniper whispered. Then, in a louder voice, she said, "Do something, Twyla!"

The sky darkened then, or rather, many black birds, big shiny ravens, blotted out the sun. The gunmen looked up, while the helicopter maneuvered away from the birds and took off. Panda stayed in her position, arms raised, as ravens organized themselves around her in a circle.

Twyla said, "I don't think she needs any help."

The security people lowered their guns and walked back to their car, stepping over birds. Juniper saw Panda slowly lower her arms and appear to speak to someone they couldn't see. Ravens covered the Tahoe's windshield and packed themselves tightly around the vehicle. Not a shot was fired.

They could hear sirens in the distance. "We need to leave," Twyla said, "It won't do for all of us to be arrested."

"None of us are going to be arrested," said Juniper as she fired up the engine and floored it back down the road toward the helipad. All the while, Panda walked unharmed through the birds. There were so many! Thousands upon thousands in the biggest show of force Juniper had seen since that old black-and-white Hitchcock movie. It was still dark as night, with occasional rays of sun shining through gaps between flapping wings. What a sight to see. Panda was partway down the street when she stopped. Twyla opened the door, jumped out, and led their trance-like friend back to the passenger seat. The door was barely shut when the Citroen took off.

***

"Oh my god, are you okay?" Juniper looked worried. She had seen her wife in a state like this once.

"Just drive," I said.

Twyla was looking out the back window. "Lucky the ravens are keeping the cops from having helicopters in the sky. There's a good chance they won't find us."

"We need to go to Namibia quickly while *Lupus Imperium* is still headed to Tanzania. Their leader was in that helicopter," I said calmly. "He was going to stop here in Merryville and kill us all first, but the ravens showing up changed his mind."

"How do you know all this?" Juniper inquired.

"A little birdie told me." Suddenly, I felt elated and did a crazy little laugh. I felt dreamlike yet laser-focused. Was this what life was going to be like from now on since the ravens were keeping me informed?

"What about Mitzi?" Even Twyla was confused. "Ekk and Elsa?"

"She'll be fine. They're *all* fine now and on their way to Africa. Now get me home so I can pack and take a nap. I'm exhausted."

I fell asleep in the car and awoke as we pulled into my driveway. I jumped out of the car and rounded it to talk to them through the driver's window. "You two go home." I ordered. "Juniper, keep Twyla with you twenty-four seven, or better yet, go back to the reservation and hide at Etsi's house."

"Are you crazy? Things are blowing up here. We need to stay together." Juniper's red hair looked as frazzled as she sounded.

"Juniper, Twyla, listen to me." I felt like Superman. Confidence flowed through me. "I've got the ravens. They're helping me— us. Did you see that helicopter turn tail and run? The supreme leader of the *Lupus Imperium* was on that flight! Ha!"

"Well, you certainly did call the birds." Juniper was capitulating. "But I do remember hearing Ekk say the ravens are fickle."

Twyla stared at me in awe.

"Not right now, they aren't. Did you see what just happened? They told me Mitzi is already on her way to Namibia with Ekk. She's fine. Lulu's being debriefed in the Garden. Mitzi will be waiting for me when I land. In the meantime, check in with Ali Badawi down at Taggart's, and keep your new intern close by." I pointed at Twyla. This made the fairy guardian beam.

Juniper relaxed a bit. "What a day."

"You really did call the ravens. It gave me goosebumps!" Twyla sounded awestruck. Her words felt so good after many months of doubting myself. "You okay, Juniper?"

"I guess. I'm staying in Merryville though. There's too much to do at the museum." She laughed. "Well, this is what we've been waiting for, right?" She grabbed my arm and shook it. "Raven Caller! We will check in with Ali and Puddle at the store." She was still holding onto the steering wheel with her other hand like it was a lifeline.

I laughed and leaned through her window, kissing her on the cheek. "You can let go of the wheel now. And you don't need to do anything. Just stay safe yourself. Juniper, for the first time, I'm confident going on this mission. I'll get the neighbors to feed Brutus. It's probably best you keep to a normal routine. With any luck, Mitzi and I will be home by Christmas."

"I bet you can't wait to talk to Mitzi."

At that, my bravado fizzled a little. "I have to pretend like I don't know her for now. More will be revealed later. I'm supposed to get my new reservation today."

"Okay, you know Val and I love you two. We're sistas!" After more assurances, Twyla and Juniper left, and I was alone in our house. It warmed me that Ekk and Lulu were fine, and Mitzi was now on her way to our mission. I was finally a raven caller! Brutus complained, of course, and as I fed him food from the purple bag, I explained that his mother and I would be gone for a bit. Then, I headed to REI for some serious safari shopping for Africa.

Chapter Nine

At Sea

Unfortunately, Mitzi, Lulu, and Elsa were, in fact, not fine. Although out of their makeshift cell, they still had to find Jack and Ekk. The three made their way quietly down the corridor outside the cabin, Elsa in front. "Do you sense anything?" Mitzi knew Elsa had many magical abilities. Even if she baked like a grandma, she still was a guardian.

"Yes," was all she said.

The ship creaked, and Lulu jumped. Her landing was loud. She whispered, "Sorry."

Elsa turned around and said quietly, "I will always know where Ekk is. This is the way. We must be stealthy."

Lulu had picked up the steel bar from the ground outside their bunk room and held it tightly in her hand. "I wonder how many are on this ship."

"Modern ships have hardly any personnel," Mitzi answered. "I saw that on *60 Minutes*. Almost everything's run by computer."

"Well, that Viktor creep couldn't have packed too many on his helicopter, but who knows? I'll take out as many as I can." Lulu was clutching the bar so tight her knuckles were white.

"I wonder how they figured out we were in the container," Mitzi mused idly.

"I know. Do you think—"

"Shh!" Elsa turned around and chided them. "We're getting close. You two need to zip it."

They continued to creep along in the semi-darkness. Below deck, only every other light was on, and it was dim. Elsa led them up some narrow stairs after taking off her shoes. Mitzi and Lulu followed suit. Soon, they were on a level with regular lighting. Stenciled signage indicated four more levels above the water line. According to the directory, they were somewhere mid-ship. This didn't help much because one hall looked very much like another. They stopped as one at the sound of a handheld radio squawk. Lulu raised her bar, ready to crack someone's skull.

"They have to be close," a man's voice said, and immediately, heavy footfalls came down the hall they were just in.

Elsa, Mitzi, and Lulu flattened themselves against the wall of an intersecting corridor as two of Viktor Volkov's uniformed men ran past them toward the room where they'd escaped. Elsa jerked her head for them to go in the opposite direction from which the men had come, and they moved fast toward a double watertight door with a wheel-locking device on each side. An empty chair was positioned in front of it, and Mitzi figured this was probably where the one with the radio or his partner had sat, guarding the men inside. "I'll handle this," Mitzi said confidently, but her surge of griffin strength had passed. Lulu handed Mitzi her makeshift weapon, grabbed the wheel to open the door, and swung it wide before a discussion could be had.

Inside, they discovered twelve sailors with Jack and Ekk. Mitzi could see Jack had cleaned up a bit, although dried blood remained on his collar. Ekk ran forward. "Elsa! Good job getting free." He turned to the group. "These were the people I came with." Then to Elsa, "This is most of the crew."

Jack pointed. "Smitty's the Chief Officer."

"Two more of us are on the bridge, including the captain," Smitty said. "The communication equipment is up there. I'll take you."

Jack limped to Elsa and said, "Once on the bridge, I can call in the cavalry, if you can hold these guys off."

"How many are there?" Mitzi asked.

"There were at least five we saw," Ekk responded. "The man they call Sergei is in charge." While they talked, the rest of the crew members, eager to get out, caused a clatter that reverberated down the hall and drew the attention of their pursuers.

"There they are!" yelled one of Viktor's men, and a shot rang out, ricocheting off the metal walls. "Back, back." Ekk shepherded the sailors back into the room they were trying to escape. A Samoan crew member with big hair pushed forward to the threshold. "I don't know what this is, but I'm security. The name's Fetu. Let me help." He pulled out a Glock handgun. "This was hidden under my bunk. They missed it."

Lulu said, "I'm a police officer. Give that to me."

He looked at her, not unkindly, but said, "Nope." Another shot hit the door, making a dent on their side. Fetu fired around the open metal door that served as their shield. "I'll hold them off."

"Mitzi, let me have that bar." Lulu reached out her hand. "We might need it if Fetu here runs out of bullets." Mitzi handed it to her as she took up a position next to Fetu behind the door. Lulu said to him, "We will hold them off."

Jack said to the men remaining inside, "Stay put while we get help." Mitzi was glad the men acknowledged Jack as being in charge and obeyed him.

"Uh, Feta," Jack said, "I want to know about the Glock pistol. How did you get it on board?"

"It's Fetu. Feta is a cheese." He looked hurt. "I've got permission. Too much piracy is happening at sea. I was an ordnance specialist in the Marines."

"Apologies about the name." Jack asked, "Are there any other weapons?"

"Just my Glock. Everything else is under lock and key on the bridge."

Jack patted him on the shoulder and thanked him.

The soldier fired another shot at them after Lulu peeked through a crack in the hinge of the door. She yelled over her shoulder, "You boys gonna chat or get to the bridge?"

Mitzi hesitated. "Maybe I should stay here."

"We'll hold them off. Now go!" Elsa was fierce. "Jack's going to need you, and you need to get outside."

Get outside. Her wings! Surely the situation was serious enough to help her fly.

Lulu held the bar with both hands while Fetu kept up the gunfire. Elsa slipped into the room where the rest of the crew was gathered.

"This way." Smitty took off down the corridor, looking right and left at every juncture. Mitzi and Jack followed. Jack limped but did not complain, and Mitzi helped him up the seemingly endless stairs they needed to climb. It had been so long since she flew that she had almost forgotten it was a possibility once they were outside. Her wings would sprout, and she could fly for help. Wiry and fast, Smitty put a hand down behind him to halt their progress. "Wait. The next set of stairs will put us on top deck. Are you ready for this? We don't know who might be up there."

"Uh, I may have another way to get help," Mitzi said quietly, not sure how much else to say.

"Any way onto the bridge without going out in the open?" Jack was sweating and didn't look too good.

"Not really. This ship isn't battle-fitted. It's only for commerce."

As they continued talking, Smitty climbed the ladder and was near the top when a voice said from behind them, "Just in time."

Two hairy arms reached down and grabbed Smitty, pulling him through the hatch. "Got 'em!" a gruff voice from above said.

Mitzi turned and recognized the soldier who had crushed her cell phone under his boot heel before locking her and her friends in the berth below deck. Another of Victor's men joined them, and a face from the hatch above poked through and announced, "Smitty won't bother us anymore."

Jack shook his head, spitting mad, and yelled, "You guys have no idea the trouble you're in. Before I left, my own security team was to send in the Coast Guard if they didn't hear from me."

The *Lupus Imperium* men didn't seem worried. A soldier mocked him. "Ooh, the Coast Guard coming for the billionaire!"

"Tape his mouth," said Sergei, as he climbed the ladder. "Her, too, but first make sure her wings can't deploy."

Mitzi was shocked. They knew about her wings!

A soldier put tape over Jack's mouth and poked him with a gun. "Stay put."

Mitzi was trussed up like a mummy and couldn't move her arms. "How do you expect me to climb out?" The soldier didn't bother to answer and roughly taped her mouth. He and the man on the deck lifted her up. She could hear Jack being ordered to climb.

Once on deck, Sergei walked forward, lowering his radio. "Viktor says no more executions until we get the camera going. They'll be bringing up survivors soon."

This sent a chill down Mitzi's spine. Anymore? Who had they killed?

A soldier grabbed her arm, and she and Jack were led on deck to a row of chairs. She had to walk like a Geisha with all the ropes they trussed her up in. Jack's hands were tied behind his back. The attackers were taking no chances that Mitzi's griffin side would appear and she would fly away.

A cool breeze hit her face, and Mitzi could see fluffy white clouds. Her shoulders ached to let her wings deploy.

Noticing, Sergei said, "No sky for you," and laughed at his joke as he sat her down on a chair facing the starboard side of the ship in full view of the ocean. Her stomach lurched. The stage was set for an old-fashioned walking of the plank. Viktor's men had bolted an actual wooden plank on deck, which hung out over the sea, the surface of which was at least ninety feet below. Jack was pushed down to sit next to her. She hoped Jack had not been bluffing about his men calling the Coast Guard. Looking around, she saw a GoPro-type camera duct-taped to a pole and aimed toward them. She had no doubt this new *Lupus Imperium* would show the film to her father and Panda. Tears ran down her face as she thought of her wife and wondered where she was at that moment. She hoped with a vengeance that her friends below deck had won their battle against the ones shooting at them.

***

Down below, Elsa helped the crew members leave the room as Fetu sporadically fired. A lucky shot took out their attacker's radio, and Lulu cheered. The departing sailors were each told to find a place to hide on the large ship. One by one, they snuck down corridors and melted into cabins, the engine room, and other spaces known to them. Spread out, they would be much harder to recapture. Finally, only Lulu, Fetu, Ekk, and Elsa were left. They were almost out of bullets. Ekk implored Elsa to go, but she would not. Her spells would help slow the inevitable until help came.

***

On a Mission

Believing my wife and friends were safe, I whistled on my way to the airport. An email had delivered my new ticket, and I felt snazzy, decked out in khakis and boots newly purchased from REI. No doubt Mitzi would have tempered my choices, but I was happy with them. Ali and my sister Puddle had been at the house to see me off. "You look like Indiana Jones, Panda. How rustic is it where you're going?"

"I'll take that as a compliment, Puddle." Ali put her bag in the back of the Lyft, and they hugged one more time.

"Let me know if you hear from Sally. I've left several messages, but she hasn't called me back."

"Okay. Did you get your satellite phone? I'll monitor your regular one."

"Yes, but don't forget if you have to reach me, I'm Dr. Hannah Panover, an anthropology adjunct professor." I laughed. "I'm meeting Charlie Potts at the airport. He's my traveling companion. They must be short on guardians." Charlie and I had a history. He'd investigated me for murder. He would not have been my first choice for a traveling companion, but this was tempered by the thought I would see Mitzi when we arrived in Namibia.

"What's his name?"

"Charles Copley, philosophy professor. They probably let him keep his real first name because he's not very creative." I adopted a snooty pose. "Apparently, we are a scholarly bunch on this tour."

"We'll keep an eye on the Goodens and your house," Ali said. "Any news about Aurora and Ralph?"

"I haven't heard a thing since Ehren and I spoke. I was so excited about scaring off Viktor Volkov with the ravens that I forgot to ask him where my Land Rover was. Would you ask if you talk to the Garden?"

"Will do. I guess we stand by 'til we hear something. Safe travels." Ali had his arm draped around Puddle; they were becoming inseparable.

Even with the light banter, we all knew this mission was serious business.

After I arrived at the airport, it didn't take long to spot Charlie at the gate. He was wearing worn jeans and one of those vests with many pockets. "Hey, Charles. It's been a while."

He looked me over. "You look like you're auditioning to be the new Indiana Jones."

I started feeling insecure. Had I overdone it? Childishly, I lashed out. "You look like you're going fishing."

"I wasn't going to spend much money on new clothes." He looked at his watch. "About time you got here, Hannah. The plane's boarding."

I smiled. "Then let's go." He was grumpy today. He was a former police officer, and even though I could see why the Garden picked him to be my travel companion, it was going to be a long journey if he didn't lighten up. "How's Alexandra?"

He slung a carry-on over his shoulder and folded up his NRA magazine.

"She's fine. They've got her busy in the Garden helping mediate some unrest on the council. Now stay in character, Professor."

"Shouldn't you be reading something a little more...um, scholarly?"

He growled and tossed the magazine into the trash. "When we get on board, I'm going to tell you about the history behind the place we're going."

Our group was called, and we had no more time to chat until we were seated in Economy Plus. "No business class?"

I was being facetious, but Charles responded. "What did I say about being Dr. Panover? Academics don't fly first or business class. *Capisce*?"

I was silent, clicking my seatbelt and arranging my bag under the seat in front of me. "*Capish* is not a real word."

Charles gave me an evil look. "It's *Eye-talian*," he said as if speaking to someone dim.

"I'm an academic and was simply being academic. Good grammar, you know?" I said in defense. He was not going to harsh my buzz. I was on the way to join Mitzi.

"You're supposed to be an anthropologist, not an English professor."

"Fair point." This was going to be a miserable flight.

The flight attendant came down the aisle and told him to buckle his seat belt. He had trouble adjusting it over his girth, and I feared another grumpy outburst. Instead, he said, "It's Italian."

"Okay, I believe you." I wasn't going to argue.

As the plane taxied for take-off, our silence morphed into a truce.

"I heard your wife ran into trouble—she okay?"

"Yes, thank God. She'll be there when we arrive. Ekk and Elsa too. How much do you know?" I was eager to know the details myself.

"Not much. I overheard Alexandra and Ehren talking. She's a trained mediator, and he's been really uptight over some guy on his council. He said, 'My daughter was held captive.' I asked Alex about it after they met, but she said she couldn't talk about it."

"Well, I don't know how she got out of it, but she and our guardians were put on a container ship."

He was surprised. "What? How did they get off the ship? Who took her? Oh wait, I can guess." His jaw tightened. "Those bastards."

I looked around to make sure no one was listening. "Charlie, I can call the ravens now. They saw the whole thing and told me Mitzi, Ekk, Elsa, and one other you don't know were rescued. It's driving me crazy not having all the details. Obviously, I can't wait to hear the whole story. She should be waiting for us at Walvis Bay."

"Glad to hear it." He took his attitude down a notch now that we'd talked about Mitzi.

"Now I'll tell you the story," Charles said. "First, I gotta tell you, though, I hate flying."

I bit back a smart-ass comment, realizing he was actually communicating. "Lots of people do. No shame in that."

"Pan—I mean, Han—nah,"—the look he gave me would have shriveled most people—"I wasn't discussing my feelings. I just hate being in the air. Tactically, you're cut off for too long."

"Oh." This guy was prickly. I decided to change the subject. He and my old criminal defense attorney, Alexandra Stephanovsky, had moved to the Garden in Germany after retirement. "How do you like living in the Hercynian Garden?"

He finally smiled. "It's good. This was my last trip to Merryville. We finally sold the house. I'm going to miss it a little, although the fishing in the Garden ain't bad. I was also sorry to miss all the action around you guys with finding the Winter Stone. We couldn't believe all the pictures of snow in our old town."

"That was crazy." I recapped for him the events that resulted in Aurora and Ralph needing to go to the Garden for their safety and how Aurora was the key to much of what happened with the Winter Stone being activated. "She's the Garden's only lead to finding the other stones."

"So Gary Smithers was extorting Ralph all along. That makes me so mad. He's quite a guy. I'm stunned our fraud unit didn't pick it up."

"Well, who would think a sitting city council person would do that?"

The flight attendant pushed her tray to our aisle. "Something to drink?"

"Coke for me." I put up my index finger.

"Sounds good, Coke." He tilted his head. "Can I get a little bourbon with that coke?"

"Certainly, sir."

I wondered if he would be drinking if Alexandra was with him. I also noticed he had something square in his shirt pocket that looked a lot like a Marlboro box. It showed when his fishing jacket brushed back as he retrieved his credit card for the booze. Too bad. It was big news when he and his wife quit smoking together. It was also not my business, so I let it go.

Soon, we had our drinks, and it was story time. "Turn of the century." He sipped his drink and did that wince thing people do with alcohol. "In the late 1880s, Namibia was a protectorate of Germany."

"Germany colonized the area in 1882, and I did read a little. This was bad news for the Herrera and Nama people."

"Are you finished?"

"I am an anthropologist. I read all about the genocide."

"Did anyone ever tell you it's rude to interrupt?"

His question was rhetorical, so I sipped my Coke and stayed quiet.

"Anyway. Turn of the century, 1908. The Germans had colonized Namibia and built a railroad through it. They gave jobs to the locals, but they saw none of the wealth. In 1908, one of the workers dug into the sand with his shovel and found diamonds. They didn't even have to build a mine. For a while, it was the richest country in all of Africa but forbidden to Africans. It's the final stop on our tour."

"What's the name of the town?"

"The Germans named the main town Kolmanskop, and all the money went to a company in Berlin."

"What's the town like now?"

"It's a ghost town. Shifting sands have now reclaimed it, but back in the day, it had a thriving bunch of businesses. People moved there from Germany and lived it up."

"This is the new intel?"

"Yes. Aurora has been a treasure trove of information, but it's old. The Summer Stone may or may not be there now, but we're pretty sure it was at one time. Our job," he took a deep draw on his drink, "is to check it out."

Chapter Ten

Walking the Plank

It had been at least an hour, and Sergei was nowhere to be seen. Before leaving, he had told his men, "Watch them." Almost as an afterthought, he'd commanded, "And clean up your mess."

Jack, his mouth taped shut, had both hands tied behind his back. Bloodied and beaten, he put his head on Mitzi's shoulder. She had been numb and stoic until then, but this slight tenderness broke her. Her biggest thought was that she had let everyone down. She had not taken the threat seriously enough and was worried about what that meant for Valerie, Juniper, Ali, Puddle, and her precious Panda.

Being helpless was humiliating, and she felt it was a self-inflicted wound. Here she was, the daughter of the leader of the world's free creatures, trussed up and ready to star in a snuff video for *Lupus Imperium*. She knew Jack was trying to comfort her the only way he could, and she finally understood why Sally loved him so much. He was quite a man. If she thought the situation could not get any worse, however, she was wrong. The sun was getting hot as it climbed in the sky.

"Time to clean up our mess," said one of their captors. He and another man carried Smitty's body to the ship's railing and, after saying, "one, two, three," tossed it over. It took a long time for the splash, and looking over the rail, one said, "Oh!" and the other said, "Wow, that's going to look great in our little movie." They high-fived and smiled at the camera.

She racked her brain. What could she do? Struggling against her special wrapping seemed to make it tighter, and she wondered if some dark magic was involved. *Lupus Imperium* had its wizards too. She concentrated on her octopus pendant and prayed to whoever would listen. Panda had her sky god, and she really didn't have one.

A clatter made her turn her head to the hatch, and what she saw made the blood drain from her face. Jack was looking, too, as Sergei poked Ekk in the back with his gun. "Hurry up. You've made us late." With hands tied behind their backs, Ekk, Elsa, Lulu, and Fetu were shoved into chairs next to Mitzi and Jack.

"We've wasted enough time. They took out Hans. Let's get this rolling."

"We're already live, sir."

"Fine." Sergei walked and forth in front of Jack, Mitzi, Ekk, Elsa, Lulu, and Fetu, as if studying them. He had his hands behind his back and said to the camera, "Ahh, yes, let's do the fat one first."

His radio squawked. He brought it to his ear, and laughed. "Of course, sir. We'll go with the very fattest first." He jerked his head toward Fetu. "Him."

It took four men to wrestle the former marine onto the plank. "Now. Let's play dignity or no dignity."

Fetu's face was red, and Mitzi finally understood the phrase "if looks could kill." Sergei poked him with a gun, and he walked slowly down the plank, positioned over the cold ocean waters far below.

"No," Mitzi screamed against the tape on her mouth and with every cell of her body. The others were struggling similarly against their bonds.

"Hurry up!" Sergei called. "Be a man." When Fetu wouldn't move, he said, "I don't have time for this," and shot him. The bullet caught the big man in the shoulder, and he spun around into the sky beyond the plank. After a devastatingly long time during which they could only hear the wind, a mighty splash told the story. Fetu was indeed going to Davy Jones' locker to join Smitty.

Mitzi felt something then. She didn't know what, but it felt like a surge of magical power. Her wings were trying to break through the wrapping so hard! A tug of war was being played on her body as her wrappings got tighter, and her nodules pushed back.

"You next." Sergei went toward Lulu until he noticed Mitzi struggling. At that point, he almost lost his footing as the ship dipped suddenly to one side, sending the chairs sliding a bit. They all turned to see what happened, and Mitzi saw two enormous tentacles reaching over the side of the vessel. Sergei remained frozen until one wrapped around him and lifted him from the deck. He gave a strangled scream and dropped his gun, which clattered on the deck. His men shot at the sea creature, but the tentacles moved faster than they could aim. Mitzi heard a Russian voice from the radio clipped on Sergei's belt. The octopus's other tentacle wrapped around the plank and split it into pieces, popping the bolts that had held it to the deck. It grabbed the closest man shooting at it and flipped him out to sea.

As Sergei was squeezed, his face turned purple, and his radio skittered on the deck during the struggle. Suddenly, Mitzi felt her wrapping give way, and she knew Sergei had been using some sort of magic to keep her from using her powers. Wasting no time, Mitzi stood up and used her returning strength to remove her restraints. Another of Sergei's men ran toward her, gun pointed at her head. Fortunately, her wings picked this moment to deploy violently and knocked him over. The other two hostiles were busy fighting the octopus. Mitzi locked eyes with the fallen man for a moment until he cowardly scrabbled away from the fight zone. She quickly untied Jack and ripped the tape from his mouth. Despite her earlier fears, she had not forgotten how to fly. Wasting no time, she went straight up, then down over the ship's side. There were gasps. Her friends and the confused guards didn't know where to look—the flying woman or the monster swinging their boss around with its tentacle. Jack hastily untied Elsa and Ekk and ran up to the bridge.

The elves pulled the tape off Lulu's mouth, and she immediately asked, "Is Mitzi going to save Fetu?" Her chest was heaving as she shook her head, tears running down her cheeks. "What they did...that was the meanest thing I've ever seen."

"I don't know." Ekk ducked under a tentacle and went to the side of the ship. "Lulu, get a life preserver!"

The scene was chaotic and would have resembled a Hieronymus Bosch painting if someone could have stopped to take a photo. Shots rang out as Sergei's remaining men tried to kill the beast. They were no match for the giant octopus and soon turned their guns on the captives. Sergei was still being whipped around, and he yelled something in Russian, which drew their attention. Jack ran forward and knocked the gun out of one man's hand, using it to shoot another. The last man, mouth agape, was encircled with a tentacle like his leader. Both were flung, one by one, so far and fast out to sea they became tiny specks on the horizon, their screams fading quickly.

Looking over the side of the ship, Ekk spotted Mitzi in the ocean, holding Fetu's head above water. Her wings were sodden and she was crying as she yelled, "Pull us up!" Lulu threw the life preserver with astonishing accuracy given the pitching boat and waves. Mitzi grabbed it and barely managed to hold on to Fetu. Having the float helped, but she was still struggling. The two crew members who had come from the bridge must have seen it all from their perch above the deck. They joined Ekk, Jack, and Lulu, and everyone strained to pull Mitzi and Fetu up to the deck. Even with everyone pulling on the rope, both the pitch of the boat and the weight of Fetu made it impossible to pull him and Mitzi to safety.

Once more the octopus came to their aid. Using a tentacle, the octopus scooped up both Mitzi and Fetu and gently laid them on the deck of the ship. Mitzi finally getting a close look at the head of the octopus and its intelligent eyes, mouthed "thank you" to it, although she had no idea if it understood. Then, its job done, the creature sank below the waves out of sight. Mitzi, cradling Fetu's head in her lap, said, "He's still breathing." She looked cold and in shock.

For a few moments the wet and exhausted group tried to process what they'd seen before Jack yelled, "Medic, we need a medic."

One of the men returned to the bridge, and the public address system blared, "There is one hostile person on the ship. The rest of the threat has been neutralized. We need a medic on the main deck, STAT."

Ekk picked up a long splinter from the broken plank and walked to a place directly below the GoPro camera. "Hope you enjoyed the movie, you piece of *shiza*. Free creatures forever!" He then used the stick to knock the camera down, pocketed the SD card, and ran back to the action.

An hour later, a medivac unit landed to pick up Fetu. Paramedics ran out from beneath the blades with bags and soon had the big man on a backboard with his face covered by an oxygen mask, ready to go. "We've got room for one more. Anybody?" One of them yelled over the sound of the copter. Lulu jumped at the chance and said to Mitzi, "I know you've gotta go, uh, do what you do, but I'm going with Fetu and will make sure his family gets notified." She looked at the helicopter and then back at Mitzi. "He saved my life down there. When the dust settles though…"

"I understand we'll need to talk. You know where to find us." They hugged.

"Don't take off yet. I'm coming!" Lulu ran to get on and ducked her head way more than necessary to avoid being decapitated by the blades, which were speeding up. Once she was buckled in, the medivac lifted off. Mitzi watched them fly away and smiled at Lulu's thumbs up. She was quite a woman.

The empty sky filled with another helicopter approaching.

"Looks like LAX," Ekk observed to Elsa. "Are you ready to go?"

"More than ready." She looked ragged. It had been a rough forty-eight hours.

"We'll be leaving soon, but I need a minute," Jack promised. He walked to meet the men from the bridge who must have seen the whole thing.

Their faces were hard. "We have questions. Lots of them." Bridge officer Liam looked at Jack's expressionless face. "A giant octopus?"

He fixed his blue eyes on them. "I know that strange things happen on a boat, and you already probably realize this is bigger than just you, me, or this boat. This is a national security issue here, and Coast Guard will contact you soon."

"What about the two attackers who survived? We've got 'em in the brig now."

"The only reason the Coast Guard isn't here now is that they had to get a boat big enough to handle the bodies and the Russian prisoners."

"Will they be able to answer our questions?" Liam was like a dog with a bone. "Why don't you tell us what you know?"

"All I can tell you now is that the Russians have a new weapon. It plays tricks on the mind. A giant octopus? Really. What you think you saw was an illusion."

"What about Smitty? Was his death an illusion?"

"No. He's gone. Going to sea can be dangerous, and pirates of all kinds are out there. We were attacked, and I can't tell you how sorry I am about that." The two men didn't look satisfied with that explanation.

"A giant octopus saved us," Brice, one of the officers, said.

Jack tried one more angle. "If you or any of the men tell the press or anyone else that you saw a giant octopus, you will lose your license to operate this or any other boat. They will think you're crazy." He softened his voice a little. "The enemy was human with guns, things turned dangerous, and for that, I am sorry. Smitty was a good man and a good Captain. I can't change what happened. The home office will send a speed boat with a new Officer in Charge to take over for the rest of the trip. You will keep on the same route. I also arranged for hazard pay for everyone on board. Did he have a wife?"

"No. He was married to his job, but we'll send the contact info to your office."

"Copy that. I'll make the calls. Under no circumstances is this to be leaked to the media. Understood?"

The men nodded yes.

Jack's six-seater helicopter landed. He shouted over the engine, "This is us," and Mitzi, Ekk, and Elsa ran toward it with their bags, which had been brought up from below deck. Jack was the last to go.

As he walked toward the helicopter pad with Brice and Liam, Brice asked, "Er, are you coming back anytime soon, sir?"

"No." He gave them a sad smile.

"No offense, but the men will be relieved to hear that, sir." Brice's face turned red when he said it. "And I hope we never see the likes of that creature again, but it seemed to be helping you all."

"You won't see it." He paused as he climbed aboard, wind from the propellers whipping his black hair. "And did you really see it?" Jack scratched his chin.

"Is that thing one of *our* weapons?" Brice was curious.

"Sorry, can't hear you." Jack tapped on his earphones and took his seat.

As they lifted off, Brice commented to Liam, "Billionaires."

***

Sally Johnson was waiting for them in the parking lot, standing next to a Johnson Roofing van. "I hear you are going to need a ride," she said mischievously. "This one has plenty of seats." Jack was already getting in the driver's seat.

Ekk and Elsa introduced themselves and put their bags in the back of the van.

"Sally." Mitzi hugged her friend from the Merryville Horticultural Society. "I'm usually not at a loss for words but, I don't know what to say. Is there anything else I should know about the garden club?"

"Not really." She was back to typical Sally, who seemed to be on her own wavelength. She turned, but Mitzi wouldn't let it go.

"Okay, but..." Mitzi gently put her hand on Sally's arm.

"Let's just be like before." Sally reached out and gently squeezed Mitzi's hand. "It's better."

Jack called out, "Let's get you all home."

Ekk, climbing in the vehicle, got Mitzi's attention by laughing and shaking his head. "Hey, Mitzi, who's going to tell Panda her beloved Land Rover's on its way to another continent?"

Her hand went to her face. "Oh my gosh, with all that's happened, I didn't even think about it." Then Mitzi laughed, too, almost hysterically, and Elsa joined in. Sally looked from one to the other.

"You have to understand," said Mitzi, gulping for air. "She waxes that thing like once a week."

Sally smiled. "I get it. Jack's pretty fond of his trucks."

He put his arm around his wife, kissing her head. "I missed you more than my trucks. How are you, babe?" he asked.

"Fine now that you're here." She made a face. "But ew you stink!" More laughter followed.

"Let's blow this popsicle stand," Ekk said. "I'm ready to go home and take a shower."

***

After ravens forced him to abort his landing at the San Pedro landing pad, Viktor sat in the back while they flew over Los Angeles, thinking about how hard these bitches were to kill. The agents at LAX had failed to capture Mitzi's guardian elves. His right arm, Sergei, and another of his men were squeezed and then flung into the sea by a giant octopus. He'd come to bring Gary Smithers back to home base for debriefing, but being in Merryville had been too tempting. As the new leader of *Lupus Imperium*, what a feather in his cap it would be to take out Ehrenhardt Winter's only daughter.

He wasn't worried about survivors. They knew nothing, really. This was good in a way. He'd learned valuable intelligence about the enemy. On camera, he now had actual footage of Mitzi Fowler flying. He saw everything that happened before that little elf bastard knocked the camera down. Ekkehard Schmidt would pay in due time, but he was an afterthought. Viktor had been recording the transmission from the GoPro on his end and could edit it to put the fear of God in those ridiculous "free creatures." He resolved to twist this fiasco into a success somehow.

"We'll be landing in five, sir," he heard the pilot say through his headset. "Any special instructions? Can't go too far. Fuel was only to San Pedro. We're running low."

"Drop me at the private hangar in Burbank," Viktor said. He decided Gary Smithers could stay where he was for the time being until more agents arrived. Instead of this experience defeating him, he would use it to be ready for the next time. Yes, this was merely an experiment to test his prey's limits. It would be more satisfying, anyway, to get rid of that little fat wife of Mitzi's at the same he annihilated the half-griffin. They would never see it coming. He eagerly picked up a call from Germany. "Oh, I was waiting to hear from you. So where are the targets headed?"

***

Hercynian Garden

The Black Forest was in Germany, the Hercynian Forest was within the southern part of that, and the Hercynian Garden was the magical hidden headquarters for Free Creatures inside the forest. At the lowest level underground was the Garden Library, officially the Scriptorium. No one knew how old it was, but all agreed the library had been in its present location as close to "forever" as anything on this old earth could be. Scribes contemporaneously recorded the histories of the Hercynian Garden and, indeed, much of the world and sent them here. The scrolls were stored in a temperature-controlled space underneath the keep for future reference. The scribes themselves had come and gone, of course, but the librarians endured, for death had not separated them from their holy mission of minding the priceless records throughout the history of the world. Ehren stood and stretched in the library after spending hours reading about any reference to the Circle of Stones.

Shrumm picked up an armful of incredibly old scrolls he'd already examined and walked back to the junior archivist, an Italian who had worked at the Malatestiana Library in Cesena, Italy. He said in Latin, "Thank you, Adriano. I don't suppose your team has found anything else?"

The shade shook his head no. "We will, of course, keep looking." He started to fade.

"Is Enid in?"

Adriano returned to solid form. "Enid is deep in study. We have an order here, and I am the current official librarian of the Keep."

"Please take no offense, but Enid is from Wales. Ehrenhardt asked me to inquire because sometimes local knowledge holds a clue. The Circle of Stones is said to have been assembled in Cornwall, but the magic is rumored to be of ancient Welsh origin."

"Are you sure?" Adriano looked uncomfortable.

"About the rumor or whether or not we want to speak with Enid?" Shrumm almost laughed at the shade's reluctance. Although only serving in the Keep library for over a century, Enid had a reputation for being difficult.

"As you wish." Adriano turned into a bluish smoke and disappeared into the books.

Enid Hughes, the aforementioned Welsh librarian, materialized before him. She appeared fully human and appraised him coldly through wire-framed glasses.

He spoke at once, knowing she had little patience. "Ehrenhardt Winter has asked me to call on you because of your expertise on the Black Book of Carmarthen."

"What do you want to know?" She spoke in her native language, but the Garden provided that everyone would understand all languages. Her hair was wound in an immaculate bun, and she wore a dress with a large brooch and comfortable shoes.

"We are searching for anything related to the Circle of Stones."

She gave a curt nod. "I was wondering how long the current leadership would take to see me. But I will only speak with Ehrenhardt."

"He sent me—"

"When it's important to him, he will seek me out. Until then." She left, only a whiff of Ambergris perfume in her wake.

Shrumm returned to Ehren and found him standing, ready to leave. "I can't look at one more document, and the council is meeting in a couple of hours. Anything?"

"Adriano said there was nothing more, so I asked for Enid."

Ehren stood up straighter. "And?"

"She will only speak to you."

He cursed and appealed to the ornate ceiling. "Enid." Ehren was torn but said, "I'll come back tonight. I have another meeting."

Although it wasn't apparent to the creatures living in the Keep, other than to his closest advisors, Ehren was troubled about many things. First, his daughter's fate. He had heard nothing since being informed of her and her guardian's capture. Jack Johnson had been activated but had also failed to check in. Then, there was Alaric involved in the search for the Summer Stone. The research was supposed to provide clues that might help answer questions about the Stones, or at least distract him, but it had yielded nothing so far.

His thoughts churned as he and Shrumm walked up marble steps to the main floor. Why was there no word from Ekk, Jack, or Mitzi? Why couldn't the stone fragments have just stayed buried? His life would be much easier.

While Aurora had given them information, it was intel at least sixty years old. He was frustrated that he didn't understand the technology involved in Aurora's treatment and felt in his gut that Alaric was at the root of something nefarious. He sought out his husband, Jay, who brought him calm, and found him leaving his coffeehouse, *Wirtschaft*. Instead of speaking, he held out a hand, and the other man took it.

"How nice to see you!" Jay bubbled. He wasn't a classically handsome man, tall and gangly with a bit of scarred skin, but he had the kindest eyes and always made Ehren feel better.

Ehren loved looking into those eyes. "Let's take a walk."

The Hercynian Garden was utterly beautiful. The sky was always blue, and flowers of every kind lined the paths. Lots of streams with crystal clear water provided a soundtrack to the walk. The best overall description would be perpetual spring.

"Husband, I can tell you are troubled. Please tell me about it." Jay picked up a rock near a stream, and they sat for a time, pressed together in silence, watching butterflies and holding hands. Ehren's hands were beautiful, like a surgeon's or musician's, with long fingers. Jay lifted one to his lips and kissed it, before drawing bony knees up to his chest.

Ehren loved how Jay knew not to rush him. He understood how hard it was for Ehren to share inner thoughts. Finally, he said, "It's Alaric."

"Oh, your *wunderkind* on the council." Jay nodded, no doubt remembering how everyone gushed about how Alaric, in his mere thirties, like a toddler in Garden years, was going to bring the aging council into the technological age. He was brash, handsome, and a good talker. Ehren knew Jay didn't like him at all.

"There's something not right about him." Ehren tossed a pebble into the stream.

"I trust your instincts, but there must be something concrete you've noticed."

He was about to answer when his satellite phone vibrated. Eagerly, he removed it from his waistband and connected to the caller. Very few had this number.

On the screen, Ekk was, in effect, doing a selfie. Standing behind him was Elsa with her black eye and, most importantly, Mitzi, soaking wet with a blanket draped over her shoulders. She looked different, and not just because one strand of her beads was gone. She looked both beautiful and serious.

"Ekk, Elsa, daughter. Someone tell me what's going on."

Jack came into the frame. "I hope you're sitting down. We're sending you a video."

Chapter Eleven

Panda Undercover, Namibia

I slept fitfully for the next ten hours, tortured by nightmares about forgetting how to control the ravens. In the dreams, I waved my arms and shouted, but they ignored me. The ravens all had opened beaks and shrieked so loudly I had to cover my ears. They were trying to tell me something urgently, but I had no clue what it might be. Upon waking only a few hours before landing, I started to doubt everything. Our instructions, now that this mission was actually happening, seemed impossibly sketchy. Go to some ghost town in Namibia on the other side of the world and "check it out."

With Mitzi at my side, I wouldn't have worried about much other than my usual anxiety. She always took care of the details. Now, there were lives at stake. It hit me how astonishingly selfish I had been and how much pressure my fears must have put on her. In contrast, my traveling companion must have taken something because he looked incredibly docile while asleep, like a huge baby dressed in fishing gear.

Charlie—I couldn't think of him as a Charles—had some more time to sleep before we landed and met up with our tour. It dawned on me that this was how our cat Brutus must feel before making biscuits on my stomach to make me get up. With a smirk, I shook him awake.

His blue eyes opened and he looked alarmed, scooting his body fully up in one motion. "What? Is everything okay?" When the white noise of the plane and the darkened cabin indicated nothing had changed, he reasonably asked, "Why did you wake me up?" He seemed more mystified than mad, and I couldn't blame him.

"I thought we should go over our mission before we land."

He rolled his eyes and stretched. "You remind me of Alexandra. She can't stand it that I sleep like a baby on long flights. I'll be back in a minute." He unbuckled the seatbelt and went to the loo.

A booklet came with my ticket, and I read it over again. Our tour guide would be Mitzi, and one of our last stops would be

Kolmanskop. As Dr. Hannah Panover, I had to pretend not to know her. It seemed silly to play a role, but Ehrenhardt thought it was best to avoid detection. Two American women traveling together would alert *Lupus Imperium.* I didn't know who else would be on this tour besides Charlie and me, and I hoped my role as a professor wouldn't fall apart.

Charlie returned and said, "This is the fun part of the adventure, Pan—I mean Dr. Panover. No plan. We make it up as we go." I had never pegged Charlie Potts, who as Dr. Copley, philosopher, was an adventurer. We had much to learn on this trip, and the thought of seeing my wife soon perked me up.

When we disembarked, it felt good to stretch my legs after such a long flight. The noise level was loud. People from the U.S. and other countries mingled with locals. I could hear many languages. We retrieved our one bag each and soon were outside in the heat looking for Mitzi. It was so chaotic. So many voices were calling for our business: "Taxi!", "Come tour with us!", and "I'll take you to your hotel—discount!" bombarded my ears.

Charlie spotted a woman holding a sign that said "AZARI SAFARI."

"Right there, *Hannah*. That's us." Charlie pointed to the woman and walked toward her.

This felt wrong. "No. Mitzi's supposed to be here." I stood where I was stubbornly, hustling drivers jostling me. Charlie kept walking. We were in danger of the aggressive crowd separating us, so I followed. My bag tipped so that I was dragging it instead of rolling it, not a great start, and panic took over. "Maybe this lady will know something," I called after Charlie, but he either couldn't hear me over the din or didn't care.

"The lady" turned out to be our tour guide and was not Mitzi. Her name was Dominique. She had frizzy black hair, a gap between her two front teeth, and wore several colorful bracelets on her thin wrist. She had a deep tan, but her voice was pure Australian. Wearing khaki-colored shorts and a matching shirt with Azari Safari stitched in green, she reminded me of a zookeeper at a national park. I must have been staring because she waved us toward the curb energetically. "It's best to keep in a tight group. Did you lose something?"

"In a way," I said, and my heart sank.

"Sorry, love. Traveling can be hard." Seeing my disappointment, she said, "Don't worry, we'll learn lots and have fun! Welcome to Namibia." Several disappointed hustlers turned away. Her driver got out of the air-conditioned van and opened the back door.

"I want to make sure we're on the right bus. We were expecting a different tour guide." Mitzi had to be here somewhere, maybe on a different bus?

Charlie looked impatient.

"Something came up at the last minute." Dominique said this absently as she flipped through her clipboard. The driver began loading our sparse luggage.

"Wait," I said.

"You are…" Dominique was trying hard to help.

"Dr. Hannah Panover."

"Yes, you are on my list." Her head popped up as she scanned us. "And Dr. Charles Copley?"

"Charlie, please." He gave her a lopsided smile.

She grabbed his arm in a friendly way. "You and I are going to get along great."

"Shall I put it in or not?" the driver asked.

"Yes, load it up," Charlie and Dominique said in unison.

I'm sure I was sporting an unwelcoming facial expression, as I was still trying to figure out why Mitzi wasn't the tour guide. *Fantastic. I probably look like the problem academic, and he gets to be good-time Charlie.* First impressions were essential.

"Johannas, let's get a move on. We're already a couple of minutes behind."

"But—" I said, wanting to ask more questions.

Charlie pushed me toward the running board. "Let's go, Hannah."

As we went from strong sunlight into the van, it took a minute for my eyes to adjust. Two people were seated in each of the rows in front of us. A sweating male in his sixties sitting in the middle row said, "Yay! Finally!" and fanned himself with a cowboy hat. The woman I assumed was his wife offered a wan smile. She was pretty but a little wilted in the heat.

Two elderly British women in the front said with far too much enthusiasm, "Welcome, Yanks." As the last ones to board, we had to sit in the last row. I tried to talk to Charlie, but he put up a finger and shook his head. The driver pulled away from the airport curb into the swirling, crazy traffic, and Dominique turned around to address us.

"Okay. All accounted for. As I said, my name is Dominique, and our driver is Johannas. We will be with you the whole tour. Let's introduce ourselves. I'm told some of you are on a mission…"

I felt a frisson down my spine and snapped my head quickly to look at Charlie, who ignored me. Did she know?

"…to learn more about your respective areas of study. You will meet with local experts in each part of the tour, as promised. We have"—she extended her hand toward the women in the front row—"Drs. Edith Roswell and Lorelei Pinck, Namibian studies." One answered for both. Edith had a cherubic face and thinning hair like white clouds. Lorelei was much younger and had straight, jet-black hair, cut in a modern style. "I'm here for the Cheetahs!" Her London accent was enthusiastic. Everyone laughed politely.

"That's right!" Dominique picked up on the comment. "Namibia has the world's largest population. Good on ya." Her flattened vowels always sounded like a lazy British accent to me.

Dominique motioned toward the second row. The man in his sixties with a deep tan drawled, "I'm Dr. Richard Bush." He looked around the van and waggled his Stetson. "Texas." The woman next to him was much younger and heavily made up. Her hair was piled up in a chignon. "Rick's being modest. He's a top professor at A&M."

He looked toward the ceiling in mock modesty. "I study rocks. Professor of Geology. This is my wife, Rena." He had his arm around her and smiled. "She's my lucky charm." She beamed at him. "We are on our honeymoon."

"Aww. Congratulations!" Dominique responded as everyone clapped.

"And in the back?"

Charlie looked at me, but I wasn't in a talkative mood. "Dr. Charles Copley, but call me Charlie." He motioned to me and said,

"And this is the illustrious but grumpy Dr. Hannah Panover, UCLA."

I knew I should stay in character, but my anxiety was high. Great. From now on, I was the grumpy professor. "I'm not—"

"Okay!" Our guide cut me off, keen to keep the energy up. "We have a couple more in our group at the hotel waiting for us." My hope soared at her. Maybe one of them was Mitzi.

"It's a twenty-minute drive, so enjoy the air conditioner and the sights through the window while I introduce you to Namibia. How much do we already know, anybody?"

Dr. Edith Roswell put her hand up. "It's a large country with a fifteen hundred-meter coastline, but its population is approximately three million people."

"Okay. Namibia is about half the size of Alaska and seven times that of Pennsylvania." Dominique sat on the arm of the front passenger seat, clipping a little microphone to her collar. "Walvis Bay, where you just arrived, is Namibia's second largest city and its primary coastal city for business. See the ships to your right? That's where we'll have our farewell dinner, a cruise on our last evening. Walvis is the biggest port in the country and is vital. Rail connects ships to take imported goods to Namibia, Zambia, and the Democratic Republic of Congo."

"Don't forget Botswana." Edith Roswell was an apparent fan of Namibia.

"You are right!" Dominique tipped her head with its frizzy black hair toward the women in the front row. "I can see who is going to win any quizzes this tour. But for now, we're on the way to the Comfort Inn, and I know you're all tired. After we check you in, you can rest a bit, and we'll see you at our meet-and-greet dinner in the hotel restaurant. Sound good?"

Among the yesses, Dr. Bush grunted and said, "I'm looking forward to the Skeleton coast. Can you talk a little about that?"

"Rick," Rena chided sweetly, "I'm sure she'll get to that."

"Yes, we will! As a person who studies rocks, I think I know the kind you want to hear more about—diamonds! We are going there in four days. Anyone else?" Dominique started to unclip her mic.

An elderly woman in front asked with a crisp English accent, "I hear you serve tea? And are there any other academics on the tour?"

The tour guide, ready for any question, answered, while holding her mic before her lips, "As part of the commonwealth of nations, you will find your choices very cosmopolitan. I'm sure we can find you some PG or Earl Grey." She lifted her voice. "And the answer is yes. We have two men, a couple of herpetologists, waiting at the hotel. So we have many areas of study represented here, and each of you will find something to take back to your class."

I couldn't see Dr. Bush's face, but he did not comment. It would take a few days to learn more about those on the trip and whether any were involved in *Lupus Imperium*. From what I had seen so far, that was doubtful. Dominique spoke a bit more, and I heard none of it, instead staring out the window and wondering where Mitzi was.

***

Black Forest, Germany

Jay had lived a good while in the keep and had set routines by now. After his duties at the coffeehouse, he often sought out Ralph, another nonmagical creature, and took walks. Aurora had started to join them on their jaunts.

The Hercynian Garden leadership was buzzing. After delivering coffee and baked goods, Jay met Ralph and Aurora to walk the halls and entertain themselves while Ehren and his council poured over Alaric's new technology. As they approached the "war room," they heard, "That can't be right!" Through the open door, Jay saw Woda with both fists on her hips, directing a hostile stare at Alaric. He shook his head. This had been going on all morning.

Alari raised his hands in a protective manner. "No magic! Come on. This is science, Woda. I think—"

Jay heard whirring and clicking sounds in the background and watched as Ehren took a sip of his coffee and lifted his eyebrows at him.

"Wait, wait! I have more printouts." Shrumm wiggled between Alaric and Woda and spread a large piece of paper on the table. Ehren gave Jay a tired smile and waved at Ralph and Aurora before lowering his gaze to review the new data with the rest of those present.

"They were at it last night too," Jay said. "Learning that the stone was probably in southern, not eastern, Africa was a big deal." Jay was in the know. "Panda's probably there now. I think Mitzi is on her way too."

"Let's get out of here," Ralph said, grabbing his wife's hand. "Coffeehouse?"

Ralph and Aurora looked at each other and then back at Jay. "No offense, but we're feeling a little cooped up, and I've already had too much caffeine." Ralph shuffled a little in place. "Before you suggest it, I've fished, which was great, and walked the paths. You can only do that so many times. Anywhere else to go?"

"I understand the cooped-up feeling." Jay paused and thought. "When Ehren first brought me here, everything was so new. Starting the coffeehouse took up much of my time. Now that the locals are taking up the slack, I have more free time but haven't left the Garden." As they went further down the hall, the conversations from the war room faded.

"I feel like a well-kept prisoner." Ralph shook his head.

"The magical folks want to ensure we stay safe. *Lupus Imperium* is still out there."

"Are they?" Ralph snorted. "I'd like to understand more. We were so rushed getting out of Merryville that it's all kind of a blur. I still don't know what's going on. All I've seen is the inside of the hospital and streams in the keep garden. What is this place, anyway?"

"From what Ehren has said, the keep is all that is left of a medieval castle and is the strongest part. It's his residence. These walls," Jay pounded a bony fist on a stone, "are at least fifteen feet thick."

"What happened to the castle?" Ralph was studying the workmanship. "I'd like to know more about this place."

"I don't know." Jay scratched his head.

"I'm here, you know." They stopped and stared at Aurora, who seemed to be entirely present at the moment.

"I know you're here, sweetheart. Where would you like to go?"

"See Enid."

Both men said, "Who?"

"Is there a library?" Aurora didn't speak much, and it surprised both men. She wore a flowered dress and some sketchers. Her gray hair was down and pulled back in a braid. "Enid." She said it as if they were both hard of hearing.

"I don't know who that is, baby." Ralph smiled widely. He loved that she was taking part more in conversation.

"Ah! The Scriptorium." Jay smiled wickedly. "I have been listening and learning. That's what they call the library sometimes. We could try there and ask about Enid. Ehren is so busy lately with this search for the Summer Stone…" His face fell. "You can only work so much at the coffeehouse. "Let's go find it. I think I know where it is."

Aurora's eyes lit up. "The Scriptorium."

Ralph linked his arm to hers and said, "Lead on, Jay."

***

Council Meeting

The whole council was present: Alexandra, Woda, Alaric, Heloisa, Dr. Mot, and Karla, the chief historian and scribe. The wooden table was covered with maps, both hand-drawn and computer-generated. After hours of discussion, the evening was upon them. Ehren had just returned to the table after communicating with Mitzi.

"What did your daughter say, sir?"

He ran his hand through his thick brown hair, a tell for when he was tired or worried. "She said Victor Volkov is the new Wolfrum. After a quick debrief, she went directly from the ship to the airport. She's in the air on her way to Namibia."

"Where is Ekk?"

"He and Elsa are to regroup at home. The situation was very traumatic. I told them to stand by."

Shrumm, smartly dressed in lederhosen, asked if anyone needed anything, and he put a small plate with a selection of meats and cheeses in front of Ehren. As the first person, he was a conduit to the leader of all free creatures. Nonetheless, he would serve snacks in highly confidential meetings, seeing to the most minor details.

Alaric raised his eyebrows at Shrumm's traditional outfit and looked at Dr. Mot, who smiled. Alaric was Elvin, too, but much younger than Shrumm. He was wearing a white shirt and black pants and, other than his height, would have blended in at a Silicon Valley company board meeting.

"I'll have whatever he's having." Alexandra said, while continuing to stare at the map. "I still don't understand...why Namibia? Didn't we hear from Aurora that the stones came from Cornwall, England? Then we heard they might be in Tanzania?"

Ehren munched his snack and turned to Alaric, who launched into his report.

"So according to Aurora's information and the information gathered by our historian—"

"I'll speak to that in a minute." Karla, also young in Garden terms, wasn't rude, just keeping Alaric in his lane.

"The forbidden area of the Namib Desert," he tapped a little harder than necessary with a pointer at a map from one of his computers printouts, "appears to be the place where the Summer Stone is probably buried. Record high temperatures are being recorded there now as we speak." Alaric was standing, and his head was the same height as Ehren's, who was still seated.

Heloisa was standing in a corner, radiating impatience. "That's a vast area. Having a few agents on a tour bus isn't going to find something buried for hundreds of years. No offense, Alexandra."

"None taken," Alexandra replied. "Part of me hopes Charlie, Panda, and Mitzi have an uneventful trip." When they all stared at her, she said, "This is just me, the wife, talking. I'm sure you feel the same, Ehren. I never saw the need to put our families in harm's way."

"Mitzi is half-griffin, don't forget, and Panda now has a special ability to call the ravens. Charlie couldn't be safer, but, fair point, Heloisa." Ehren leaned forward, holding a toasted piece of bread with sliced salami. A crumb fell on the map. "Namibia has a vast desert, and it's always hot. What say you, Alaric?"

Shrumm quickly swiped away the crumb.

"This is where science comes into play." Alaric smirked at Woda. "When Mitzi joins Azari Safari, she will be wearing a special device that, wait for it, detects the minerals only found in one of the powerful stones from the Circle. She will take over for the current guide, Dominique, and is set to be the guide to Kolmanskop."

"Where is the device?" Heloisa almost looked hurt. "How come I wasn't told about this?"

"Need to know, Heloisa." Alaric tried to keep his face neutral but failed. He was enjoying being "in the know."

"This is as good a time as any for your report, Heloisa. What's security like?" Ehren wiped his mouth. "And don't worry, you and I will be briefed about this device at the end of the meeting." To Alaric, he said, "Heloisa is chief of security for the Hercynian Garden. She *always* needs to know."

"My bad." Alaric was flippant.

Heloisa answered Ehren. "So far, so good. I've had to rely on locals, and our network isn't tight in Namibia. If I had more notice, we would be better situated. As it is, our resources have been busy with the decoy search going on in Tanzania. Let me tell you, *that* has attracted some attention." Her bronze face was animated. Heloisa was made for action, not paperwork.

Alaric looked surprised at this new information. "Nobody told me."

"Need to know only." Heloisa's smile at Alaric was wicked.

Alaric stiffened and said. "All I have ever tried to do on this council is use science to help achieve the Garden's goals. I need information to do my work."

"There is no time for discord." Ehren smashed his fist on the table to punctuate his comment. The man had a mercurial temper people often forgot. They all snapped to attention. "As we discussed, this Namibia exploration was intended to be low risk since Mitzi is involved. If she, Panda, and Alexandra's husband find anything," he nodded to Alexandra, "we are counting on Heloisa's teams going in for retrieval." He leaned back in his heavy wooden chair. "And everyone in the council needs to be briefed on everything. Let's hear from the others." He turned to his right, where Woda sat.

"My team has been busy too." She had been noticeably quiet, which was unlike her. "We have a group that does nothing but monitor security in the Garden. My team has sensed a mole, or maybe even more than one."

Alaric looked uncomfortable and walked over to the printer, a new addition to the war room. Shrumm stopped moving around and adjusting the maps on the table, listening intently.

Ehren said quietly, "Who?" It was deceptive, like the quiet before a storm.

"I was going to say perhaps we need to strengthen our skies. I'm worried about the ravens. Lately, we've allowed them to come and go. Although Schwartzwald Castle has been quiet since Wolfrum was taken down, they are nearby, and ravens visit them too."

"They monitor them for us," Ehren said, giving Woda all his attention.

Alaric, curious, returned to the table with another map.

"Yes, they've kept us abreast of some things. But apparently, they told Panda that Mitzi had been rescued, which is why she's now in Namibia."

Woda took the floor and magically threw a timeline on the wall. A pointer appeared in her wizened hand. "When the ravens appeared to Panda, Mitzi was still on the boat with her guardians and that security guard. The rescue hadn't happened yet. Why?" She returned to the table. "Maybe we let them in our airspace too soon."

"But are you sure?" Dr. Mot finally asked. "Time works differently between the worlds, you know."

"Of course we know that!" Woda spat. A tense silence followed.

Breaking the silence, Shrumm, always deferential, bowed his head slightly toward Ehren. "Sir, when Ekk was temporarily in charge, a raven came to him unbidden with a message. They seemed able to penetrate our skies at will, even before our new treaty."

Ehren's face turned almost purple. "Why was I not told of this immediately by my council?" He glared around the table, and Karla, frail and scholarly, seemed to shrink.

Shrumm was loyal to a fault but spoke truthfully. "Sir, you were in Merryville and quite occupied with the threat there."

Ehren stood and walked to a window. He was filled with emotion. Turning suddenly, he exclaimed, "Heloisa, gird the skies!" With a nod, she raced from the room, finally prompted into action.

Karla ventured to say, "Historically, any change in—"

"Not now, Karla. Alexandra, go and call your husband. Panda needs to know."

Chairs scraped on the floor. Alaric began to roll up his computer-generated maps.

A wooden pointer smacked on the map he was rolling. "Leave it." When Ehren was in this mood, they all knew to disappear.

"Woda, I need you to stay." As the others hastened to leave, Ehren said, "We will meet again soon. In the meantime, review everything you know and see what you've missed."

When the door closed, he turned to Woda, who said, "Alaric—"

"Not now. I need you to tell me what it would take to change from a human back into a griffin. I want to fly to Raven's Den."

Chapter Twelve

Namibia

Once our tour van arrived at the Comfort Inn, Johannas began unloading bags, and we registered in groups. Since we were in the last row, Dr. Bush and his wife beat us to the hotel's front desk. Dr. Edith stayed outside and engaged our driver in conversation, smiling broadly. Her travel partner was already on the phone, leaning against a wall in the lobby while everyone checked in. I walked around the parking area and looked around the lobby before standing in line. Suddenly, my safari outfit felt a little like a costume, as most wore ordinary street clothes. Charlie stood calmly in line, holding his one small bag, as the Bushes took their time and exchanged dollars for local currency. The clerk smiled broadly and upgraded them to a better room after they told him it was their honeymoon. I didn't remember Charlie being so patient before when he was a cop. Maybe living in the Hercynian Garden had mellowed him. For the first time, I wondered if that was a possibility for Mitzi and me, although living so close to her father was not a selling point.

"Dinner in thirty minutes," Dominique cheerfully sang out, grabbing her bag and heading for the hotel restaurant, no doubt to update those waiting for us. I set my bag down and followed her. My heart sank when I saw her walk over to a table with two men but didn't see Mitzi. Where the hell was she?

I turned back to the lobby and got back in line. I wanted to ask Dominique about the "other tour guide" but didn't want to raise suspicions. I was here as an anthropology professor and needed to act like it by asking questions about the culture. Dinner would have to be soon enough. Charlie and I rode up the elevator with one of the Brits, so we had to stay in character. "See you in a few," he said as we parted and actually smiled and whistled, walking down the hall. Did he think this was a vacation?

In a foul mood, I opened the door to my room and was pleased to see no netting over the beds. Namibia was not a malaria area, thankfully. I plugged in my satellite phone and lay on the bed near the window, hoping against hope I would get a call. A sound in the bathroom made me start. Did someone next door flush, or was that my bathroom? Was I sharing a hotel room or bathroom?

I had been so exhausted and worried about Mitzi's whereabouts that it never dawned on me that I could be in danger here. Now, I felt fear and searched for a reasonable explanation. Mitzi had taken me to Bali once, and the monkeys got in our room. Was it a monkey? I sat up. The bathroom faucet was turned on and off. Yep. That was my bathroom.

I jumped off the bed and looked around for something to use as a weapon. There was no need. The bathroom door opened, and in the doorway stood my wife. Mitzi was wearing jeans and a khaki shirt. Her hair was sticking up with gel, two beaded braids framing her lovely face. Her eyes had bags underneath, but she gave me a tired smile. "Hi."

I burst into tears as I ran to her, practically knocking her back into the bathroom.

"Whoa! I'm here, I'm here." She laughed, the most beautiful sound to my ears.

Staring straight into her brown eyes, I said, "I wasn't sure I'd ever see you again."

She shivered then. "Actually, you almost didn't."

"Why didn't you call?" I grabbed her tight and put my hand on the back of her head, holding her close. "Tell me everything." We parted, and I grabbed both her hands, dropped them, and hugged her again while I cried. "Oh my god! I was so worried!"

She grabbed me by the hand and dragged me to the bed where we sat. "There's a lot to tell you, but only a little time."

"I don't care." I started crying again. "I'm so glad you're here." My face was buried in her shoulder.

"Panda." I was kind of crazy. "Panda!" She said more firmly. "First, we don't know each other." She wiped my eyes and said gently, "Stop crying."

"Got it." I sniffled. "Sorry."

"Panda, you have to be able to pull this off. I am joining the tour as an additional guide. My name is Miranda. Tonight, love. We have to go to dinner now and meet the others. You'll be meeting me for the first time. Okay?"

"Okay." I was not okay. I was still clinging to her.

She removed my hands comically. "I'll sneak in after everyone's in bed."

I sat straight as a new thought dawned on me. "You mean we're not sharing a room?"

Mitzi turned her head sideways and bit her lip. "Darling, think about it. I'm your *tour guide*. That would never happen. Whatever you feel, you must remember why we're here. This is only for now." She kissed me. "I love you." Probably sensing my volatility, she held my face and stared into my eyes. "I gotta go. See you downstairs."

"But we have a couple more minutes." I followed her as she got up.

"As a guide, I need to meet with Dominique." She shook her head and said fiercely, "You have no idea what and who we are dealing with. Suck it up, buttercup!" She was probably trying to be funny, but somehow, that penetrated my Cancerian-wet mess of emotions.

"Mitzi..." The door closed. She had gone. My insides were raging. So many questions! I was really mad at Ehren for making us come here. What was she talking about? I couldn't stand not knowing what happened and resolved to pin Charlie to the wall. He must have known somehow that she was here with that smirky smile. Then that passed, and I was just grateful she was alive and here. I used my last minutes before dinner to quickly shower and dress, before going downstairs to meet the others as Dr. Hannah Panover.

***

"Did you know?" That was the question I asked "Dr. Charles Copley" in the elevator while going down to dinner. Charlie was dressed in jeans and a collared shirt, and his hair was wet from the shower. He smelled of freshly applied Old Spice. The mirrored elevator walls and tight space put him on the spot as I grilled him.

He shrugged. "Alex called me while you were wandering the parking lot. I wasn't sure when Mit...Miranda would show up and, obviously, I couldn't talk about it in the lobby."

"What about when we walked down the hall to our rooms? You had to know I was dying. I still haven't heard what happened to her." I caught my reflection in one of the long mirrors and tried to dial my facial expression back a few notches.

He smiled and exhaled. "That's her story to tell, and I don't even know it. Come on. It's showtime." The doors dinged open, and he led me out of the elevator toward the sound of clinking silverware and cooking smells. I entered the room, which was decorated much like an American hotel, except for some African mask wall art.

"There they are!" Dominique, frizzy hair captured in a scrunchie, was holding court at the head of the table. Seated around were the two British women who waved at us, Dr. Rick and Rena, sharing champagne, and two fortyish men, one of whom must have been the photographer mentioned by Dominique earlier. Next to Dominique sat Mitzi, who said, "Welcome! Come join the group!" as if we'd just met.

Dominique gave some sort of hand signal to the kitchen, and as a server brought bread to the table, she said, "Come and meet Miranda, an expert on diamonds;. You are all very lucky. Azari Safari is letting me stay until Kolmanskop, so you'll have two tour guides." She had us all introduce ourselves to "Miranda," much like we'd introduced ourselves on the tour van. An expert in diamonds?

The new tourists were Geoff and Simon, brothers from Australia, who were interested in lizards. I had hoped they were a gay couple. Edith had to share what she knew when she heard the word lizards. She asked them, "Are you looking for the shovel-snouted lizard? We cover that in one of my classes. I'd love to see one."

Simon answered when his brother stayed silent. "We're interested in all of them."

Dominique offered a lizard fun-fact. "The shovel-snouted lizard is also known as the dancing lizard. With the desert heat, they lift their little lizard feet every ten seconds or so to cool them off."

"And they burrow in the sand if it gets too hot. I hear that is happening a bit more lately." Edith had to have the last word. Her comment about the heat made me think about the Summer Stone, our reason for even being here.

I noticed Geoff had finagled a seat next to "Miranda" while I was at the end of the table as the "latecomer." I struggled to find the proper facial expression.

Everyone seemed a bit tired, and the vibe was anticipatory as we chowed down on the decent hotel fare. I kept quiet, taking in my new surroundings and listening to the others. Charlie was a natural at this, and I wondered if he had gotten the skill of pulling information from his previous career as a detective.

A bit before midnight, Mitzi finally returned to my room. I let her in, and we hugged. "I'm so tired, but I have to know."

She put her finger in front of her lips. "The walls are thin." We crawled into one of the twin beds, where she whispered out her story until she fell asleep. I held her, and despite my exhaustion, I was still wide awake, trying to picture a giant octopus, as something niggled at me. Perhaps tomorrow everything would make sense. What was I missing? But I was so glad to spoon her warm body and have her safe with me. Sleep came.

It seemed like two minutes later when my phone alarm went off. Mitzi, of course, had slipped out before dawn, and I was on my own again. With so much to think about, I welcomed being alone. As I showered, the shock of learning of Viktor Volkov, the new bad guy, and of having a name started a new train of thought. So was *Lupus Imperium* a Russian thing now? How big was this organization that was trying to stop all Ehren's free creatures? As far as I knew, we good guys only had the one Hercynian Garden as our headquarters. The water turned cold, and this got me out and toweling off. It wasn't all that hot here for summer. I dressed in safari gear again. If Mitzi had helped me shop, my wardrobe would not have looked like a twelve-year-old boy had selected it.

Wait a minute. I was so high on that trip to REI because I knew Mitzi had been rescued. Last night, she said something about that timeline, but she was dead on her feet. We both were. Tucking that away for a later conversation, I hung onto the fact that I was here, she was here, and heck, we had a vacation, sort of. I only needed to pretend like I didn't know her. Weird, but this was our life right now.

I heard a knock on the door. "Hannah, breakfast!"

Opening the door, I took a good look at Charlie. He had lost weight. "I must say living in, er, your cottage in Germany has been good for you."

He said in a slightly louder-than-normal voice, "That was a great VRBO. I might go back someday."

"VRBO?"

"Vacation Rentals by Owner." He looked right and left over his shoulder and made his eyes big. "Dr. Panover, let's get some breakfast." Doh. If any other folks on this trip were part of *Lupus Imperium*, we didn't want to link any of us to Germany. I thought the chances of this were low, but I mouthed "sorry" as we waited at the elevator.

The Texans came around the corner and joined us. I smelled Rena's perfume first, it was so strong. Rick Bush looked hung over, but they were holding hands.

"Mornin' California.," Rick said with a grunt.

"Mornin' Texas," Charlie responded, matching his accent. "How was that champagne?"

Rena looked fresher than her new husband. "It was good. I told Rick to slow down." The gentle chide didn't sit well with him, if his facial expression was any indication.

"Coffee, I need coffee." The elevator dinged open.

"I'm with you," I said cheerfully.

Breakfast was a blur as Dominique and "Miranda" talked about our first day's adventures. "Today, we visit the bustling city of Windhoek, capital of Namibia," Dominique began.

"Miranda" picked up the narrative. "We wanted to give you all a chance to adjust to the time zone. This is modern Namibia, much like Western countries. If you need anything," I thought she zeroed in on me, "we will have lots of shopping opportunities."

Dominique picked up the tour patter as if they had practiced. "It's not all like home. You will see plenty of Herero women in traditional dress. We'll meet up for lunch at 12:30 p.m. Now if

I'm not mistaken, our larger bus is waiting outside. Miranda, will you check everyone in?"

"Miranda" waggled her clipboard and headed out of the café. I smiled, never having seen her do a tour. When we traveled, we were vacationing.

I was first out the door of the hotel and approached the big bus with AZARI SAFARI on the side. Mitzi stood with her clipboard, wearing the shirt with her name stitched over her pocket, part of the khaki shirt and short set, radio on her belt, and boots. She looked really cute. "Hey Miranda, will we—"

She glanced at me. "Dr. Panover, gotcha." She checked off something on her clipboard and said in a friendly way, "Take any seat you like." Her radio crackled softly, and she turned it down with a practiced move.

"We're here!" Rick pulled Rena with one hand on her arm while still wiping his face from breakfast. Others followed, carrying backpacks and coffee in disposable cups. After being checked in, the Bushes looked up expectantly, and I realized I had frozen with my hand on the bar. "Anybody seen Charlie?" I asked lamely.

He hollered from the front of the hotel, "Get us a seat. I brought us coffee." This whole charade felt weird, and I wondered if this was some kind of joke Mitzi's father was playing to put me in my place. Did Ehren think I wasn't good enough for his daughter? What was the purpose of acting like we didn't know each other when we were really just on an information-gathering trip? It didn't feel dangerous at all so far. Being first, I climbed onto the empty bus and found a seat by the window near the back. If Mitzi was going to ignore me, I didn't want to sit close to her and watch the Australian men flirt with her. This day was going to suck.

***

The Hercynian Garden

"You want to transition?" Woda tilted her head and uncharacteristically whispered the question, disbelieving.

Ehren was on a roll. Lately, he had eschewed wearing purple all the time, something his council secretly discussed as "the Jay influence."

"We're changing, Woda. As a human, I am losing my control...distracted. Alaric's introduction of social media hasn't helped either." He walked to the mantel. "If it were only me, I wouldn't care. But there are thousands of free creatures under my protection." He looked at her with his piercing, dark eyes. "In some respects, I'm happier than ever since Frederick died, but the people aren't. I get regular reports with a summary of what's being said."

He motioned with a big hand, as if throwing something at the wall, and a map of the nine provinces appeared. "Northern province says I don't visit enough, Southeastern says I favor only the creatures who live in the keep, Western is doing whatever the hell it wants." He turned toward her. "Do you know they've started an informal shadow council? It's as if they all just discovered they are different."

"What is this shadow council doing?" Woda looked alarmed.

He laughed. "They argue that maybe the unicorns should be moved to their own space."

"Well, unicorns aren't the easiest to live with." Woda referred to their messy ways. "How would transitioning back into a full griffin solve these problems?" She was patient, wanting to hear his logic.

"As a griffin, nobody asked me impertinent questions!" He sat and adopted a stare as if looking beyond the walls. "I flew in unexpectedly, and I saw respect in their eyes."

Shrumm opened the door and poked his head in. "Do you need me for anything, sir?"

"No. Um, actually, yes. Bring me an aerial map of Hollental."

This made both Woda and Shrumm to pause for a millisecond. Shrumm swallowed. "Hell's Valley, sir?"

A steady stare answered his question. Although human, Ehren still had the power of the eagle's eye. "Yes."

"As you wish." Shrumm left to pursue his task, leaving Ehren and Woda alone. She wasted no time trying to dissuade him.

"Ehren, we discussed this when you transitioned from griffin to human. It's dangerous enough to transition once, but twice? I don't even know if you would survive it. Every system in your body is affected. And Hell's Valley? Very few who enter it return."

"Of course I know that, Woda. I'll be flying over it."

"So that's your goal." Woda was very old and wise. "What's really going on? Have you spoken to Jay about this?"

Ehren would have roared at her impertinence if she hadn't been in his court as long as she had. As it was, he answered truthfully. "He knows something's up. I've been restless."

They stared at each other. He treated her as an equal, something he never did when he was in his griffin form.

"I'm frustrated, Woda. This news about the ravens is troubling, and the only way to get to the bottom of the lie about my daughter's rescue and the security breach no one informed me about is to go myself and meet with Rayva. I'm ready to fly to their roost on Falkenfelsen." He put his arms out and presented his human self. "And honestly, I'm enjoying being human but miss the flight." He now smiled, showing straight, white teeth.

"But you do have flight." Woda looked astonished. "Didn't you tell us in the debriefing after your trip to Merryville about jumping out that hotel window and flying to a sanctuary?"

"Yes." He smiled. "That was the last time. The authorities from U.S. Customs are after me, so being human no longer helps me go to Merryville. I'm on a "watch list" in Mitzi's world and can't travel. The reasons for staying in human form are diminishing." He walked to the sideboard and picked up the coffee carafe, but it was empty. "Except for Jay. Where is he, by the way? It's not like him to run me out of coffee."

He put the carafe down so hard that it cracked. "Now I know why Mitzi has been a bit frustrated. In human form, you don't get to choose where and when you fly. There must be some threat nearby for your wings to deploy."

Woda stood, a powerful, motherly presence emanating from her. "Come with me."

"Where?"

"To the library. As minister of magic, I can sense where everyone is as long as they are in the Keep. Jay didn't bring you coffee because he is headed to the library."

"Why? What could he possibly need down there?"

"That, I don't know. A good book to read? He gets restless too now that the *Wirkshaft* is practically running itself." Woda risked putting her hand on Ehren's hand. "By the way, those of us on the council think things are changing well since you became fully human."

"You've been talking about me?" He looked ready to be angry again.

"Talking about the boss is natural when they're not around. We're all hearing from our constituents who live in the Garden. Trust me—they've always squabbled. They were too afraid to tell you about it. It's been hard for them with war outside our magical boundary." She risked saying even more because he didn't shut her down. "By the way, the free creatures approve of you being with Jay, Ehren. They feel more comfortable speaking out with you as a human and..."

"You may as well finish."

"You might even let him help you more with official business."

"Let's go to the library." On the way out the door, he grumbled, "Maybe they have coffee there."

Woda followed, smiling.

The good vibration was interrupted as Shrumm knocked and brought in an old, rolled-up map. "Sorry, sir. It took me a minute. It was under a pile. No one's looked at it in a unicorn's age. Do you still need it?" Woda looked at Ehren with questioning eyes.

"I do. Please put it in my study."

Chapter Thirteen

Downtown Windhoek, Namibia

Our bus pulled up in front of the Hilton Windhoek, and again, I felt silly about my outfit. Everyone else on the bus had apparently gotten the memo and wore street clothes that would have been appropriate in the States. I was wearing a safari shirt, vest, and pants with the one pair of boots I brought. Windhoek has a decidedly European feel, which made sense because Europeans built the buildings.

When we were all off the bus, standing in our little group, Dominique said in her Aussie accent, "Okay! We'll meet back here for lunch at 12:30 p.m., and as I'll say several times, don't be late! But first, I'm taking most of you for the historical part of the tour, and since we are blessed with a second guide, Miranda will be taking our Aussie boys to the reptile museum, which is quite a walk from here."

"I like reptiles," I said lamely.

Rick said, "You look like you're about to wrestle an alligator," and the group laughed.

Rena hushed him. "Don't worry, Hannah. I'm sure one of the boys will find lizards for ya in the desert." The remaining tour group followed her as I watched my wife leave for the reptile museum with Geoff and Simon. I was irritated at Dominique's use of "boys" to describe what were two grown men and hoped Mitzi would be safe with them.

Simon and Geoffrey, smiling, followed Mitzi down the street in the direction opposite us. My heart sank. "Come on, Hannah," Charlie said, pulling at my sleeve. I had no choice but to pull up the rear in our group and listen to Dominique gush. If she used the word "artisanal" one more time, I would barf. After an hour, we were released to shop on our own. My mood wasn't great, to say the least.

"I'm going back to that hunting shop. Wanna come?" Charlie was like a little boy when we were in the store full of spears, masks, and local fishing gear. "I'm interested in those African fishing poles. Wow!"

"Really? Who could tell?" I remarked, deadpan. "No, you go on ahead. I need to do a little shopping." I was feeling pretty low. We had walked through a crowded market and had been jostled several times as if invisible. I felt unprotected and out of my depth, and I longed to be at home petting my cat. Then there was my ridiculous outfit, which now felt like a costume as everyone else was dressed for the city. Edith from our group was older and wore khakis, but she'd paired it with a colorful silk blouse and scarf. Lorelei, also from England, was younger and thinner than Edith. She wore a muslin top that went down to her knees with blue form-fitting capris underneath, and had topped that off with some ethnic chunky jewelry. The locals, Herero women, were in Victorian-type dresses, flowing and colorful, a riff on their European-influenced past. Rena Bush took the cake, however. She was slender and wore a summer dress with big flowers, makeup carefully done, and looked like a model. Her hair was shiny and pulled into a chignon. I felt like a different species beside her and wished Mitzi was there to discuss it. I went into one of the stores I had seen, deciding to look a little less Indiana Jones and a bit more feminine. As a Chapstick lesbian, this was not always easy. A saleswoman watched me as I went up and down aisles.

"What are you looking for?" She asked in her soft accent. In my mood, I almost snapped out something sarcastic, but I could tell she was sincere and said, "An outfit for the cities."

"Come with me." She was young and had kind eyes. She smiled in a friendly way. I followed.

She led me back to a section with lots of colors. "You will find something here." The bell over the front door tinkled, and she left me to my shopping.

I appreciated her brevity and studied the selections. After trying on some native-sewn outfits, I bought a bright blue blouse and earrings. My safari shirt and vest were stowed in a bag, and I prepared to leave, feeling more appropriate for this part of the tour. My salesperson appraised me carefully. "Good choice, but you need something more." She walked away. Worried about getting to lunch on time, I checked my watch. When I looked up, she had returned and presented me with a lovely yellow necklace. "This will look good on the blue."

I put it on and looked in the little round mirror on the counter. "I believe it does, thank you!" After paying, I left the store and walked back toward the Hilton.

This experience made me think about what I had learned on the reservation when trying to call the ravens. My internal homophobia was a block to being free and magical, and it had just reared its ugly head. Suddenly, I felt the urge to call Valerie and talk to her about what happened. I had brought a regular cell and a satellite phone and patted my pockets while trying to figure out which one to use. My wallet was in my back pocket, but no phone. My other clothes were in the bag, and my vest had many pockets. Stopping at a planter, I rustled through the bag and the pockets, which contained only my safari clothes and a receipt. Both phones were gone. Returning to the store where I bought the blouse, my salesperson helped me look in the changing room. Nothing. Dammit, all that jostling at the open market...I was mooning about Mitzi and my outfit while my pockets were being picked!

I walked back to the market entrance with the half-baked thought of looking for my phones or finding a lost and found, but one glance told me the effort would be futile. Watching the ever-changing, chaotic swirl of the crowd made it clear that my phones were gone forever. Charlie would need to call the Garden and let them know about this.

I arrived at the hotel to find the others seated around a long table in the Hilton café. Dominique was frowning, but it turned into a smile when she saw me, "There's another wanderer! And look at you, lovely blouse and necklace."

Lorelei joined in. "Love the color!" The group was in high spirits, clinking glasses and talking excitedly, but I didn't see Mitzi or the "boys."

"Hannah! I saved you a seat." Charlie was already halfway through a beer.

I sat beside him and whispered, "My phones were stolen."

"What? When? Where?" His good mood shifted to concern, and he started patting his own pockets. "We need to call the Garden."

"It must have happened at the marketplace. Remember how crowded it was?"

He stopped patting. "Shit."

"What?"

"Mine are gone too." We stared at each other, as a server brought several appetizers to the table, and our group cheered.

***

Aurora led Jay and Ralph the last twenty feet. The floor to ceiling door leading to the Scriptorium was locked with a large iron ring. It looked impenetrable. Jay gave it a pull. "No way it's going to budge. Well I guess that's that. Maybe we can return with—"

"Hold on, son. Wait 'til you see this!" Ralph looked at Aurora and motioned to the door.

Aurora lifted her hands casually and said, "Kowlleski." The door unlocked and opened about two inches.

Ralph said proudly, "She's got her magic too."

"What language was that?" Jay's mouth hung open.

"Welsh. It means open. Now help me get this bad boy to move."

The two men pulled on the ring, but the door swung open quite easily, knocking Ralph down. "My hip!" Jay helped him up, and thankfully, nothing seemed broken. Aurora had already walked inside.

The room was dark as she entered, but lights began flicking on as she walked. "Who goes there?" Adriano's shade appeared suddenly, making Jay and Ralph jump.

"Aurora. You are Adriano?"

The Italian ghost nodded, surprised that she knew his name, and asked, "Who are these men?"

Jay stepped forward, cleared his throat, and said, "I'm Jay Winters, Ehrenhardt Winter's husband, and this is Aurora's husband, Ralph Brown."

"Why do you call upon us?" He spoke in heavily accented English.

Ralph was unnerved. He stood in the semi-darkness with his wife while conversing with a glowing, floating ghost. He was about to suggest they go when Aurora said, "I need Enid."

If you've never seen a ghost pale, it was quite a sight. "That is irregular, only—"

Almost instantly, Enid Hughes, the aforementioned librarian, materialized before Aurora. She appeared fully human and opened her arms, smiling and eyes crinkling through wire-framed glasses. "Aurora, *fy mhlentyn gwerthfawr.*"

Aurora went to her, and they hugged. Ralph didn't know what to do, but the energy seemed safe enough, actually loving, so he looked at Jay and shrugged.

Jay seemed fascinated.

They stood quietly and watched while Aurora joined Enid in her light bubble and conversed in what he assumed was Welsh. Enid's presence seemed to intimidate Adriano, who had shrunk and dimmed but remained in the room.

After only a few moments, Enid embraced Aurora again, nodded to Adriano, and, with a small "pop," disappeared.

Aurora looked unsteady on her feet and ready to fall. Jay and Ralph rushed forward to catch her. At the same time, a clatter was heard at the library door, and they turned to see Ehren and Woda walk in, looking mystified.

***

"What's this?" Ehren asked. "Jay, what are you doing here?"

"I'll tell you, but Aurora needs to rest first." When her eyes closed, Ralph panicked.

"Baby!" He turned to Ehren and Jay. "Help her!"

"We need to get her to the hospital," Ehren said his demeanor serious.

Woda created an invisible stretcher and called Dr. Mot by using magic. "Lift her gently and place her here." She motioned to what seemed like thin air.

"She'll fall!" Ralph exclaimed, frantic.

"No, she won't." Ehren moved forward and helped the men put Aurora on the "stretcher." The woman's body was invisibly supported, and she started relaxing. Woda began walking with her hands raised toward the stretcher, moving it down the hall. The men followed as Aurora floated toward medical assistance.

"How did this happen?" Ehren was angry now. His heavy boots echoed as they walked.

"It's my fault." Ralph looked like he might cry. "I asked Jay to take me and Aurora someplace different and—"

"Aurora wanted to see Enid," Jay said to clarify.

Ehren interrupted him, his mind working furiously, as he exchanged a look with Woda. "She specifically asked for Enid?"

"Yes! She appeared, and that other ghost looked frightened or something, but the ghost lady held out her arms and hugged Aurora." Ralph said this with his eyes on his wife as they navigated the corridor's twists and turns. She looked peaceful.

"Enid hugged Aurora?" Woda asked sharply. "That's bad."

"Oh my god." Ralph looked even more worried.

"So anyway, they talked in another language," Jay said. "Ralph said it was probably Welsh because he's heard it before." Jay started to get defensive. "They were both smiling. I don't know what happened."

"I'll tell you what happened," Woda said as they approached the hospital opening. "When an earthly creature, even a magical one, has extended contact with someone visiting from another world or plane, it's an extreme energy drain. She needs medical and magical attention immediately."

Alaric was standing at the door, looking rumpled. His coat jacket was off, and his sleeves were rolled up. He looked at Aurora and ran a hand through his thick hair. "I heard the call. Dr. Mot's not here. Can I help?"

"This is a medical emergency. We need a doctor, not IT." Woda's voice was sharp.

"I tried calling him, but he's not answering."

"I'll see if I can locate him." Woda stepped aside and closed her eyes, concentrating. Ralph, Jay, and Alaric moved Aurora to a solid medical bed, and Woda turned her magical talents to scanning the keep for Dr. Mot's location.

"We need to hydrate her and keep her from going into shock. I can do this." Alaric moved to get a bag of saline. "Nurse! Bring me a line." An elf in nurse's garb entered the room and started setting it up. "You know, if her brain is—"

Woda's eyes flew open. "Don't you dare talk about doing anything with her brain." She was almost as purple as her dress and held up her index finger as a warning. "She's had the life force sucked out of her. She needs medicine and magic, not more testing." Turning to Ehren, she said, "I need to get my circle of healers here."

Alaric yelled at Woda, "I do have training in regular medicine, too, you know."

Ehren looked at both and said in a quiet, growly voice, "Stop bickering. Alaric, finish what you started with the saline. Woda, find Dr. Mot."

"He's not in the Keep," Woda said, then called her circle to join them in the infirmary.

Just then, Shrumm came running to the door. "Ehren! Quickly, to the war room!"

"What's happening?" He was torn between Aurora and this new emergency.

"Best kept in the war room. There's something you must see."

"Ralph, stay with your wife. Jay, come with me."

Jay and Ralph had been watching all this, which only took a minute. Ralph said, "I'm staying here." Jay looked confused.

Ehren put out his hand. "Jay, join me in the war room."

"Do you need coffee?"

"No." Ehren grabbed his hand and, upon leaving with Shrumm, said, "I need an ambassador."

Jay smiled with surprise, eyebrows raised, and kept pace with Ehren as they ran toward the war room. "Whatever you need."

***

Soon, five energy workers from Woda's special healing brigade entered the infirmary. After a brief explanation of events, they circled Aurora's body and closed their eyes. Their lips moved, but no words could be heard, only a humming. Alaric ensured the drip was placed correctly in Aurora's arm and said,

"You might as well sit down, Ralph. This will take a while." His tone had softened. He really did seem to want to help.

Woda concentrated outside the circle until, startling them all, Aurora shouted, "It's a trap! The ravens know. The ravens know! Get them out of there!" She then fell silent.

Alaric felt her pulse, "It's reedy. She needs to rest."

"My magic—"

"Is taxing on her, like the tests were earlier."

She said nothing but capitulated, telling her circle, "Only one of you stays here with low-level healing. The rest need to find Dr. Mot."

Woda said, "One of us must tell Ehren." Alaric looked at Woda, who said, "Go. We will make sure she has hydration and quiet." He ran out the door to deliver Aurora's urgent message to the council.

***

Alaric's dramatic arrival at the council meeting made everyone look up. Karla, Alex, Jay, Shrumm, and Ehren were present. He delivered the message.

"A trap?" Alexandra paled. "How did they even know Charlie and the girls would be in Namibia?"

"The ravens tricked us again. I will personally go to Rayva and find out what's been going on behind our backs." Ehren punched the table with a fist. "Shrumm, message Heloisa. She needs to come down from Tanzania." Ehren was angrier than Karla had ever seen him. "I want someone to tell me how the leak happened. Now."

Everyone looked at Alaric.

"Don't look at me!" He held up his hands.

"Alaric, ever since you joined the council, *Lupus Imperium* seems to know where my daughter is." Ehren seemed to grow as he glowered at the elf.

Karla wasn't even the target of Ehren's anger, and she was shaking. Jay took a step back. The energy in the room felt dangerous.

"They've been one step ahead of us in a way that would only be possible if someone in the know was working with them." Ehren walked menacingly toward Alaric.

Woda arrived in time to hear the end of the tirade and said, "Ehren, it's not Alaric."

All heads swiveled to look at her. Woda filled the door with her ample frame, wearing a solemn expression.

The young elf looked relieved. He said, "Ehren—"

"Silence!" Ehren focused on Woda. "What do you know? Quickly, Mitzi's life is in danger."

"And Panda and Charlie," added Alexandra, frowning.

"It's not Alaric. It's Dr. Mot." Woda must have run because she took a moment to catch her breath. "My gut was trying to tell me earlier when I came and got you, but I thought it was Alaric who was disturbing the magical signature in the hospital. After he left to deliver the message from Aurora, I was still in the infirmary, and nothing changed. The evil lingered over Dr. Mot's study. To be sure, I went in, and the stench of evil was on everything. He must have used a spell to contain it. I came here immediately."

Shrumm, charged with being parliamentarian, had to say, "Without a warrant?"

"Exigent circumstances work here like in the States." Alexandra was an attorney, after all.

Woda sat. "It was an emergency. What now?"

"First, we deal with the current emergency. Shrumm?"

Shrumm looked grim. "This arrived fifteen minutes ago." He pointed at the wall, and a screen descended. "This video came on a thumb drive delivered by a raven. One was dropped in the Western province, and someone there shared it widely on social media."

Everyone was seated. There was no sound. On the screen, they saw Mitzi, Ekk, Elsa, and others with their hands tied behind their backs, two men throwing a body overboard, and a large man being made to walk a plank. The man was shot and spun over the edge. The video stopped, and a message floated on the screen like in the silent film era: "Your leadership is weak." A silhouette of a raven filled the screen before the image faded.

"This was shared in all the nine provinces?"

Shrumm nodded. "Representatives are on their way to the keep for an explanation. The Garden is roiling with fear and anger."

"Wartime propaganda," Karla said. "This tactic is used to demoralize an enemy. In 1538—"

Alexandra shook her head, and Karla caught the cue to stop talking. Ehren seemed distracted, probably trying to remember the chain of events about the video.

"Mitzi didn't talk about it, but Ekk said something."

"When I spoke to Ekk, he said there was a camera, but it got destroyed. He kept the SD card." Shrumm showed signs of strain. "Mitzi and Ekk both told me about the giant octopus being activated by her pendant. This appears to be only a portion of the story."

"Shrumm did give it to me, but it was a different version." The others gave Alaric a side eye as he spoke. Woda's declaration alone that the traitor was Dr. Mot would not clear him of suspicion. "This video must have been edited." Alaric was on firm ground now. "It's easy to do."

"Show me that video." This was not a question. Ehren stared at the screen, ready.

"I don't have it." Alaric, for once, didn't have a smart-aleck comment.

"Where's the SD card now?" Alex asked the obvious question but did not seem perturbed.

They all looked at Alaric again.

The elf was pale. "To be fair, Shrumm only gave it to me yesterday while we were focused on Aurora. I had it in my computer room, but now it's gone. I discovered the computer I downloaded it to was smashed, and I was trying to figure out what to do when you all arrived at the infirmary." The room was silent. "I was looking for it."

"Did Dr. Mot have access?" Ehren asked.

"Yes." He hung his head and used two fingers to pinch the top of his nose as if he had a headache or was trying not to cry.

"Did you at least make a copy?"

Now he smiled sadly. "No, I hadn't had a chance."

"Then it's a good thing I did." Alex sipped her coffee.

"What?" Alaric's head popped up.

"You've been on our radar for a while, Alaric. I've heard you even question the way we govern here." Ehren shook his head.

"And by the way, we weren't helpless when you joined the council," Woda stated. "We still have our magic."

"For your information, I lived in California for years and used computers daily in my law office," Alexandra explained. "Shrumm brought the SD card to me to look at before taking it to you. When this is over, the entire chain of events must be reviewed."

"But, my work..."

"Alaric, for the foreseeable future, you are off the council and going nowhere near the TMT. I hope you're telling the truth, but until we've investigated, you'll stay with these gentlemen." Ehren rapped on the heavy wood table, and two keep guards burst into the room.

Briggam and Tuk, both pretty beefy, entered quickly and moved toward Alaric, who raised his hands in alarm. "You're lucky he's putting you in a keep guest room and not the brig. Come on."

"I'm not a traitor," Alaric yelled as they led him from the room.

"Shall I play it now?" Shrumm asked.

Ehren nodded, and all eyes went up to the screen. They saw what was on the unedited video. When the octopus tentacles appeared over the ship's side, even this group, which had seen so much, let out oohs and aahs.

Ehren exhaled heavily. "Shrumm, put this on social media, but we need more. We must find Dr. Mot." He turned to his husband. "Jay. I need you to be my Paul Revere."

"Who?" asked Shrumm.

Karla was happy to show off her historical knowledge. "He was a man who spread the word that the British were coming during the United States Revolutionary War. He also made gunpowder and created the first currency." She took a deep breath and was about to launch into more facts when Alex cleared her throat. Karla looked at her briefly and said, "There's more. Would you like to hear it?"

"Thank you, Karla, I think they get the gist," Alex whispered. She had been working with Karla on her social skills.

"I'll do whatever it takes, but don't you have an announcement system?"

"We do, but I'm learning that the people of the Hercynian Garden don't want text messages and emails." He looked at Woda. "Times are changing." He looked lovingly at Jay. "I can't think of a better person to communicate with and invite calm. You would be the Garden's first official Ambassador while I'm away."

Now Jay looked confused. "Where will you be?"

"After dealing with the representatives in the throne room, I will see Rayva, queen of the ravens." Ehren got up. "That is all."

The council erupted in talk at these dramatic events. As she prepared to leave, Alexandra announced, "I'll call the elves and catch them up."

Chapter Fourteen

Undercover

That night, I readied myself for a visit from Mitz, brushing my teeth and straightening the room. She had come back today almost at the end of our lunch, laughing with Simon and Geoff, which made me jealous. I was fed up with the undercover scenario and needed to tell her that. At about 11:00 p.m., she knocked on my door. After a quick kiss, she said, "I can't stay; Dom and I are rooming together."

My smile dropped. "The thought of being able to hold you is the only thing making the mission bearable." She hugged me.

"You have no idea who we're dealing with, Panda. They killed an innocent person on the ship, gave Elsa a black eye, and made another innocent walk the plank, but I think he'll make it. They would have killed all of us if the, you know, octopus..."

"You didn't tell me that last night!" My heart thudded.

"Honey, I know how you are. How long have I known you?" Tears were in her eyes.

"What about the elves?" The thought of anyone harming them was horrifying.

"They were going back to the house. The whole thing was pretty traumatizing." She must have seen my expression. I'm known to have meltdowns. "We have to be brave, Panda. We're in the middle of a mission." She kissed me softly. "Now, have you noticed anything weird on this trip?"

I swallowed my anxiety. "Something happened at the market today—"

A knock on the door interrupted me. We froze in place. "Who is it?" I asked.

"Hannah? It's me." Charlie.

We let him in and quickly closed the door. "There's something fishy going on with those Australian guys. They're supposedly tourists like us and don't know anyone here, right? But about five minutes ago, I went to the coffee shop to fill up my water bottle for tomorrow and saw Simon being dropped off at the front door by a car full of locals." He walked to my window and looked out without moving the curtains. "Can't see who was driving, but it's not a taxi. I think they're still in the parking lot." He asked me, "Did you tell her about the phones?"

"I was just about to." Holding Mitzi's hand still, I said, "Charlie and I had both our satellite phones stolen at the market today. That can't be a coincidence."

Mitzi's face clouded. "That's not good and means we've been found out. We need to get word to the Garden. I was counting on you guys to be my conduit. I even tried to use the "business center" to check on the elves, but the one computer was out of order. Let's find a phone in Luderitz tomorrow." She checked her watch. "I've got to go."

"Be careful, love." I kissed her quickly, and she left. Charlie and I were alone.

"We are now on our own, cut off from the Garden, and almost ten thousand miles from home."

"Aren't you a ray of sunshine? Alexandra will raise the alarm when she can't get in touch."

"Any ideas?"

"I would fake being sick and fly home early, but that would leave you two without backup," Charlie said, but even as he said the words, the idea was dead on arrival. "Think, Panda."

"I'm wondering how *Lupus Imperium* even knew we were here." I started to shiver. "Do you think it's the Australians? I haven't liked them from the get-go."

Charlie shrugged. "I hate to say it, but it's like somebody at the Garden is leading us by the nose. First, we're going to Tanzania. I was looking forward to Serengeti. Then we're sent to Namibia. Then our phones get stolen."

"If someone is after us, this mission is no longer simply intelligence-gathering. We need to be on our guard more than usual." I sagged. "I'm going to bed."

"See you at breakfast. We'll talk tomorrow. Goodnight."

My mind spun as I closed the door, but I did my usual nighttime ritual, hoping to sleep. Cut off from communication with those at home and in the Garden, I lay on the bed, fully clothed, feeling abandoned. As I watched the moon through threadbare curtains, I realized I hadn't seen even one raven since arriving. Did they even have ravens in Namibia? They were my alleged superpower—what a joke. My hubris in not correcting Twyla after she told Ehren about me being able to call them seemed not only foolish but highly dangerous. We would be defenseless if I tried to summon the ravens help and they didn't come.

***

While Charlie and I stood in line at the breakfast buffet, Dominique stood near a window on her cell phone, her finger on her free ear. She paused to say, "Okay, folks, eat a good breakfast. It's about a five-hour drive to Luderitz."

She returned to the table. "Sorry, folks. I'm merely lining up some wonderful surprises for us. We'll spend the night in Luderitz, then go to the Skeleton Coast tomorrow."

Mitzi was already eating and had her professional smile on. "Dominique and I think you will all appreciate the cooler temperatures in Luderitz."

Rena fanned herself. "It has been hot."

Rick said unnecessarily, "It is Africa, honey."

"Actually, the summer temperatures arrived early this year." "Miranda" jerked her head up. I knew she was thinking what I was, *the Summer Stone*!

"Edith can't wait to see the shipwrecks." Lorelei had her plate filled with a traditional English breakfast. I sat down next to her.

"Baked beans?"

"You should try it, Hannah. Great protein."

"Thanks, but I'll stick with my hash browns." The banter was light and friendly.

"The seaside, thank goodness! My skin feels so dry I could be one of the Aussie boy's lizards!" Rena fluttered her lashes at Simon, flirting shamelessly. Rena was not turning out to be one of my favorites. Her world seemed to revolve around men. Also, calling grown men boys was a pet peeve.

Charlie looked at my plate and saw I was ignoring my sausage. "You gonna eat that?"

"Have at it." I started wondering what was in the sausage and longed for Elsa's cooking back home.

Edith had finished eating and sat with an elbow on the table and a cup of tea. She gestured toward Dominique. "There was a small museum when I went to Luderitz years ago. Is it still there?"

"Yes!" Dominique looked excited. Of course, she seemed excited or interested in everything—essential for a tour guide. "That's on the agenda. And for those who like beer," she looked at the men, "this town takes its ale seriously."

After returning to the table with a second laden plate, Simon celebrated with a "Huzzah!"

Charlie said, "I'll drink to that."

Wanting to be able to speak to my wife, even in her undercover role, I asked, "Miranda, I would love to visit with the locals. Is there any chance we can do that?"

"That's right, you're a professor of anthropology." Dominique showed interest, which engaged some others at the table.

Mitzi smiled at me. "Anything is possible, but we don't have it specifically on the itinerary."

Edith said, "I would love that too. In our Namibian studies semester, we will be covering the Skeleton Coast. Now you've got me curious. Dr. Panover, what does anthropology have to say about the Himba people?"

"Hannah, please." My mind went blank. I was supposed to be an anthropologist here, but Himba didn't ring any bells. "The Himba are a people who need to be studied more."

Thankfully, Edith saved me by agreeing. Thankfully, academics love to talk about things they've learned, and she was the Namibian expert among us. "Precisely! I hope we see the tribe. The intricate way they decorate themselves is fascinating."

"Absolutely," I said, tucking into breakfast.

"Well, Skeleton Coast sounds spooky to me. Kolmanskop is the main reason I came on this trip," Rick said, busy picking his teeth with a toothpick. "Miranda, what can you tell us about diamonds?"

Rena smacked her husband with a napkin and said, "Let her eat."

He smiled at the table. "I might find a diamond for my bride." This made Rena smile.

Mitzi said, "I'll be giving a presentation once we hit Kolmanskop, and as Dr. Panover said, anything is possible."

Simon and Geoff took the news in stride. "Plenty of reptiles on the beach and in the desert," said Simon.

"Suits me," said Geoff.

After a fifteen-minute opportunity to ensure everyone was checked out of the hotel, we loaded onto a bigger bus this time. "Since our drive time between sites is over five hours, the Azari Safari folks have provided more space for your comfort. Feel free to spread out." She climbed aboard, leaving Mitzi to check us off, as if there weren't only eight of us. Dominique seemed a bit off her game, but once she clipped on her microphone, she went into tour mode, describing the coastal town of Luderitz and its attractions.

***

Burbank, California

"Report." Viktor Volkov leaned back in his chair and waited. He was still watching his new recruit, fresh from *Lupus Imperium* where he trained in Italy. Otto was in his twenties and very fit. He had not told him what had happened to Sergei, but their security officer needed to be ready for anything, and he specifically asked for someone who could handle himself.

"We've been tracking them since they left Walvis Airport, sir." Otto stood in front of Victor Volkov's executive desk.

Victor sneered. "They're like children, these people. Our source tells us the 'big plan' was to have Mitzi Fowler act as a tour guide, with her fat wife as a tourist, and we would *never know*."

Brother Bruno from Schwartzwald Castle was on the open speaker and laughed. "I'm sorry, sir. It just seems so ridiculous."

"No, it is. They should be laughed at. I don't know why Wolfrum had such trouble dealing with them." This was a touchy subject for Brother Bruno, who had been Wolfrum's second in command.

Otto gave a tight smile. "May I ask what they hoped to accomplish with this ruse?"

"We have agents worldwide, while they have a dwindling collection of outposts full of misfits they call 'Free Creatures.' They use what they have and are trying to find the Summer Stone in Africa. This was the best they could come up with. Imagine, the Hercynian Garden against *Lupus Imperium*? What a joke."

"They do have the Winter Stone, sir." Brother Bruno had to get that in.

Viktor's face clouded. "That's on Wolfrum. He's not your boss anymore. I am."

"Yes, sir. It's surprising how easy this whole infiltration has been. Our mole is on the council, in the room with Ehrenhardt."

Victor said, "Let's not waste this opportunity. We take out Mitzi Fowler at Kolmanskop, then move on to the Garden with all your German forces."

"What about Panda Fowler?"

"My colonel on the ground will probably shoot her and leave her baking in the sand. She's worthless, and I don't care what he does with her as long as she's gone."

***

The Hercynian Garden

After being rescued from the container ship a few days earlier, Mitzi left to join the Azari Safari tour, which was already in progress. Ekk and Elsa stayed behind in Merryville to regroup in the little house on Thistle Drive. Like nonmagical people, they did laundry, emptied trash, and went through the mail before sitting down for dinner. Unlike nonmagical people who can let themselves get hungry, elves must eat, or they fade and disappear. This happened to Elsa once, and the experience was so painful that she could be excused for keeping herself and Ekk a tad plump. Elsa ensured they had plenty of hot comfort food, and for these German elves, this meant the table was laden with currywurst, sausages, pretzels, and Black Forest gateau. Dinner was quiet. They were bone-tired after the events on the container ship, but as agents of the Hercynian Garden, they had one job to do—keep Panda and Mitzi safe. Elsa commented, "It feels like we're not doing our jobs. I'm not used to being so far from our charges."

"When I talked to Ehren, he assured me this was a low-risk intelligence-gathering trip, almost a vacation for the girls. It's not like they're alone. Charlie Potts went too." Ekk leaned back in his chair in the girls' kitchen. The elves loved their treehouse, but the kitchen in the main house was the heart of the Fowler's home. In that space, the two empty dinette chairs punctuated the comments.

"Well, Charlie's something of a guardian but has no magic." Elsa pushed a half-eaten sausage around her plate. "I miss them, but that's not why I'm worried. Victor Volkov caught us by surprise. That shouldn't have happened."

"I'm feeling it too. We should be doing something." He balled up his napkin and put it on his plate. "*Lupus Imperium* is as aggressive now as they were under Wolfrum, maybe even more. Our orders right now, however, are to stand down. I'm going to bed." Ekk kissed her and left to find the kitty.

She watched him through the Dutch door leading to the backyard oak tree as he carried Brutus up the ladder to their little treehouse nest. Elsa surveyed the mess in the kitchen. She had cooked, and usually they both cleaned. Things were out of sync, though, and it had been a busy day. She locked up the main house and climbed the ladder herself. Soon the three were fast asleep, exhausted after their experiences and the work they did upon returning home.

Ekk was sleeping, snuggled up against Elsa's back in bed in their treehouse the following morning when Elsa's cell phone rang. The Fowler's big Bengal cat was lying on his back on their bed with all four paws up and didn't stir.

"Ekk." Elsa jostled her husband with one hand.

He made a snorting sound and opened one eye. "Yes?"

Elsa was sitting up, cell phone in hand. He rubbed his face. "What, love?" Seeing she was on the phone, he shook off his sleepiness and sat up, too, disturbing the cat.

"It's Alexandra. I'm putting her on speaker." She punched a button on her cell phone, and their friend came through.

"Sorry to call so early, friends."

"*Guten morgan.* What's happening? You wouldn't call otherwise."

"I have been meaning to call anyway, but yes, things are happening. It may be nothing, but we're out of communication with Panda, Mitzi, and Charlie. Of course I'm worried. Panda and Charlie had satellite phones when they left. Mitzi was supposed to be able to communicate through them."

"Oh no." She sat up straighter, becoming fully awake. "What does Ehren say?"

"We've had very sketchy reporting from the ravens, and he's frustrated about that. If you recall, the ravens first reported Tanzania as the possible place for the Summer Stone and Heloisa is there now. We only recently learned about Namibia through Aurora. Ehren's going to talk to Rayva directly. He's on his way to Falkenfelsen soon."

Ekk burst into the conversation. "Rayva? Wait, he's not in griffin form anymore. He's not thinking of going through Hell's Valley, is he?"

"He is, and he's only taking one of Heloisa's warriors with him."

"What should we do?" Elsa asked.

"We need to go." Ekk was already out of bed, looking for his pants.

"To Falkenfelsen?" Elsa was confused.

"There's more. You haven't heard the rest. At our last council meeting, Alaric came running in with more news from Aurora, who met with Enid."

"*Gott in Himmel*!" Everyone in the Garden knew about Enid, and no one talked to her unless it was a matter of life and death.

"What did she say?" Ekk was frozen in place, listening with every cell of his little body.

"She said that Kolmanskop is a trap."

"Elsa, pack a bag. We're flying to Namibia." Ekk's voice was sharp.

"Listen, I didn't intend for you two to be the ones to go."

Elsa gave a little laugh. "Of course you did, but it's okay. We've known each other too long. Alexandra, you were right to tell us. Last night, we felt something was amiss and couldn't put our finger on it. We need to protect our girls," Elsa's voice was trembling, "and your husband."

"Thank you, thank you a million times. Let's not tell anyone at the Garden yet. There's turmoil here, and we had a leak on the council. Please call me as soon as you know anything about Charlie." Alexandra's voice broke on his name.

"Say no more." Elsa's voice was firm and clear. "We are trained for this." Over her shoulder, she asked, "Ekk, do we still have our old satellite phone?"

"Yes."

She handed him the phone. "Give Alex the number. I'm jumping in the shower."

***

Day two of the Azari Safari Tour felt like a vacation, even with the disturbing events. You can only stay alarmed for so long, and sensing no immediate danger on the bus, I zoned out. During the nearly five-hour drive, I looked out my window at the vast desert and dramatic landscapes while napping off and on. Charlie had moved a couple of rows up and was seated across the aisle from Rick, our Texas rockhound, talking endlessly about hunting and fishing. Rick's wife, Rena, sat beside her husband, working on some needlepoint. She would have made a great TikTok advertisement for Tradwives.

Mitzi, Dominique, and the Australians traded stories about their past trips at the front of the bus. Edith was deeply involved in some picture book, making notes in the margins. During an awake moment, Lorelai came down the aisle and sat across from me, offering dried fruit. "Hello, Hannah, hungry?"

I'm always like the cat that, while sporting a sour attitude, still can't turn down a treat. "That looks good." I took what turned out to be a dried prune, which looked like a giant raisin. "Are you enjoying the trip so far?"

"Mostly. The good stuff is coming up though. Do you know much about the Skeleton Coast?"

I sat up from my slumpy position. "Not really." I caught myself. As a professor of anthropology, that sounded dumb. "I mean, I study people and…there aren't too many…people…there." I ate my prune. Maybe I should have just stopped at not really.

Lorelei laughed so hard that she almost fell off the bench. "You are a hilarious Free Creature, Hannah."

My eyes got wide, and I started chewing. "Oh?" She said free creature.

Lorelei leaned forward and said in a low voice, "I am on this trip for the same reason you and," she smiled, "Dr. Copley are." The constant engine noise covered our conversation.

"Where are you from?" I asked.

"London, clearly."

She looked mock offended, but I didn't know enough about England to figure out that calling a Londoner a non-Londoner might be an insult. "Oh."

"Look, I just wanted you to know you have an ally on the trip. I studied at the Hercynian Garden, but they aren't the only outpost, you know."

"What?" I was still so shocked that my cover was blown. All I could do was say one-word responses.

"Word of advice? Edith is exactly what she appears to be and has no idea there is anything otherworldly about me. Don't bring up Namibia unless you want to be grilled. It was clear at breakfast you were fudging."

"And here I thought I was so slick." Curiosity struck me. "Are you magical?"

"Isn't everyone from London?" She laughed. "Can't stay back here too long. Let me know if I can help in any way." She got up to leave.

"Thanks. I have lots of questions."

She paused and smiled. "I'll meet with you tonight." I watched her stagger down the aisle across from Charlie and Rick and offer her dried fruits. The roads were rough, and walking on the bus was challenging. Could we trust her?

I wanted to tell Charlie and Mitzi about having an ally, but there was no way. Both enjoyed their roles and conversed with others as we bumped along. There was no internet or phone to play with, so I pulled out my tour book for Namibia, found the Skeleton Coast, and got to reading. The pictures were haunting. Namibia's coast was about three hundred miles long, beginning at Angola and continuing down to another German colonial town. Before prepping for this trip, I had never heard about the German colonization of Namibia and wondered how much of Africa's history I didn't know. The coast was littered with bones of seals and whales, punctuated by the "skeletons" of shipwrecked vessels. Because of the desert climate, the bones and boats made for poetic silhouettes in the sand. Portuguese sailors called the place the "sands of hell."

This made me want to know more, but the tourist book was limited. I resolved to buy a book in Luderitz about the Himba people so that I could play my role successfully. Eventually, the hum of the motor, the sun through the window, and sheer boredom lulled me to sleep.

Chapter Fifteen

Ehren and Jay's Private Chambers

Ehren lay on the bed and closed his eyes. "I leave before dawn tomorrow."

The chamber was ornate, with a large comfortable bed and a window looking out over the fields beyond the keep. When Jay had moved in, he was given his own valet and all the clothing he could request from the Garden tailors. Even so, he had simple tastes and didn't take up much room either physically or with his demands. Ehren's personality was larger than life, so it worked for them, although it was somewhat out of balance. The elephant in the room was Ehren's upcoming journey to confront Rayva, leader of the ravens at Falkenfelsen, a dangerous nest.

Lying next to his husband, Jay finally spoke up about his feelings. "Look, I'm not a hysterical person. I think I've been a pretty good sport following the love of my life to a magical world, but you want to go somewhere that people often don't return from?"

"Jay, my Jay." Ehren opened his eyes, turned, and pushed some strands of Jay's hair behind an ear. "I must. I'm the one who believed the ravens and convinced Panda to harness her abilities to call upon them. My daughter's life is in danger now, partly due to this decision."

"But they have Alexandra's husband Charlie with them. He's a big, strong guy. You don't think that's enough?"

"He's also a normal human. Zero magic."

"You just described me, too, love." Jay crumpled. "I've been here a couple of years now and, as a normal human, I wonder where I truly fit amongst these amazing creatures. You have unicorns! Trolls! Elves!" Jay exhaled and sat up on the bed.

"What?" Ehren looked shocked. "Haven't I given you everything to make your life comfortable? Has anyone treated you poorly? I'll have them beheaded." Jay knew Ehren was kidding. His sense of humor was always a bit dark. He probably did have the power to have someone beheaded, however, which was also a nod to the power he wielded in the Hercynian Garden.

"Yes, we—I am privileged, to be sure, especially compared to some out in the provinces, but that's not what I wanted to talk to you about." Jay was tall and thin, and some might say skinny. He didn't feel he was particularly handsome, living with scarring from childhood acne, but Ehren always called him beautiful. "Ehren, what happens to me if you die on this mission? I don't have my old life in Merryville. Even if I moved back and got a job at the coffeehouse again, how could I live there, knowing this place exists?"

"Jay, you have a life here with me, and I fully intend to return." Ehren scooted over, swung his legs around, and held him close. "But if I don't, there is a succession plan. Ekkhard Schmidt did a good job running the Garden while I was in Merryville. He's probably the leading contender to take over for me. Heloisa would be his right hand like she is for me. Alexandra is helping me plan for these contingencies."

"I heard you asked Woda about transitioning back to being a griffin."

"I did."

"Would it be safer than going through the Valley of Hell to get to Rayva as a human?"

"Hell's Valley." He booped Jay's nose. "And, maybe."

Jay was an ordinary person, but a person who loved an extraordinary partner. He realized that Ehren had an important role in the larger world beyond their relationship. "If that is safer for you, then I want you to do it."

Ehren pulled back his head in surprise. "I'm not sure you know the implication of that. Have you ever seen a griffin? I have the head of an eagle, covered with feathers; my talons are sharp. I could never hold you like this. Our lives would vastly change."

Jay shed a single tear and put his head on Ehren's breast. "I know, love. I also know we're not talking about only us. We're talking about the balance of good and evil in the world and the fate of so many in the keep and the larger world. I can't stand in the way of that."

"You." Ehren lifted Jay's chin with a finger and looked into his eyes. "I vow to return. I shall stay as I am because I would rather die than lose you."

"Then take me with you."

"No." Ehren sighed. "You have to hold up the kingdom while I'm gone by going to each province, remember? This is vitally important to me."

"I wish I had a motorcycle. I've never ridden a horse and certainly not a unicorn," Jay blurted.

Ehren looked thoughtful. "Talk to Shrumm about it. You need to be yourself and connect with the people."

Jay, a lifelong biker back in California, perked up considerably. "I won't let you down."

They were both aware that time was fleeting. "Now help me pack," Ehren said.

***

Once organized, the elves were unstoppable as they raced to Namibia. "Did you call Jack?" Elsa trailed behind Ekk as he marched to the ticket counter.

"Yes." He turned so fast to face her that she almost walked into him. Smiling, he said, "I turned off the coffeepot."

She had to smile back. She got anxious about little things when they left for a trip, and she always worried that the coffee was left on. "Puddle would have caught that anyway." Puddle was going to stay in the house and watch Brutus.

"Jack Johnson has moved mountains to get Panda's Land Rover to Walvis Bay. I don't know how he did it, but we should have wheels when we arrive." He turned back and walked, trailing a rollaway carry-on. "I can't wait to see Panda's face when we drive up." They both laughed at that.

They didn't speak of the mission until they were seated on the plane. "Alexandra got me an update. The bus is on its way to the city of Luderitz. I don't know if we can catch them there, but they go to the Skeleton Coast next, then Kolmanskop."

***

The Azari Safari bus finally reached Luderitz but had to park two blocks away due to the size of it and of the old European-style streets. After directions to the hotel, we all walked. I fell in step with Mitzi. Conversations and street noises surrounded us, as she asked quietly, "What's up?"

"I'm about done pretending we don't know each other. We've been busted. Lorelei told me she's part of the Free Creature movement in London."

Mitzi stumbled, then steadied her rollaway and continued walking. "This whole mission feels totally out of control." She looked ahead and shook her head. "What should we do?"

"I think we talk more and have Miranda and Hannah get to be friends. You avoid me too much right now. It sounds like everybody, well, a few know who we are anyway. I hope they don't know Charlie is part of the Garden."

"Fat chance. They took his phone, right?"

"Oh. Yeah."

"By the way, I got a chance to look at the tour book on the Himba people. They are nomads and color their skin and hair with ochre, which can be pale yellow, deep brown, or red. They eat meat almost exclusively and go back and forth between the Ka—shoot! I forget the other place—and the Skeleton Coast. They have done that for centuries. Hope that helps."

"Thank you." I guess my wife was paying attention at breakfast.

As we turned a corner, Mitzi exclaimed, "Wow! This is gorgeous." The Nest hotel faced the Atlantic Ocean, which sparkled in the setting sun. Her eyes lit up. This kind of beauty was what drew her to travel. "I love it." She smiled at me. "Duty calls."

Dominique stood on the steps of our hotel, the Luderitz Nest. "Where's Miranda?" She shielded her eyes from the intense setting sun. "There you are. Okay, cue up at registration, and Miranda will help you with any issues. Dinner at six. I'll get our itinerary sorted for tomorrow, the Skeleton Coast." Some in the group oohed and aahed. I guessed everyone had seen the dramatic silhouettes of shipwrecks in the brochure, and anticipation was high. I saw Lorelei and Charlie talking to one another. Charlie had a twinkle in his eye as he smiled at me before mounting the steps to reception. Lorelei must have told him, too, that she was an ally. Even with zero evidence, it made me feel a bit better. She returned to where I was and said, "I looked over Edith's shoulder. She's been reading all afternoon about the Himba." When I opened my mouth, she said, "Just listen. They are matrilineal and polygamists. Most men have two wives, and they have large, extended families. I hope that helps." She rushed up the stairs, probably not to be seen with me. I wished I knew the whole story about many things, but the Himba had never been on my radar.

As usual, Rick and Rena Bush were first at the registration counter, not too happy about having a queen-sized bed. Rick said nastily, "I need a king-size bed. Do you see how tall I am?" I waited patiently and tuned them out. Edith got in line behind me and said, "I was reading up about the Himba. What's your take on their family structure?" She studied me with pale blue eyes through rimless glasses. This was a test.

"What part?" I asked. "They're polygamists." So much was at stake, and this lady was busting my chops like I was part of her class.

"But that is somewhat of a paradox, right?" She thought she had me.

"Oh, you mean because it's men with multiple wives, even though they're matrilineal? That's probably due to the tribe's survival in harsh conditions."

She looked surprised. "Yes, with such small families." The Bushes left the counter, and we moved up.

"Small?" I said, feigning shock. "Their families are large and extended." When her face fell, I said, "If you see a group with ochre-dyed skin, you've found them. Now, if you'll excuse me." Thankfully, my turn had come to check in, as that was the full extent of my knowledge.

Grasping my old-school metal key after getting my room assignment, I walked away smiling. I didn't know why keeping up the charade was so important, but it felt good to hold up my "Dr. Panover" guise. Lorelei was now at the counter with Edith, checking in, and no one would ever guess how she'd saved the day. Mitzi and Charlie were elsewhere, and I was alone until dinner. My room was small but charming, and the sliding door opened onto a balcony. Still having an hour before dinner, I relaxed into a wicker chair on the third floor and looked out over the ocean. I was tired and intrigued by the idea of other "good guy" outposts. With all that had happened since I'd discovered Ekk hiding in the bushes at my workplace, I assumed the Hercynian Garden was it. The breeze was heavenly, and thinking out loud, I asked, "Oh where, oh where, Ravens, where are you?"

Almost at once, three birds that looked like ravens but had a white band around their necks landed on the railing. They lit only for a minute or two, but an exchange of sorts happened between us. They knew I was only testing them, and when satisfied there was no good reason to stay, they took to the sky. I took this as an excellent sign.

***

Ehren left the Garden before dawn, accompanied by Bur, Heloisa's most highly trained guard. He left in secret before others were aware, so nothing could be done about it.

Jay went to see Shrumm and asked about a motorcycle. He felt silly now, as motored vehicles were highly uncommon in the Hercynian Garden. Most people walked or rode horses and unicorns. During the late afternoon, they walked down a path he had taken with Ehren many times before. It followed a river that turned into a creek and led to the trees. "Where are we going?"

"You'll see." Shrumm had seemed surprised at Jay's request and only asked, "Ehren told you to ask me?"

"He did."

Shrumm and Jay finally got to a place of overgrown bushes, although he could see the path once wound through it. Shrumm said, "This way." He waved his hand, and the bushes parted. An old wooden structure about fifty feet ahead of them came into view. It had a front door and rustic walls made of grape-stake wood, with gaps in them. Vines grew around it and through the gaps as if trying to reclaim the structure, which resembled a barn. They approached, and Shrumm turned, a concerned look on his face. "It's been a long time since we entered here. Ehren used to come here and sleep sometimes after a sad time. It's...kind of a sacred space." Shrumm lifted a piece of wood holding the double doors in place and swung them open.

Jay stared at the dark interior, lit only by shafts of light coming through the gaps in the wooden walls. The only thing in the room was a ghostly piece of furniture covered by a sheet. Dust motes swirled, and as his eyes adjusted, they gave the place an otherworldly feel. "Why all this mystery?"

Silently, Shrumm led Jay into the shed, where he approached a covered object. He pulled off the sheet, revealing a vintage motorcycle.

"If I'm not mistaken, that's Galahad green. I can't believe I'm seeing this!" Jay ran forward and fell to his knees, almost fondling the bike. "It's an Indian 440. I've only seen them in magazines." He turned to Shrumm. "Wait, this belonged to Frederick?"

Shrumm nodded sadly.

"I can't. I mean, this is too special." But his eyes kept returning to the bike. Shrumm patted Jay's shoulder since Jay was still squatting. "I'll need some tools."

Shrumm walked to a dark corner, taking an old canvas off a scratched and worn red tin box. "All right here."

Jay walked over to the toolbox and lugged it into a light beam. "Sweet. If you give me a few hours, we'll know if she'll run." He finally stopped looking at the bike and tools and looked at Shrumm. "You sure it's okay?"

"Ehren wanted you to have it. Frederick used to tear up the place when he wasn't at sea. It was a source of great joy, although some in the keep complained. I've always wondered if that isn't what caught Ehrenhardt's attention when you met. Didn't you ride a bike in California?"

Jay stood, dusting off his jeans. "Well, yeah. I've ridden, like, my whole life." He looked at the bike longingly. "Is there a gas station in the Garden?"

***

Jack Johnson was true to his word and, upon the elves' arrival, had a "Johnson Global Shipping" representative on-site to help them navigate the tricky import and government systems to get the Land Rover. That was the easy part. Getting the Code Three license to drive a US car on Namibian roads took a half-day.

152

Thankfully, Panda kept the Rover's engine in tip-top condition, and finally, the officer doing the review closed the hood and announced it was ready to go.

Leaving Walvis Bay, Ekk drove while Elsa navigated. Because the Namibian coastal roads did not have reliable GPS, they headed straight to Luderitz using paper maps after gassing up. "Have you heard anything from the Garden?" Ekk was getting anxious.

"Nothing." The satellite phone rang at that moment. "Maybe that's them. Hello?"

"Elsa, it's Heloisa. Where are you?" Elsa put the call on speaker.

"We're on our way to Luderitz. Are you getting close?" Ekk slowed to check a sign, then sped up again.

"No. I'm still back in Tanzania, but we've got a problem. Ehren's disappeared."

"He hasn't disappeared. He went to see Rayva to sort out the raven issue." Ekk was surprised Heloisa didn't know this.

"No. You haven't gotten the update. He left for Falkenfelsen with Bur, one of my best men. Bur returned without Ehren and said that shapeshifters had taken him. I'm leaving for Germany now."

"But Heloisa, Mitzi and Panda are in grave danger here, as is Charlie Potts. We're in Panda's Land Rover on the way to Luderitz. If they're not there, we're going to Kolmanskop."

"Then you will have to be enough, little ones. I must go. Godspeed."

Elsa clicked off the call. "Can't you make this thing go any faster?"

***

Dinner was festive, as we were finally leaving civilized Namibia and on the cusp of the wild. Dominique said she had a treat for our tour group, so no one should go to their room after dinner. I sat next to Charlie, with Edith and Lorelei at the other end of the long table, lest Edith quiz me again. At our buffet bar, I chatted casually with Mitzi, commenting, "I didn't know there were ravens in Namibia! Three of them landed on my balcony. Isn't that cool?"

She raised her eyebrows and smiled. "Very!" It was enough to communicate my connection to the ravens was working, even in Africa. Things were finally looking up.

Simon and Geoffrey entered, and Simon cut in line to be near Mitzi. "How ya going, mate?" I wanted to smack him with my tray. Geoff grabbed an apple off the end of the buffet and found an empty chair.

"Come on, Simon and girls. I have a surprise!" Dominique said this as she dragged an unusual-looking man to our table. He was Caucasian, but his deep tan and wild hair made me look twice to figure that out. She had pulled him from his table, a half-eaten plate of food still in his hand.

After the long day on the bus, we were ready for some entertainment. At least I was for sure.

"I was hoping we would run into Paul, one of the best storytellers on the coast. He has agreed to tell us a few after dinner. You are in for a treat," Dominique gushed.

I saw Rick roll his eyes, but Rena looked interested. I know I was.

The man sat and gave a Stone Age hand lift in greeting. "I have been here so long the native people have given me a name, *Wit Storieman.*" He had a voice you couldn't ignore, like what you would think Moses would sound like. Very portentous.

Dominique said, "I met *Wit Storieman* years ago. You never know where he will turn up." She was clearly enamored of him.

"Is his name in the local language?" Rena inquired.

Edith beat Dominique to the punch. "It's Afrikaans for White Story Man. English is the official language." With a quick glance at Dominique, she said, "Although Afrikaans is also spoken here."

"You speak Afrikaans?" Mitzi was impressed, or maybe it was part of her sleuthing.

"I've been to Namibia six times in my twenty years of teaching. It's handy to know." Edith was full of surprises. *What made this pale, elderly English woman so obsessed with this place?*

The man was heavily tattooed, and his faded khaki shirt was unbuttoned to show a necklace of shells on his hairy chest. After wolfing his food, he stood and invited us all to the beach after dinner. "I shall go now and start a fire." He fixed his dark eyes on each of us at the table. "You will learn what to do," he paused dramatically, "and what not to do on this trip. It may save your life, " he said mysteriously before leaving the dining hall.

"Isn't he terrific?" Dominique asked. She was always trying to make sure we were engaged.

"Terrific," Rick commented sarcastically. "If it's all the same to you, I'm turning in after this."

"No, I want to hear!" Rena was excited.

"You can go if you want." Rick gave his wife permission to go. Ugh.

Her eyes were shining. "I'm in!"

"Sounds like a laugh." Simon took a big bite out of his apple. "Geoff, you in?"

"I hear an ale calling me." He put a hand up to an ear comically.

"Oh, join us. It'll be fun," Lorelei implored. "Miranda, will you be there?"

My wife was daintily patting her lips with a napkin. "Wouldn't miss it." She gave the table one of her engaging smiles. It was weird. I missed her so much even though she was right in front of me—so near, yet so far. "Hannah?"

"I'm coming," I said.

Charlie asked Rick, "Why don't you and I go to the bar and join Geoff for an after-dinner ale?"

"Suits me." Rick kissed Rena, and the men headed off after we finished eating. Lorelei, "Miranda," Dominique, Rena, and I— "the women,"—and Simon headed for the beach.

Simon made some dumb comment. "I guess I'm the guardian of the ladies tonight. Ha ya!" He made exaggerated karate moves. Lorelei giggled. Mitzi fell to the back with me, and we walked side by side. The party spirit was high, and I was looking forward to a good story.

"This will be so much fun," Dominique said, ramping up our enthusiasm. We walked along a torch-lit path and soon saw and heard the waves lapping the shore. *Wit Storieman* sat in the lotus position, face eerily lit by the bonfire he had made. I hoped it wouldn't be too cheesy. It wasn't.

Once we were all seated around the fire, he waited until we were quiet, then lifted his head, eyes fixed on something in the dark behind us. "First, we ask the spirits of those sailors who lost their lives here to join us, for the land God Made in Anger belongs to them." He shut his eyes, and the giggles stopped as the dark pressed in. The breeze off the Atlantic Ocean became a few degrees cooler, and my skin prickled. Mitzi jumped when he said in a distorted voice:

"I took to the sea, o most beautiful souls
A free creature was me 'til we stuck in the shoals
Greeted by sand and more sand and the heat
We had drunk ourselves dry and had nothing to eat

The red creatures found us but didn't bring us scones
They left us to die and we sing with our bones
The wind whistles through them
The crabs they did eat
Beware my intruders

Beware..." As he said these last words, he raised a rattle over his head and started chanting. It was riveting. He began his first story.

"In 1860, an unnamed ship was wrecked offshore. Later, twelve headless skeletons were found in the sand. Whaling used to be an industry here until it was outlawed in the 1980s. Some say the spirit of the whales whose bones litter the coast had had enough. Some say it's the Himba, red-skinned nomads who have been known to attack and behead—"

"Bullshit!" Surprisingly, this came from Edith.

"Don't enrage the spirits. This is not a joking matter!" *Wit Storieman* looked furious.

"Well, you at least are right about that. I'm Professor Edith Rosell, and I've studied both the Skeleton Coast and the Himba people for decades." She stood. "You, sir, disrespect the local culture. The Himba survived the German genocide and are now struggling for survival against our encroaching, so-called modern ways and development. I can't hear one more word from you!" She started walking back to the hotel.

Wit Storieman looked stoic, but that had to be embarrassing. Dominique tried to salvage the situation. "Sorry, folks, but storytelling takes some liberties. I'm sure he has another one." But the mood he had set was irretrievably broken.

"I'll go with her." Lorelei reluctantly followed Edith, and Simon said, "I'll escort them and return."

"Well, that was rude," Rena said.

Wit stood. "I'm afraid I can't help you. God be with you on the rest of this journey. You'll need it."

Rena practically ran after the others as he said this. Dominique stayed to talk with him, and I casually asked Mitzi, "Walk on the beach?"

She exhaled. "Sure."

We walked on the deserted beach, lights from the hotel in the distance. "That was interesting," I said.

She drew me behind a shipwreck monument and kissed me. "I've been dying to do that," she said.

We leaned against it, watching the moon shine over the ocean, and I spoke poetry to her. "Here is a poem I wrote. It's an antidote to being in all these romantic places and unable to be with you as my wife."

"So now it's your turn to be cheesy? Do you have a special name?" We both laughed.

"Here goes:

"Watching the ocean one night in its bed,
Hypnotically rocking, it lulled me to stay
Where the cool salty spray blew right through my head.
I was one with the sea and just blowing away;
Soon I could see that the seagulls of past
Were really soft angels with lights in their eyes.
I knew I was seeing the true sea at last;
The moon shone down blurry through dark velvet skies."

"That's beautiful," she said, head on my shoulder.
"I didn't want you to go to sleep thinking of death and bones."

"And I appreciate that. Let's get serious. Is there anything we need to do? So you can call ravens?"

"If they have white rings around their little birdy necks, I think that's what they are." I shrugged.

"I'll take it. We better go."

I felt better at that moment than I had since we'd arrived. As we walked around the monument, Dominique jogged toward us. "There you are. Time to get all the little duckies in." She fell in beside us as we walked back to the hotel. "Don't you think Edith was rude?"

Mitzi shrugged. She hated to criticize anyone.

"It's her thing, the Himba," I said. "It's her field of study."

"Maybe that was a miscalculation. She is rather passionate about everything Namibia," Mitzi said.

Dominique looked puzzled. "It was merely a bit of entertainment to set the mood for the Skeleton Coast. Tourists usually eat it up."

"These are academics," Mitzi said.

"Yes, we're weird," I said. When they both looked at me, I added unnecessarily, "It's our big brains and all."

"You're funny. You don't seem like the others." Dominque laughed. "Even with your big brain." Mitzi joined her with a gut laugh.

"Let's just turn in." Now I felt silly.

"Right. Tomorrow is a big day." Dominique squinted toward the hotel. "I hope the rest of the group isn't turned off now. I have several stories about the coast, but I will leave it factual. It will be a long bus ride if they are in a sour mood."

"That's a good idea, Dom. We can talk about Kolmanskop," Mitzi said, putting a friendly arm around her fellow tour guide.

"By the way, be careful walking in the dark like this. Even though Namibia is mostly safe, it's like any city at home. Women must be careful."

"Yeah, where was our big protector, Simon? I thought he was coming back."

Entering the hotel, that question was soon answered. The men must have snagged him because we could hear a drunken chorus from the song "Africa" by Toto coming from the bar.

"Good night, ladies," Simon called out.

"Good night." I fell asleep quickly, happy at having a few stolen moments with my wife. I vowed never again to take time with her for granted.

Chapter Sixteen

The next morning was quiet, with Rick, Simon, Geoff, and even dear old Charlie nursing what must have been epic hangovers. As we filed onto the bus, Rena stopped and complained to Dominique. "That man scared me! What did he mean, beware?"

"Oh, it was just part of his storytelling show. The bones we'll see have been on the coast for ages, and explanations exist for them all." As Rena and Rick climbed aboard, Dominique asked, "Did you know that whaling was a big industry until the 1980s when it was outlawed?"

"Several times. That weirdo last night told us. Let's get on with this," Rick snapped and walked down the aisle to the seat they had claimed for themselves the whole trip. Once, when Rena had gone elsewhere to sit, Rick sat near the window and pointed to where she was to deposit herself. It appeared the trip was not as conducive to newlyweds as they'd hoped, and I wondered how long Rena knew him before saying "I do."

I was last on the bus, having one last run to the bathroom. It was sensible when you knew you're going to be on the road for hours. As I walked down the aisle, I could see that Edith was still frosty, although Lorelei was doing everything but using shadow puppets to draw her out. Simon was chatting with Mitzi again, and the Bushes were arguing. Dominique did her best to smooth things over with the English professor after the fiasco at the fire.

"So, you see, there is science, and there is poetry. As you view these haunting images out the window and reflect on some of the real shipwreck stories you have heard, perhaps you will say a little prayer for the souls lost far away from home. I'll leave you to it while Miranda and I prepare for Kolmanskop. Trust me, it's worth the long drive. We will spend the night at the lodge and go first thing tomorrow morning."

We were on a particularly barren stretch of road, so I settled in next to Charlie and asked, "And how was *your* night?"

He was wearing sunglasses and moved painfully slow. "The ale went down so easy. It's some crazy good artisanal brew that knocked my socks off." He scratched his head and yawned widely. "That Rick is something else. He talked all night about his investments and what a big shot he was. Thank God there was a soccer game on the big screen. Geoff was drunk and trying to get with the girl serving in the bar, and Simon came in and told us all about Edith blowing her top about the story man." The bus hit a particularly large bump, which made him wince in pain. "That's about it."

"No secrets of the universe revealed?" I grinned. The noise from the big Mercedes engine drowned out any soft conversation between us.

"Only that Namibia has a hell of a soccer team. They ate Mozambique for lunch."

After a couple of hours, we stopped at an outpost for food. Since gas stations were few and far between, we were advised it was wise to keep the tank full—meaning vehicles and people. We were the last patrons served in the café, and the employees locked the door as soon as we left.

***

Mitzi heard Rena let out a scream. Everyone except Panda had boarded the bus already. Some were standing to adjust things they'd bought into the overhead storage when she did this. She pointed out the window where one of the Namibians who had helped us lay bleeding on the ground next to the gas pump. The other gas station attendant boarded the bus and ordered the driver to close the door. "Sit down, everyone." Then, to the driver, he yelled, "Go."

They were all in shock. A somewhat dull stop for food and gas had turned into a hostage situation. "Do as he says," Charlie bellowed. As a former cop, he knew this fellow wasn't playing.

Dominique said, "Maybe we can work this out. We have money." She looked so frail next to him, wearing her little AZARI SAFARI shirt. To Mitzi, it felt like she and Dominique were San Diego Zoo employees in charge of a tour that had suddenly turned deadly.

God bless Dominique, who did take her job seriously. She looked at her group. "Can all of you just empty your pockets?"

"Shut up! I don't want your money." The man held what looked like a small machine gun, waving it around as he spoke.

He was dressed like the other gas station attendant lying on the ground. The expression he wore on his scarred face was blasé, which made the whole experience more terrifying.

"Now see here," Rick Bush started to rise, and the man shot out the window next to his head. Rena ducked, but a piece of glass embedded in Rick's ear, which began bleeding profusely.

Amid screams from everyone, their captor waited calmly as the driver drove them. "Listen to me, and you will survive. It is Mitzi and Panda Fowler that we want."

"There's no one by either name on this bus," said Charlie in a non-confrontational voice.

Mitzi had a choice to make about whether to stay silent. She was about to open her mouth when Rena shouted, "It has to be one of them," pointing at the English ladies, Dominique, and "Miranda."

Until now, Simon and Geoff, seated on the same bench seat, were silent, watching events unfold. Geoff finally said, "Leave the ladies out of it."

Their attacker turned to him slowly, like a snake coiling for a strike. "You, first handcuff your boyfriend to you." He reached into his pocket and pulled out a set, which he tossed to Simon.

Simon caught the handcuffs. "He's my brother."

"Whatever. I'm told there are some unnatural things about some of you. I'm here on the Lord's work. You do what I say, and some of you will survive." Simon cuffed himself to Geoff, who now had nothing to say. "Here is what we are going to do. There are some people that want these two women. You give them up, and we will let you go."

"There isn't anyone with those names on this tour. I'm the tour guide, well, Miranda and I are." Dominique babbled.

"Driver, is everyone here that you have been driving around?"

"I didn't notice, sir." Mitzi quietly thanked him for not mentioning that Panda wasn't on the bus. She hoped that Panda might be able to call the Garden somehow.

"Liar!" He swung his machine gun to Mitzi's face. "How about you? Is there something you want to tell me?"

"No, sir, I think you have the wrong bus." She was trembling. Simon lunged forward, and the man used the butt of his gun to knock him out. "I could have killed him, but that is for the people we are going to see. Anyone else want to test me?"

Everyone stayed frozen. The only sound was Rena sobbing softly.

He slapped Mitzi hard. "You will tie everyone up now."

"With what?" Her voice was like ice.

He reached into his pocket and pulled out a ball of twine. "Everyone needs their hands tied tight behind them." To the driver, he said, "Kolmanskop is our destination. Don't try anything, or I will start shooting the men one by one."

To her credit, Rena didn't give up the fact that "Hannah" wasn't on board. Whether she'd found some shred of courage or was just too freaked out to remember, Mitzi was grateful for it. As a half-magical person, she felt the buzz of another magical person when tying Lorelei's hands. She purposefully tied her hands loosely, as she did to Charlie's hands too.

The man stood resolutely in front and watched Mitzi like a hawk. The only sounds were the drone of the large Mercedes engine and the wind. Hot wind swirled around the bus from the shattered window. Finally, Rena said, "My husband needs a bandage, Dominique. Do you have one?"

"You, tying up the people. Get her a bandage. Can't have anyone bleed out before we get there."

Dominique said, "Under the front bench, Miranda." Mitzi staggered as the bus hit a pothole but managed to pull out the first aid kit.

"Slowly."

Mitzi dragged the first aid kit in front of their hostage-taker and opened it slowly. She pulled out a piece of gauze and some tape, using blunted scissors to cut an ear-sized bandage.

"Make him stop bleeding."

She walked, hands in full view, and did what he asked. Rena tied up, sobbed, and said, "We don't deserve this. It's our honeymoon."

Rick was stoic but winced when Mitzi taped the bandage to his ear. "He's going to need a doctor. Can we move them to the back? I'm afraid the wind might blow off the bandage, and there's glass all over."

The man seemed torn, then motioned with his machine gun for her to help them relocate to the back of the bus.

Once this was done, he put the gun under his arm and tied Mitzi's hands behind her back. "Don't even think about it," he said as Simon awoke, shaking his head. Soon afterward, he sat at an angle where he could watch over them as the bus roared to Kolmanskop.

***

I had been dawdling in the dusty gift shop behind the gas station when I heard the big bus engine fire up. I hurried out and saw it leaving at full speed down the road without me. How could this be?

Surely, Charlie or Mitzi would notice I wasn't on board. Frantic, I went to find someone to help me. The man who helped us with gas was lying in an unnatural position by the pumps. I ran to him and felt for a pulse. It was thready, and he had a gash on his head. What should I do? Something bad surely had happened to him and those on the bus. How could I have missed this? No one else was around the gas station.

I ran to the café, which was locked, and returned to the gas station. I found a phone still connected to a wall. As I picked up the receiver, I realized I had no idea who to call. It was like a nightmare. The realization that this was a completely different country and that I was helpless landed on me hard. Just then, a Land Rover pulled in, and I ran out to ask whoever it was for help.

My jaw dropped to see Ekk behind the wheel. Was I hallucinating? "Elsa?"

Elsa hopped down and ran to the man on the ground. "Panda, help me get him inside." This snapped me out of my shock.

Without questioning, still wondering if this was a hallucination, Ekk and Elsa took the man's legs on either side, and I lifted his torso. We carried him out of the sun and laid him on a small couch in the gift shop area. Elsa used her satellite phone to call for help. She then filled the room with the healing scent of eucalyptus.

Ekk went outside and topped off their vehicle's tank. Freaking out, I yelled to Ekk, who looked very serious. "What the hell, Ekk?" I walked outside and put my hand on my head, looking at the direction the bus had gone. "Mitzi and Charlie are on that bus. Is this—?"

"*Lupus Imperium,* for sure. We found the mole, Panda. It was Dr. Mot on the council in the heart of the Hercynian Garden."

"Dr. Who?"

"Dr. Mot. Listen, we must get to that bus."

Elsa exited the gas station and said, "He'll have a headache, but he'll be all right. I called Luderitz police. They're coming, and we can't be here when they arrive. Come on." When I didn't move, she said, "They'll think we did it."

"Of course we didn't knock him out. Did you tell them his coworker hijacked our bus?"

"Not exactly, but if we don't go right now, even if they believe us, it will take ages to sort out. We have no time, Panda." I was glad she was thinking things through. I wasn't.

"Oh. Right." I put my hand out for the keys. "How did you guys get here?"

"We'll talk on the way." Ekk was all business.

"I'll drive. Wow. That Rover looks exactly like mine."

The elves looked at each other. "Um, it is," Ekk said, stepping up on the running board to remove his adapters so I could be unimpeded while in the driver's seat.

"What? How?"

"Patience, Panda, patience," Ekk said, throwing his adapters in the back.

"How did it get that scratch along the driver's side?" Neither elf answered.

I hopped in the driver's seat and drove my Land Rover like a bat out of hell on the deserted road. "Everybody buckled up?"

"Yes."

"Now talk to me." The tank was full, and the road was mostly smooth. I felt at home behind the wheel of my car, which was made for all kinds of roads and even no roads.

We hit a large bump, and everyone's butts lifted from their seats. I felt my head touch the roof of the car.

"Panda, slow down. If you kill us, we can't help anybody." Ekk was wide-eyed.

"I don't even know where I'm going!"

"Kolmanskop is fifteen minutes from here." Elsa was looking at a map. "That must be where they're going. The Summer Stone?"

I had almost forgotten that was the point of this mission. "Somebody better fill me in." I kept my eyes on the road.

"I'll start." Elsa was in the back seat, and I looked at her. She looked stressed and tired. "There has been no time to catch you up. Alexandra told us you weren't answering your phones."

"That's true. Somebody stole them at a market, Charlie's too. So they know Charlie and I are here for sure. I don't know if they know about Mitzi."

"Of course they do, Panda," Ekk commented. "Ehren never should have sent you here." It was rare to hear Ekk say anything disparaging about, well, anything, but especially Ehrenhardt Winter. Stressful times, indeed.

"This was supposed to be an intelligence-gathering trip. We've been playing these ridiculous roles as if an evil empire couldn't figure out who I and Mitzi are." I was still trying to figure out how my Land Rover drove us down a road ten thousand miles from home.

"It might have worked if Dr. Mot wasn't feeding all the plans to Viktor Volkov." Elsa dropped this bombshell.

"What?" I almost veered off the road. "That's the guy who was going to kill Mitzi on the container ship."

Elsa pumped a little lavender into the car's interior, probably to calm me down. Nothing was said as I regained control, but Ekk leaned forward with both hands grasping the "chicken bar" above the glove compartment. My heart was beating fast. "Sorry. Ekk, I'm not sure where I'm going."

"Just drive. I've got a map." This was classic Elsa. Through all the shock and fear, I felt overwhelming gratitude. "You came all this way for us?"

"We are your guardians, Panda," they said in unison.

"And I thought you just liked to hang out." I scanned an empty landscape. "Why don't we see them?"

"We'll catch up." Elsa consulted her map. "You need to turn left in about five miles. It's the back road to Kolmanskop." The sun burned through the window, and I flipped down the visor and cranked up the air conditioner. "Tell me how my car is here."

The elves filled me in as I drove, a distraction from what we would find when we arrived. My imagination ran wild, and dread filled my bones. That *Wit Storieman's* "Beware!" suddenly didn't seem so silly.

***

It was late afternoon when we pulled up in front of a small wooden sign hanging on a gate. Another sign said, "Authorized Personnel Only. Private Road."

"This is it." Ekk hopped out and found the gate locked.

"No problem," I said and drove through the sand to go around.

"Where is everybody?" I asked. "Looks like a ghost town."

"Seriously?" Ekk asked, exasperated. "Did you even read the brochure?"

"I was busy reading about the Himba."

Elsa said, "Your group was supposed to do their tour tomorrow morning. It's closed now, so it was the perfect time for *Lupus Imperium* to strike. It would be hard to search for the Summer Stone when the place is crawling with tourists."

"There," I shouted. Up ahead were the buildings of Kolmanskop. Once a bustling diamond mining town, German colonialists abandoned it after removing everything of value from the sand. It reminded me of Western movies I'd seen, except for the incredible amount of golden, shifting sand. I stopped the Land Rover outside an outer building and turned to my friends. "Did you bring any weapons?"

"You have your ravens, Panda. Use them," Elsa reminded me.

"Ekk, no dagger?"

He shook his head. "We flew commercial."

I studied them like they were crazy. "Have you seen any birds, guys? Because I sure haven't. A couple landed on my balcony back in Luderitz, but they had white rings around their necks. They're probably not even ravens."

"Those are Namibian ravens. They have white rings." Ekk knew his birds.

I stopped for a second. "Well, good, but until we know what we'll find inside, I won't try to call them. Those buildings look like they have many hiding places, and we have a sandstorm coming."

"That's probably why they close early before the winds come." Ekk was still cool. I felt almost hysterical. "First, we need to confirm they're here. Let's fan out and look for the bus. Elsa, I need you to stay here and try to contact the Garden. We'll need backup if any magicals are in the area."

"No Heloisa?" I asked.

Elsa looked guilty. "She was called to Germany. We'll talk after. Be careful, you two."

Like in my FBI shows and police procedurals, Ekk and I fanned out. Me to the left, him to the right. With nods and hand signals, we communicated our intended paths. The wind was blowing harder than at the gas station, and the structures, while frozen in time, were mostly filled with sand. It's funny what came to mind at times like these. I felt vindicated in my safari clothing choices, which seemed perfect for this environment. My vest even held a compartment for a scarf, which I pulled out and wound around my face up to my sunglasses to protect myself from the blowing sand. Walking around what appeared to be an abandoned bowling alley, I caught a glimpse of the bus. Despite the wind, the heat was incredible, which reminded me that this whole thing was to find the Summer Stone, or at least a piece of it. The truth was, I really couldn't have cared less about that.

As I slogged through the sand toward it, I wished I had a hat. The bus was farther than it looked, a trick of the monotone landscape, but eventually, I reached it. Bullets riddled the side, and my heart sank. Rick Bush was the only one on the bus, still strapped into his seat. He had a bandage on his ear and hands tied behind his back. He had lost a lot of blood. I untied his hands and poured water over his lips, but he needed medical help fast. "Those bastards took Rena!" he exclaimed.

"Who did this to you? Who was it?" I couldn't help myself. The questions poured from me. "How many were there? Do you have any weapons?"

"I saw four. They have machine guns." His eyes lifted to where his Stetson hat was stowed above the seating. "Rena has a gun. I gave it to her for protection." He tried to get up and groaned in pain. "Rena's bag." It was then I noticed his leg was broken, and he likely had a bullet wound. It, too, was bleeding.

"Let's take care of you first." There were various pieces of clothing left on the seats, and I found a scarf to tie around his leg. "I'll find it."

He closed his eyes and let out a big sigh. I grabbed his hat and the tiny Derringer gun from his wife's bag, which looked like a toy. "I'll be back as soon as I can." I opened a cooler on one of the front seats, put some ice cubes around his neck, and tucked a water bottle by his hand.

"Thank you. Tell Rena I love her, " he croaked, eyes closed. My final journey to Kolmanskop began then, and his words lay heavy on my heart. This was a man who was sure he was going to die. Leaving the bus, I noticed God, or somebody, had cranked up the heat while I was inside. I returned, got as many little water bottles as possible to stuff in my pockets, and set out.

I used to laugh when a comedian, as part of the act, said exaggeratedly, "It's African hot," indicating a temperature beyond the warmest of summer days—the kind of day you must wear flip-flops because the cement was too hot for bare feet. Now in the Namib Desert of Africa, as far as I could see around me, was hot sand. The soles of my feet burned, even through my new REI boots. My legs felt heavy as lead as I slogged through golden sand toward the ghost town barely visible on the horizon since the wind decided to throw sand around. A glance at our tour bus was all I needed to spur me on. It was the only shade for miles but was permanently out of commission. The tan bus lay pitched to one side—the Azari Safari Tours sign now riddled with bullets, windows shattered, and heavy tires flat. Rick, unfortunate soul, was still belted into his seat, most likely beyond human aid. Eventually, the sand would claim the site and be his grave unless we could figure something out.

Reba Birmingham

My head hurt. I wanted to sink to my knees and weep, but I had no time for self-pity. Mitzi was somewhere ahead with the others, in the clutches of some evil men and unknown creatures. I hoped she was alive and wiped some of Rick's blood from my cheek. It had mixed with my tears. I pushed forward, wearing the Stetson hat, ringed with someone else's sweat. Under the merciless sun, my arms burned, despite wearing long sleeves, and sand stung my face. I trudged on, swatting tsetse flies, certainly not laughing now.

Chapter Seventeen

Kolmanskop was discovered after a German national found diamonds washed up on the beach. A German boomtown proliferated, creating a town with homes, a hospital, a saloon, stores, and even a bowling alley. It was quite the place to be until the diamonds started running out and prospectors found easier mining to the south. By the 1950s, people abandoned the place entirely, creating the classic boom-to-bust ghost town like the American Old West after the gold rush.

The buildings slowly filled with the shifting sands, creating an eerie but extremely picturesque landscape. Tourists started coming both for history and photography, and the Namibian government restored some of the main buildings so that people could experience what they used to be like. It all felt familiar to Ekk, having grown up in a small German town, but this was no time for sightseeing. He entered the town proper and crept from one building to another to avoid being seen. The beginnings of a sandstorm were taking hold, and he needed to find shelter soon. Luckily, he stumbled upon a structure near the main hall, now the main visitor center. Although sand drifts had made it through the openings of the building he chose, he could still navigate inside it. Edging near the opening that once held a wooden window frame, he saw movement and lights on at the visitor center. His gut told him that was where Mitzi, Charlie, and the rest were being held. The wind was increasing, so he stayed out of the wind and sat down to think and watch. Soon, a guard appeared outside the main door to the building. He couldn't tell how many were inside with Mitzi, Charlie, and the rest of the tour group. Interestingly, he picked up on a magical signature he recognized as a shapeshifter. *Uh oh*, he thought. Is Viktor Volkov there? Rumors were that he was a shapeshifter. Ekk wondered where Panda was and worried that they had no weapons, as the sand would prevent ravens from coming to their rescue.

"Ekk." He jumped. It was Elsa.

"I couldn't contact the Garden. There was too much interference." She peered carefully at the building across the way.

"So much planning, and for what?"

"Mitzi and Panda, as well as the Summer Stone, would give *Lupus Imperium* great power. I've been thinking about it. If they capture Ehren Winter's daughter, what better way to keep the Garden under control? We are the thorn in their side."

"Any ideas?"

"On the way here, I noticed no one was guarding the back of the building. There's one tiny window, probably a bathroom. It's our size."

"Shouldn't we wait for Panda?"

***

As if on cue, I walked up behind them. "I'm here, guys." Now, both Ekk and Elsa jumped. With the sandstorm's noise, it was not surprising they didn't hear me. "What's the plan?"

"There is a guard in front of the visitor's center and a window behind. That's as far as we've gotten." Ekk said. "But something unexpected happened. I think someone inside is a shapeshifter."

"Oh boy. Is it a panther like the women in Peru?" I referred to the Amazonian women of the jungle who could turn into panthers. It gave me a shiver despite the heat.

Ekk shook his head. "Not all shapeshifters turn into panthers. It can be anything, depending on the tribe."

I snapped my fingers. "It might be Lorelei, one of the professors from England. She as much as told me she's part of our good guys group, but in London. How come I didn't know this?"

"It's better to learn as it is necessary. Safer," Ekk said.

"What if the shapeshifter turns out to be *Lupus Imperium*?" The thought hit me and came out of my mouth.

"Did you find the bus?" Elsa was exasperated.

"I found the bus. Rick Bush is on it and will die if we don't get some help for him soon. I left him some water. He gave me his wife's Derringer."

"A gun?" Both Ekk and Elsa looked gobsmacked. "Is it loaded?"

My vest was packed with water, and I awkwardly pulled the Derringer out of my pocket and checked. "Yes, four in the chamber."

"You might want to leave the water bottles behind." Elsa was so practical.

"If we get anyone out of there, they may need it." I piled them in the corner.

Ultimately, we decided that Ekk would take the Derringer to distract the guard and Elsa would go through the back window. Sand had collected on that side of the building, making it possible for her to reach the window by herself. It was my job to call the ravens, but due to the sandstorm, I had no clear idea if they would or even could come.

It wasn't the best plan, but it's what we had.

After the elves left, I started with a quick meditation. Realizing that no one could hear me over the storm, I said, "Ravens come." Then I closed my eyes in the abandoned building and held out my arms, concentrating mightily.

After what seemed like an eternity, three birds flew through the opening as if shot by a rocket due to the force of the wind, crash-landing into the sand near where I stood. "This is it? Where are the rest of you?" I asked.

All three responded with irritated caws.

"Okay, okay. I appreciate you showing up. Thank you for being here," I said. "We need to take out the guard." I made up hand signals on the spot and spoke slowly to communicate. "This is so that we can rescue the people inside." I pointed at the visitor's center. Six shiny bird eyeballs studied me.

I sighed and tried again. "We must help Ekk." Here, I made a hand gesture indicating someone short. "Distract the guard." I made as if shooting a machine gun. "That's your job." I pointed to myself. "That's all our job." All three flew out the window.

Disheartened, I walked out the door and crept over to where Ekk was hunched behind a pillar. He had the gun in hand, and I hoped the birds wouldn't mistake it for a machine gun. That is, if they hadn't just left for parts unknown. I didn't see them anywhere, but it was hard to see anything with all the sand flying around.

***

Inside the building, what was left of the tour group was huddled in a corner. After being marched into the visitor's center, they were separated and questioned one by one by a soldier named Sam. The man who had hijacked their bus was called Nathan, and he watched everyone, pointing his machine gun at the captives. A Russian man entered and asked Sam, "How long can we expect this sandstorm to last?"

"It should be over soon, Colonel."

"Thank you, Sam. My helicopter?"

"Until this storm is over, they will stay in Luderitz, sir."

"So we have a little time."

Mitzi and Charlie were tied up back-to-back. Nathan had his machine gun trained on them.

"What have you learned?" the Russian man asked, holding his red beret in hand behind his back. He then walked around the group, inspecting them.

"We learned that these two are here searching for the stone weapon." Sam pointed with the barrel of his gun at Charlie and Mitzi, who were looking down the barrels of two guns now.

The Russian put out his hands, as if warming them over a fire by Charlie and Mitzi, then did the same with the rest of the tour group. "Not bad, but you missed something."

"Sir?" Nathan asked.

"There is another magical present." He put on his beret and smiled. Sam looked puzzled.

"He means me," Lorelei spoke up.

The Colonel smiled. "Surprise, surprise. Where are you from?"

"London."

Edith craned her neck around and looked at Lorelei, mystified.

"Bring her here."

Nathan grabbed Lorelei's arm, bringing her to her feet.

"What shall we do with the others?" Sam asked.

"Shoot the rest. They know nothing."

"No!" came shouts from the tour group.

The Colonel unholstered a gleaming semi-automatic handgun and held it to Lorelei's head. "Then somebody better tell me something useful, or Miss London here will lose her head." Nathan cracked a smile.

Mitzi cried out, "She's innocent. Leave her alone."

The Colonel went on. "Oh, we'll get to you, Mitzi Fowler."

Now Dominique looked at Mitzi in her Azari Safari shirt. "Her name is Miranda. She has nothing to do with this!"

"You know nothing." He used his boot to push Dominique over and watched her scramble to be upright again with her hands tied behind her back. "Although I do love corporate loyalty. I'll make you a deal." He walked around slowly. "What if I let one of you go for every piece of good information I get? Sound fair?"

Lorelei nodded, as did most of the hostages that were not frozen in place.

"You first." He pointed the gun at Lorelei again. "Where is the Summer Stone?"

"It's here. I mean, you feel the heat, right?" She looked around. "If you untie my hands, I can sense where it's kept."

"Hold that thought." Swinging toward Mitzi, he asked, "Where is your friend, Panda?"

Mitzi held his eyes with a steady gaze. "My *wife* is back in Luderitz." Dominique looked so confused.

"See how easy that was?" the Colonel said in a mock friendly way. "Let the driver go." He paused and added, "To show how sporting I am, let the old lady go too."

Johannas and Edith Roswell were untied and ran to the door. The door closed behind them, and a few seconds later, machine gun fire could be heard.

There was a general wailing from the group.

"Oh darn, I forgot to tell my man it was okay that they left." All three of the captors laughed.

***

While Edith Roswell and Johannas ran out the door, my three ravens descended upon the guard's face, pecking at his eyes, scratching, and flapping their wings, totally disorienting him. He swatted the birds with one hand while pressing the trigger of his machine gun with the other. Thankfully, it missed all of us and merely peppered the building across the way with bullet holes.

Ekk and I rushed him while he was thus blinded. I yanked his gun out of his startled hands and clubbed him with it. He went down hard.

Edith was wild-eyed, her glasses askew, and she was hysterical. Johannas grabbed her, putting an index finger before his lips and staring into her eyes. "Breathe."

"How many are inside from the tour group?" I asked Johannas.

"Seven, I think."

I pointed vigorously at the building we had used to plan our mission and whispered, "Go that way. There's water. Wait for us." He didn't need to be asked twice and dragged the elderly professor with him, disappearing into the nearby ruin. After about a minute, when no one came outside from the visitor center, Ekk and I dragged the unconscious guard to another building and used his handcuffs to secure his wrists behind him on an exposed pipe in the half-destroyed building. We stuffed one of his socks in his mouth, and I used my scarf to keep it secure, tying it in a knot on the back of his head. This would buy us some time, although it would ensure I would swallow some sand when we went outside.

The sandstorm was dying down, which meant our cover was going away. "Now what?" I asked Ekk.

"We're armed. Let's get closer."

Ekk and I crouched down and hurried to the side of the building. I followed so closely that we almost fell. Ekk was in commando mode. He turned around and motioned for me to give him space as we scrabbled to the place beneath a window. After all that work to hide under the window, we couldn't hear what was happening inside.

"Trade me for the Derringer," I said. I held out the machine gun.

"Why?"

I put on my serious face. "It's my gun; Rick gave it to me."

Ekk pulled it out of his pocket, and I handed him the machine gun. The handoff was clumsy, and the Derringer slipped from Ekk's hand and fired as it hit the ground. The window above us shattered, raining down glass. "Shit!"

***

Inside the Visitor Center

A few seconds before, Elsa had wiggled through the bathroom window and flattened herself against the inside wall, listening. She could hear quiet sobbing and men's voices. "Lorelei, where do you want to start?" a Russian-accented voice asked.

"If you untie my hands, this will go more quickly," a British female's voice responded.

"Do you think I'm an idiot?" The Russian man asked.

Elsa heard a single gunshot and glass breaking.

"Well, yeah, I do," Charlie Potts' distinctive voice said.

"What the?" A male voice said in amazement.

Elsa had to peek. She saw the tour group mainly on the floor with their hands behind their backs. Mitzi was sitting on the floor near a standing Charlie, who held a machine gun to the head of a black man in gas station coveralls. Elsa assumed the woman with her hands tied, next to the armed leader, was Lorelei. A third man turned toward Elsa and fired. Instinctively, she ducked and did what she knew to do, casting a quick freeze spell over the two aggressors. It wouldn't last long, but it might give Charlie, Mitzi, and the British woman the edge. Seizing the moment, Mitzi sprang up from the floor and head-butted the man who shot at Elsa. She caught him unawares, and the impact sent him spiraling into the guy wearing a red beret and knocked the machine gun out of his hand. Elsa picked up the gun. Red beret still had Lorelei and now held a knife to her neck when suddenly the British woman disappeared, her clothing falling to the wooden floor. A badger appeared, leaped on the man's arm, and gave it a vicious chomp. He screamed and ran from the room, followed by the animal.

"Shall I follow?" Elsa asked.

"No. Untie me, then help me untie these people," Mitzi said. "We don't know how many others are with the Colonel."

"There's only four total." Elsa jumped in, and between her and Mitzi, they untied the hostages. A dazed Dominique asked questions, but no one answered them. After two minutes, a British voice asked from behind the doorway, "Will someone throw me my clothes, please?"

The Australians looked stunned, and Simon said, "Crikey."

Mitzi, smiling, picked up Lorelei's clothing and handed them around the corner. Soon, she reappeared as if nothing had happened. Rena, the Australian men who had been utterly helpless in the face of danger, and Dominique clapped. "Good on you! I don't know how you did that trick, but it was fabulous!" Dominique said with appreciation. Mitzi thought Lorelei was in danger of being asked to entertain a future tour, knowing Dominique.

"Let's get out of here," Charlie said, tying up Nathan. He threw a rope to Geoff and said, "Make yourself useful. Tie up Sam." He and his brother did so.

***

When they went through the front door, they stopped short, surrounded by Namibian police, guns drawn. "Panda!" Mitzi called out, seeing me and Ekk in custody. It took some doing, but Charlie Potts's former life as a detective was beneficial. He could also throw around some current names at Interpol, which didn't hurt. While he talked to the authorities, officers took statements from those abducted. Lorelei had pleaded with everyone to stick to the hijacking.

Only Rena stuck with the story of a woman from England who had turned into some kind of animal, and this was put down to being overwrought due to the serious condition of her husband. Rena soon left with Rick in the medivac helicopter and went to a hospital in Windhoek. Before they left, I asked an officer to give him his Stetson back, which he did. The police had already confiscated the Derringer, which we had to say was taken from the bad guys. Rena wasn't likely to get it back anyway, and I thought that probably wasn't a bad outcome.

Nathan and Sam were packed into the back of a police car and headed to jail. The guard I had clocked was taken in another vehicle to be checked out before incarceration. The Colonel was nowhere to be found. After we were released, a new bus arrived, to pick up our tour group. I walked to my Rover with Ekk and Elsa. "Is that…"

They nodded. I ran my hand over the side. Right behind the front tire on the driver's side was a bullet hole. I squatted down and pointed to it. "Did you see this?"

"Must have been a stray from the machine gun." Ekk squatted down next to me. We couldn't help but put our fingers in it. "Hope the engine's okay." I opened the front door, climbed up, and turned the key. The engine fired up. "Yay! Oh thank God." I put my hand on my chest. "The thought of having my baby all the way here and—"

A policeman walked toward us and pointed to the bullet hole. "Did that happen here?"

"Yes, but it still drives."

Charlie jogged up. "Panda, uh, Hannah. You'll have to leave the Rover here until we can all come back to testify." He stood next to the officer. They could not have looked more different. One was tall, young, black, and slim in an impeccable police uniform. The other was an older, chunky white dude in a safari shirt with huge sweat rings under his arms. Somehow, however, they were brothers in blue under the skin.

"Seriously? How long is that going to take?"

"A couple of months." The officer answered in English with a soft British accent. "This is a serious matter that NAMPOL, our national force, needs to investigate."

"But—"

"This is the compromise we worked out with Officer Potts. Your friends can take the car back to the States and leave you here if you would rather."

"Uh, no, thank you. I'll wait." I loved my car, but not that much.

He and Charlie walked a few feet away to talk before Charlie came back. The officer left, bathed in the white and green lights from the top of his police car.

Charlie said, "Panda, before you—"

He couldn't finish because I was hugging him. "Thank you, Charlie. If not for you, we would probably be on our way to jail for who knows how long. Are you riding with us?"

"No, I need to be with the tour group and listen to what gets said."

"But you have no magical powers."

He cracked his knuckles. "I am very persuasive and will have you know that I worked undercover in my younger years. We need to know what they think they know."

"Okay. See you back in Luderitz." Mitzi came over to us and hugged him. The bus driver started tooting his horn. "Bye!"

Mitzi and I rode with the elves in the Land Rover, knowing it would be my last drive in it for a long while. A cop car escorted us, ensuring we wouldn't go four-wheeling away. We all talked over each other, since there was so much to catch up on. As usual, our affection for each other was the magic that sealed our little family, and despite the near-death experience, I was laughing soon.

"I loved it when you burst in wearing that Stetson hat! It felt like a Western movie." Mitzi curled my hair behind my ear. "But your hair is a mess."

"What about the birds? You should have seen them, Mitzi! I thought the raven thing would always look like thousands or hundreds of thousands coming. Instead, I got a fantastic little three-bird commando group."

"Did you thank them?" Elsa asked.

"Uh, no. I was a bit busy."

"I've heard that if you are lucky enough to command magical creatures, you must keep the scale equal."

"What am I supposed to do?" I was irritated. This was our triumphant debrief, and I needed to brag a little.

"I can help you with that when we return to the Garden." Ekk always had my back.

"Sure, someday. I don't know about you all, but I want to go home!" I squeezed Mitzi's hand.

There was a silence from the back seat that got our attention. "What?" Mitzi asked.

Ekk leaned forward from the back and touched Mitzi's arm. "Ehren's not in the Hercynian Garden. Your father went to the Raven's nest to clear up where the ravens stand in this fight." Elsa said.

"Shouldn't I have been consulted about this? I am the raven-master." I was still slightly irritated at Elsa, who had stepped over my story.

"Panda, you may be able to call them, but make no mistake, Rayva oversees the ravens. She is nested in a mountain called Falkenfelsen in Germany. Ehren set out with one of Heloisa's men to speak directly to her. Bur came back, but Ehren did not return."

'Oh my god!" Mitzi started shaking. "We have to find him."

"We will," Ekk said. "That's why tomorrow we need to go to Germany."

The situation finally sank in. "I'm so sorry. Of course we'll be on that plane. We can call Puddle at the hotel."

The rest of the drive back to our hotel in Luderitz was much less triumphant. After we parked, the elves, who had not had a chance to sleep since they arrived, stayed in Mitzi's room. Mitzi and I freshened up for what would be our final dinner with what was left of our tour group since, due to the circumstances, our dinner cruise in Walvis Bay was canceled.

We walked into the dining room together and got a little "yay" from those left over. Dominique informed us the Aussie boys had skipped dinner and gone on to Walvis to catch a flight home, having lost their taste for the trip. Edith Roswell, Lorelei Pinck, Dominique, Charlie, and the two of us were all who remained.

"Any word on Rick and Rena?" Mitzi asked Dominique.

"He's hanging in there, but he went into shock before they got him on the medivac. It's touch and go. Rena's with him."

This was the touchy part—how much did these people need to know?

***

Final Dinner in Namibia

The dining room staff served us a special dinner, having undoubtedly heard about "some trouble" we'd had at Kolmanskop. We kept our conversation as light as possible until dessert was brought with a lit sparkler, which was very special. Everyone was exhausted. I was wiping my mouth when, whom should Edith spy, but *Wit Storieman* coming in the door from the beach, followed by a gaggle of admiring tourists. She watched him stuff tips in his pocket and faux humbly beg off an after-dinner drink as his audience shifted into the bar.

He spotted Edith and looked ready to make a break for it. She pinned him with her eyes. Crumpling up her napkin, she scraped her chair back and said, "Mr. *Storieman*, a word?"

Dominique was paying the check, and when she saw this, she followed Edith, leaving me, Mitzi, Charlie, and Lorelei alone at the table.

"I'm glad we have a couple of private moments. What can you tell us?" Mitzi asked.

"It's a relief to talk about it. I'm with the Garden as well, from the London branch."

"Are you here on a mission?" Charlie asked.

She sighed. "Woda contacted me when she learned that Heloisa wouldn't be coming. Said it was an information-gathering trip, and you would never have known about me if it hadn't started to unravel."

"What do you mean, unravel? All I did was make Edith wonder why I wasn't a Himba expert." I didn't want to be cast as the one who blew our cover.

"Not that. When your phones were stolen, I knew you had been discovered." She could see I was about to speak again and said first, "You told me, Panda, but I saw who did it. That's what made me 'break the fourth wall.'"

"A theatrical term. Are you an actress?" I was intrigued.

She blushed. "I am. It helps when you are undercover most of the time."

"You sure weren't acting when you shapeshifted." I giggled. "A badger?"

She said, "That was weird for me as well. In England, I turn into a regular badger. Here, I was a honey badger, which was good because I had a pouch."

"Africa." I shrugged. "Where is the pouch?"

Mitzi kicked me under the table.

"Rude," she said, but she didn't seem overly offended. "May I go on? I saw a talented pickpocket wearing a traditional Herero dress take phones off both of you. Do you remember being jostled at the market?"

"Only about a hundred times." There was my grumpy old Charlie.

"I followed her." Lorelei looked around to make sure Edith was still across the room. "She stepped off to the side and handed your phones to the man who later turned out to be Nathan, our hijacker."

"*Lupus Imperium*," Charlie said.

"Yes."

"You told the "Colonel" that you could find the Summer Stone. Was that a bluff?" I asked.

"I had no bloody clue how to find it. The lie was all I could think of on the spot."

Mitzi cleared her throat. "We do owe you, Lorelei. If you hadn't bit him…Anyway, I have a device that was going off like crazy. A guy in Germany invented it. It signified that the Stone was there."

"Then we need to go back!" Charlie looked at his watch. "I bet we could be there and back in under an hour."

Mitzi looked at all of us sadly. "The vibration stopped after the Colonel got away. They have it."

"Damn," Charlie said. I threw my head back and looked at the ceiling.

We were all silent for a minute. Our new friend reached into her pocket. "No, they don't." Lorelei pulled out a tiny green bag. "From what I hear, this is much smaller than the Winter Stone fragment already at the Garden."

"How come I don't sense anything?" Usually, I could feel strong magic.

"My device isn't doing anything," Mitzi commented.

Lorelei tipped the bag sideways, and a rock about one inch in diameter spilled into her hand. "The bag hides it."

"Wow!" I felt a jolt across the table. Lorelei slipped it back into the green sack, and the feeling subsided. "That looks like the same material Ekk put the Winter Stone in!" I was excited.

"Shush!" said Mitzi, shaking her head.

"Sorry," I said.

"Oh my god! How?" Mitzi asked Lorelei.

Before answering, she handed the green sack to Charlie, who nonchalantly stuffed it in his pocket and zipped it shut.

"When I bit him, he ran. I crawled over him, and my little hands picked his pocket."

We sat, staring at her. "I learned the skill while playing in Oliver!"

Charlie put her hand in both of his. "Thank you. I was afraid this was all for nothing." He stood up to leave. "Now, if you'll excuse me, I need a cigarette."

"Yes, thank you for all you did." I finally found my manners. "I hope we cross paths again."

"You never know." She handed Mitzi and me cards. "Here's my number if you ever come to England."

Edith returned, having finished her argument with Dominique. "Thank you, Dominique, but that is how I feel. You would do better to find another storyteller."

"Well, it's been quite a trip!" Dominique had a full glass of wine in hand when she sat down. After all we'd been through, she talked of a reunion trip. "When you come back to testify, we can take a proper tour of Kolmanskop and get that dinner cruise."

Everyone had to smile. She was a trooper.

***

The Hercynian Garden

Ekk called the Garden from Mitzi's hotel room, and we were shocked and happy to find Ehren at the other end of the line. They fought over the receiver and finally put him on speaker. Elsa and I knew how to stay out of the fray, so we sat on the bed and watched them.

"Dad!" She never called him that, and it took me by surprise.

"Daughter." I wished we could see him, but this was a satellite call, not one of the special hologram calls Ekk would normally make with his dagger.

"What happened to you? Are you all right?"

"I can't say too much, but I have grave concerns about what's happening in Falkenfelsen."

"We'll be on a plane tomorrow to come see you. We're bringing you a gift from Kolmanskop."

"Oh?"

"I think you'll like it."

***

With Ehren home, Jay made his rounds with great energy, going to each of the nine provinces that formed the Garden proper. Riding a motorcycle was second nature to him, and despite the circumstances with whatever was going on with the ravens, he found happiness in the moment. He knew Ehren was resourceful and resolved not to worry until they really learned something.

One after another, he left each province sub-council with hugs, gratitude, and information, promising to make the circuit a regular occurrence. Each group agreed that their new social media had to be revamped and decided to wait for the safer version. The unicorns were the most challenging group, but with good cause. They didn't have access to the new social media due to having hooves, and Jay promised to bring this issue back to the council. One thing everyone agreed upon: no one had seen Dr. Mot, but if he showed up, he would be taken into custody at once, no matter which province.

Jay hurried back to the keep to join Ehren. Soon, Ekk, Elsa, Charlie, Mitzi, and Panda would arrive with the Summer Stone. It would be secured with the Winter Stone, which would make our world and theirs a little bit safer.

THE END.

To be continued in

Hell's Valley

Book Six
of the
Hercynian Forest Series

Acknowledgments

By now, you have probably read a few acknowledgments on book jackets from your regular authors and may be tempted to skip over this section. Please don't! Although the paragraphs sound somewhat similar in every book, no book is a solo endeavor, and the efforts of others need to be recognized. With so many characters to keep track of, it truly takes a (small) village of professional people to get the details right.

Launch Point Press owners Peggy and Jodi Zeramby support and encourage their writers in all the best ways. As their publishing empire expands, they still ensure each book from their press meets the highest standards and provide resources and guidance for their authors. Thank you so much! Thank you also to Peggy for the stunning cover of *Search for the Summer Stone*.

Then there are the editors. This year, as in the past, we have had an amazing all-female team. In addition to Suzan Twilley Gridley and Verda Foster—two very able editors and my first readers. I worked this time with editor Kaycee Hawn, who is super sharp. Kaycee gave my characters a dusting off and going over that only a new pair of eyes could have provided, and the book is better for it. Thank you Kaycee, Verda, and Suzan.

I also wish to thank my wife, Audrey Stephanie Loftin, who lets me read to her and is always honest and encouraging. Last, but never least, **thank you, dear readers**, for buying my books.

About the Author

Reba Birmingham is an American author, poet, and award-winning attorney. She is the author of the Hercynian Forest Series: *Floodlight*, *Words on a Plate*, *The Wolf You Feed*, *Circle of Stones*, and this one. She's married and lives in Southern California in an urban oasis with bunnies, cats, and fish.

Note to Readers

Thank you for reading a book from Launch Point Press. We have made every effort to edit this book. However, typos do slip in. If you find an error in the text, please email publisher@launchpointpress.com so the issue can be corrected.

We appreciate you as a reader and want to ensure you enjoy the reading process. We would like you to consider posting a review on your preferred media sites and/or your blog or website.

For more information on upcoming releases, author interviews, contests, giveaways and more, please sign up for our newsletter and visit us as at Launch Point Press: www.launchpointpress.com and "Like" us on Facebook: Launch Point Press.

Bright Blessings

9 781633 040694